SOUL SCENT

A Zackie Novel

Reyna Favis

ISBN-13: 978-1974580965
ISBN-10: 1974580962

Visit the author's website at www.reynafavis.com.

Dedicated to my husband, Rich Kliman, who makes sure I keep writing instead of making creepy collages.

Also by Reyna Favis

The Zackie Stories:

SOUL SEARCH
SOUL SCENT
SOUL SIGN

CHAPTER 1

A lot can happen in a day. You could be born in a day and you could fall in love in a day. If Maggie Pierceson had waited just one more day, maybe she would not have taken her own life. Her remains lay face down on a thick layer of decaying leaves in Worthington State Forest. Next to the body was a Sharpie, dropped after she had finished scrawling a final message to loved ones on her arm.

"Excuse me, Fia." Officer Jill Creighton pushed passed me and ducked under the crime scene tape. Kneeling near Maggie's body, Jill slipped on latex gloves and then gently eased the dead hands into plastic bags, cinching them closed at the wrists with zip ties. Maggie was reduced to being evidence maintained in a chain of custody until she reached the crime lab where they would test her hands for gunpowder residue. Her fingers curled inward as if grasping for something.

I flexed my own fingers in the stiff, leather gloves,

unconsciously imitating the rigor mortis contracting Maggie's hands. This small action did little to alleviate the discomfort in my fingers from the cold of the early morning. I had been warm enough while I tramped around the deep woods all night, but being forced to stand and wait had allowed the drying sweat to chill me. At irregular intervals, my leg muscles contracted in little spasms and I had a crick in my neck from carrying the backpack. The worst thing after an all-night search was having to struggle to put two simple thoughts together. I stood among a crowd of other searchers who were gathered outside of the crime scene tape. We were a sea of high visibility orange, ready to surge forward once law enforcement had finished processing the scene. It would fall to search and rescue to bring the body out of the woods and the mood among the searchers was somber. The search was considered a success because the subject had been found. But the fact that it was too late was heartbreaking to everyone who had worked all night to find Maggie.

The police had found the expended round embedded in the trunk of a tree near the body, but the gun itself was still missing. The force of the recoil would have sent it flying from her hand after the shot was fired. The gun was probably not very far from the body, but the fallen leaves and forest undergrowth made it difficult to recover the weapon. The officers worked methodically to narrow the search field by mapping the trajectory of the bullet. After being called out to so many searches for the missing, there were many familiar faces among the officers who scoured the area for the gun.

I sidled closer to Cam and waited with my question as he was gripped by a jaw-cracking yawn. Cam was my mentor and partner in crime. He had taught me everything I knew about surviving the unseen world. The rising sun highlighted the dark shadows beneath his eyes and he hunched his tall frame against the early morning chill. Warm in her glossy red coat, Zackie lay at his feet, mimicking the appearance of a well-trained search dog. In reality, she was neither well-trained, nor a true dog, but to the uninitiated, she appeared to be a Plott Hound, sleekly muscled and ready for the hunt.

"Did you or Zackie see her yet?" I kept my voice low, so only Cam and Zackie could hear. Still, I made sure my words were vague. With so many people around, there was no way that I could openly ask Cam if Maggie's spirit had made an appearance.

At the sound of her name, Zackie's ears twitched

and she briefly pointed her muzzle at me, but then her gaze drifted away. She displayed her level of concern for the proceedings by yawning in sympathy with Cam, her mouth gaping and her long canines exposed. Zackie's only real interest was the dead. It was her duty as a psychopomp to escort the dead to the next life and she made no secret of the fact that the living bored her. After witnessing how humans played out the same little dramas century after century, we had long ceased to be amusing to her. Because Cam and I were devoted to helping her cause, Zackie would sometimes make exceptions for us, but mostly, she made it pretty clear that we were on our own and we were not to involve her in our shenanigans.

Cam shook his head. "No, neither of us has seen anything, Fia." His crisp British accent was slurred with fatigue. Cam rubbed his face in an effort to wake up and then ran a hand absently through his mop of gray curls. Staring at the body, he frowned. "You know, it's unusual for a woman to choose suicide by gun. Most of the time, women overdose. I wonder what brought her to this."

My brow furrowed and stray locks of sweaty, auburn hair crept into my eyes, irritating me. I shoved the bangs under my baseball cap and turned my gaze to the body, trying to understand. "Do you think she was making some sort of statement by her choice of death?"

"Don't know. Pills leave the body intact, but using a handgun makes the violence of death plain to see. Maybe she felt that she had to show she suffered."

"Dying isn't penance enough?" I shook my head, unable to process what may have motivated Maggie to end things like this. Pain, depression and being ostracized by society are things I understood, but wanting to take your own life because of these factors had never once occurred to me. At the lowest points in my life, I thought I had firsthand knowledge of what waited on the other side, and the idea of becoming one of the earthbound dead was revolting. Aside from appearing as bottomless pits of pathetic need, these revenants also revealed the most horrifying aspect of life after death - being damned to constantly relive the brutality of the perimortem state. I wanted no part of either of these conditions. Instead, I endured the humiliation of being thought mad by the rest of the world because I could see the suffering dead. I had tried living separately from society, but came close to falling apart during my solitary struggle. If it had not been for Cam and Zackie, I would never have learned that the dead can move on from the earthbound state. The true afterlife was still a mystery to me, but in my mind, anything beat clinging to a half life on earth.

My navel gazing was interrupted when a low murmur erupted among the searchers. The police officers had found the gun. After another few minutes of taking photographs of the gun *in situ* and carefully packaging the weapon in an evidence container, law enforcement signaled the searchers that the body could at last be removed.

I noticed Peyton among the searchers entering the crime scene area and touched her arm in silent commiseration as she walked past me. She and K9 Simber had found the body a few hours before dawn. The light glinted off her glasses as Peyton nodded her head in acknowledgment and I saw a few small twigs caught in her flaming red hair. Simber must have taken her through the scenic route to find Maggie. Dropping her eyes and sighing, Peyton ran her fingers lightly over Simber's ears and the silver-gray fur of her flanks. Peyton was strongly built and her hands were larger than those of most men I knew, but each fingernail was painted a delicate pink and flaunted a perfect French manicure. Sensing her distress, Simber leaned into Peyton, and then began making the signature gargling, mewling sound for which Huskies were famous. Simber was a Husky-German Shepherd mix, but her vocalizations tended to favor the Husky in her, and under other circumstances, these spellbinding ululations made for high entertainment. The final task facing the searchers dampened any feelings of amusement, so there were no smiles at Simber's antics.

In the end, the carryout was accomplished with a minimum of fuss. After Maggie was packaged into the stokes basket, the searchers alternated between carrying the litter and clearing the way of brush. A carryout was exhausting work and by the time we reached the trail, my arms ached and trembled with the effort. After covering a half mile through wilderness, the waiting crossover utility vehicle was a glorious sight. We secured the stokes basket to the back of the vehicle and left it to the driver to take the litter the rest of the way to the parking area. A waiting ambulance would travel the final leg and transport Maggie's remains to the morgue.

Cam groaned as he held a bent arm over his head and tugged on the elbow to stretch out his triceps. "I'm done for. Time to go home and get some sleep."

"Love to, but I have to go and break down the

trailer first." I nodded to him and then turned to walk away.

Cam called after me. "You're young. You'll manage. I'm leaving."

Because the missing person was in my team's backyard, we were responsible for running the show for this search. Cam's team had been called in for additional support, but all they had to do was show up and search. My team ran incident command and there were laptops and printers to take down, a generator to be shut down and a radio antenna to be dismantled, among other things. Everything needed to be squared away and made ready for the next search before the trailer could be towed to Peyton's property to await the next callout.

The rest of the team was hard at work by the time I arrived at the trailer. Between all of us, we had the trailer re-packed and ready for the next callout in under twenty minutes. The last thing I did was to put the wheel chucks near the threshold for ready access. Peyton shut the door and secured the lock with her key. Satisfied that everything was locked and loaded, we began walking to our vehicles, bidding each other a belated goodnight. I had taken no more than three steps when the trailer reverberated with a loud bang and crash.

Stopping in her tracks, Peyton reversed direction and grabbed her key again. “What the… Did the wall anchors fail?” She yanked the door open to verify and I looked over her shoulder to see if there was any damage. Everything was in place, just as we left it.

I scratched my head. “Huh. It almost sounded like we accidentally locked someone inside.”

“Okay, whatever. It all looks all right. I’m locking this up again and driving home.” Peyton turned the key one more time and then stepped quickly away before anything more could happen to delay her departure.

###

Back at home, I stripped off my search gear, starting with the gloves that protected my hands from the briars and other nasty, sharp things in the woods. I looked at my bad right hand, flexing the fingers slightly and getting creeped out yet again by the discolored, putrescent skin and blackened nails. The hand belonged to a corpse and had no business being attached to me. The dead hand was like a cancer, something that used to be part of me, but was now a clump of mutated cells, a parasite that would act in its own best interest. But this was my souvenir from reaching into Zackie's domain. It was no place for the living and I had found that out the hard way. Sighing, I admitted to myself that there were times I was an idiot and in need of a refresher course in self-preservation.

I piled the rest of my clothes into a heap of dirty laundry in the middle of the floor and then located the heavy neoprene diver's glove, pulling it over the dead hand before hitting the shower. I hated the idea of that hand touching me, so I went through this ritual of protection every time I showered. Even though it was late in the season, I did a careful inspection for ticks and came up empty. Good for me. Breakfast was a sad affair, since I desperately needed to go shopping. I assembled a small plate of cheese and crackers and vowed to go to the grocery store after I got some sleep. Before consuming anything, I put a light cotton glove on the dead hand, so I didn't have to look at it while I ate. I couldn't bring myself to chow down if that thing touched my food. While I could control the hand and go about doing my normal activities using it, the hand was definitely non-self. There were occasions when it acted independently of me.

As I munched on the poor excuse for breakfast, I

checked my phone for messages. My heart beat a little faster when I discovered a missed call from Lucas. His voicemail implied that he had a job for Cam and me. Lucas's producers must have decided he had spent enough time grieving the death of his wife and that he needed to get back to work. After Hannah died, Lucas's ghost hunting show had gone on hiatus, broadcasting re-runs to hold on to viewers. The audience must have grown hungry for something new and the producers realized that to satisfy their voracious appetite for novelty, they might not care if the new thing was a fresh episode of Lucas's show or another, similar program on a different network. I wondered if the producers would be coldblooded enough to suggest that Lucas try to raise the ghost of his own wife for ratings.

I put the phone down and chewed on a stale cracker as I stared off into the middle distance. The order of the day would be sleep, shop and then call Lucas back. Because I knew that hearing his voice would bring on a hormonal tsunami, I did not trust myself to have any kind of conversation with him while I was sleep-deprived. Lucas continued to be off limits to me and I didn't want to make either of us uncomfortable by accidentally saying something unwise. He was newly bereaved and I would not take advantage of his emotionally vulnerable state. In addition to my commitment to act honorably where Lucas was concerned, an additional incentive was that his wife's spirit lingered near him and she would very likely kick my ass if I made any kind of move.

# # #

Jarred awake by the sound of Glenn Miller's *In the Mood*, I bolted upright and grabbed my phone to make it stop. Ordinarily, I found the tune upbeat and happy, but Peyton was calling and I didn't feel like I had nearly enough sleep to deal with whatever it was she wanted. I paused for a beat thinking that I might let her leave a voicemail and go back to sleep. When I considered the consequences of making her wait, answering the call seemed to be the better choice. Peyton was not known for her patience and she might call repeatedly until I picked up. If I shut off my phone, I was sure she'd make the trip to my place and pound on the door until she got what she wanted. Peyton Bell was one of these high-drive humans. She was ex-military, competed in the local Highland Games, throwing everything from telephone poles to small boulders, and was training to be a master stonemason.

I began the conversation with a whine and a whimper. “What, Peyton? It’s too soon to be calling me.”

“Fia? Can you get in touch with Cam for me? I need him to bring Zackie here.”

“What? Why?”

“I think there’s a raccoon trapped in the trailer. I need her to flush it out.”

“Can’t Simber take care of it?”

Peyton exhaled a long, dramatic sigh. “I’ve tried that. She’s showing no interest and meantime, the crashing and banging won’t stop. I need a coonhound. Zackie’s a coonhound, right?”

“No, not really. She’s a Plott Hound. They’re bred to hunt big game – bear and boar, mostly.”

“But some people use them to hunt raccoons, right?”

Rolling my eyes, I said the next bit imitating an Appalachian twang, so I would say it the way I had first heard it. “It’s a damned waste of the breed, Peyton.”

“Did I start this conversation with the words, ‘If it

pleases your majesty'?" She paused to let this sink in and then reiterated her demands. "I have a problem that might end up damaging equipment. Cam has a solution. Get him over here." As an afterthought, she added "please" and then "thank you" before hanging up.

I stared at my phone and blinked my eyes a few times before sending a text to Cam, asking him to call Peyton about a raccoon in the team trailer and providing her contact information. I filed this away in the big pile of things that were not my problem and tried to go back to sleep. It had been maybe twenty minutes and I was close to falling asleep when my phone went off again. This time it was the theme from *The Good, the Bad and the Ugly*. Why hadn't I turned the phone off after sending the text? Did I have such a huge fear of missing out that I would sacrifice sleep for the dubious honor of being included in other people's nonsense?

Fumbling with the phone, I poked the screen to accept the call. "Ugh… what, Cam?" I flopped back in the bed and wrapped one arm over my eyes to block the light, while I held the phone to my ear with the other hand.

"Did it ever occur to you that the banging about might be Maggie?" As usual, there was no greeting from

Cam. He just started right in with whatever was on his mind.

I rubbed my face, still groggy and not really thinking clearly yet. “Maggie? What would she be doing in the trailer? Wouldn’t she have stayed in the woods where she died?”

“Not necessarily. Because Peyton found the body, Maggie might have obsessed on her and followed her home.”

“For real? How are we supposed to release her with Peyton watching our every move?”

“Well, obviously I can’t do it on my own. You’ll need to distract Peyton, while Zackie and I work on Maggie.”

“Aw, crap…” I had thought I could sleep just a little during the day and we would go back to the woods that night to help Maggie. But because she’d made an appearance and was no doubt in deep distress, we needed to act immediately. I admitted defeat and got out of bed.

###

A booming sound could be heard from the driveway. If this was a raccoon, it had to be the granddaddy of them all. I was the first to arrive and parked next to Peyton's truck. I thought I'd scope out the situation and get the ball rolling before she noticed I was there. Stepping out of my car, I glanced toward the back of the property at the house. It was an old, stone structure that used to be a pump house and she was slowly restoring the building and making it livable. No sign of Peyton yet, so I stepped away from the car, leaving the door open to avoid making noise. The gravel crunched beneath my feet as I took another step and extended my feelers for anything that might indicate Maggie's presence. Suicides produced a particular sensory signature where everything was muted. Colors were leached and appeared gray or sepia. Sound lost its true dynamic range and flattened, so it was like listening to the world with water in your ears. Even smell and taste lacked sharpness and definition. All I would get was a kind of funky, mushroomy taste in my sinuses that made me want to spit.

What I actually perceived surprised me. I caught a whiff of tangy fear-sweat, and my own adrenaline spiked a notch in response. There was abandonment and hopelessness. Was that Maggie? Then I sensed confusion and a blazing anger. I suddenly felt cornered and an atavistic reflex raised my hackles and I hunched to protect my neck. Lifting my hands to fend off an attack, I barely suppressed a warning snarl. *Enough!* This definitely was not Maggie. The spirit was strong and dangerous and he was taking over my reality. I started building a mental defense like Cam taught me, envisioning myself surrounded by a shark cage that let me keep an eye on the predators swimming outside, but allowed me to remain protected within.

Isolated from the influences of the spirit, I closed the car door and stood rigidly next to it, taking a few deep breaths. Peyton emerged from her house just as my heart beat was returning to its normal cadence. I waved at her, pretending to have just arrived.

"I thought I heard a car door slam." As Peyton approached from the house, another vehicle pulled in and took the space next to me. Cam stumbled out of the truck, rubbing his face and yawning. While he opened the tailgate to let Zackie out, I suggested to Peyton that coffee might be in order. From past experience, I've learned some people get traumatized if they brush up against the dead, while others go into full-scale denial. Either way, it made it hard for us to resolve the problem.

As soon as Peyton was out of earshot, I filled Cam in on my impressions.

"It's not Maggie, then." Cam rubbed the stubble on his jaw and concentrated on something in the distance with unfocused eyes. He needed a shave and more sleep. "Did you get anything specific about who we are dealing with?"

"Other than emotional turmoil, nothing. But I think he got a little pissed off when he felt me tapping into him." As if confirming my diagnosis, another loud boom echoed through the yard. Zackie's ears perked and her head angled up as she put her nose into the wind.

"I suppose there's nothing for it. Let's go have a look." Cam stalked towards the trailer with Zackie at his heels. I followed, keeping my eyes and ears open for anything untoward. The door to the trailer had been left ajar. Perhaps Peyton held out hope that the raccoon would just wander off on its own. Cam squatted at the doorway and took his time scanning the interior. Looking over his shoulder, I did the same. We both came up empty.

Cam shrugged. "It's possible he doesn't want to make contact."

"He didn't seem like a shrinking violet to me…I don't know…" I shook my head, not quite believing that the spirit hid from us. Before I could move to check the surrounding woods, Zackie jumped up on the side of the trailer in the classic pose of hunting-dog-treeing-her-quarry, her ID for a high find. Something had manifested on the roof of the trailer.

Cam and I backed up to get a proper look at the roof. On the top of the trailer crouched a man in breech-cloth and buckskin leggings. He wore a shirt made from the pelt of some animal with the fur against his skin. His muscles bunched and he looked ready to spring. The sides and front of his head were hairless, but black hair stood up aggressively at the crown of his head. Two feathers twined into that dark mass of hair and his face was a shocking red. He glared at us wide-eyed with teeth bared. I took an involuntary step back as he smashed his fist on the trailer's roof, creating another sonic boom that made me cover my ears. Drawing a steadying breath, I concentrated on sensing past his blood-red features and snarl to see the man. Even with these features stripped away, the man was terrifying.

"I don't think he's happy to see us." Cam mumbled to Zackie and she dropped to the ground. Gazing up at the very angry Native American, Cam called up to him. "Hoy, do you think you'd like to come down and speak with us?"

The man growled a response. "*Awèn hèch ki?*"

"What'd he say?" I heard the words, but had no comprehension. Normally, my brain accommodates and senses the meaning if a spirit garbles words or speaks an unknown language.

"He's blocking us." Cam furrowed his brow, concentrating, trying to break through. "I think he's testing us with the language. He doesn't want us to understand his meaning if we can't understand the words."

"*Ahpu hèch awèn kèski alënixsit?*" The spirit pointed to us, loudly exclaiming the words.

"Sorry, mate. We can't understand you. You're going to have to try harder if you want to have a conversation."

The spirit smashed his fist into the trailer in response and disappeared, leaving us with an acrid smell of ozone, as if there had been a lightning strike close by. My heart raced, my skin prickled and I felt like I had just survived a near miss. "Holy crap," I croaked.

Cam eyed me with concern. "Easy there. It's over now."

Peyton chose that moment of unbalanced chaos to appear with mugs of coffee. Thanking her in a weak voice, I took mine and concentrated hard not to spill it. My arms contracted in a muscular anarchy after accepting the slight weight of the mug, still spastic from the carryout. But if I forced myself to be honest, it was our contact with the angry spirit that caused my hands to tremble. I stole a look at Cam as I surreptitiously took some tight breaths, trying to slow my galloping heart. His calm was contagious and my gut unclenched, allowing me to breathe a little easier. Cam has told me that my reactions might be a form of PTSD, on account of my traumatic childhood and early, uncontrolled experiences with the unseen world. This wasn't fear I experienced, but an adrenaline-charged preparation for battle that I had trouble controlling.

Peyton scrunched her face and stooped to check the power cable to the trailer. "I smell something…did that critter chew through the wiring?"

Peyton had some sensitivity if she could smell it too and Cam shot me a worried look. I had met plenty of people who had varying degrees of ability to sense these presences, and in general, those with a weak awareness had some protection. I hoped that was true for Peyton, because this was a delicate balancing act between the interests of the spirit and well-being of the person affected by the encounter.

I think this whole thing worked something like bear attacks. People like Peyton, who had some sensitivity, were like folks who were woods-aware. They made noise to let the bears know they were in the area and the animals gave them a wide berth. They don't absolutely know that there was a bear near them, but they mostly avoided being attacked. I should emphasize the word 'mostly' here. People who were insensitive were like hikers with no sense of caution in the woods. They might accidentally stumble across a bear, surprise it and bring on an attack. They had no idea about the danger they were about to walk into. The spiritually insensitive were the people I worried about the most. Then there were those of us with the highest levels of sensitivity. We were just bear bait. There was something about us that helped these spirits to charge up and manifest full-strength, so it was like we were walking through the woods in a meat suit.

Cam stalled with comments about possible damage as he grappled for a way to control the situation. “We didn’t see any obvious damage inside the trailer....” Rubbing the back of his neck, Cam looked down as his face flushed and he stammered out a response. He was failing to launch a believable explanation, so I interrupted.

“Hey, Peyton, we didn’t let Zackie flush out the raccoon because it might be injured. It would be more likely to fight than run. Best to keep clear of the trailer and maybe let it wander off slowly on its own.”

“Injured! I’ll get my rifle and deal with this. I don’t want Simber –”

“Don’t be foolish.” Cam swept his hand towards the equipment in the trailer. “The operative word is ‘might,’ so don’t go about trying to put holes in things. You don’t want to damage any of the laptops or radios, do you?” Peyton hesitated and chewed on her lip, so Cam pressed forward. “Just leave the door cracked as you’ve been doing and let it go its own way. Simber hasn’t paid it any attention, so she’ll be fine if you don’t mess with the situation.”

After a long moment, Peyton nodded. “All right, all

right. I have to go to my cousin's wedding tomorrow, so I'll just let this lie." She raked a hand through her hair and then put her hands on her hips, looking at the ground and shaking her head. "But if this thing doesn't disappear and stop making booming noises in the trailer, I'm calling in animal control to trap it. Funding's been cut, so they'll take forever to respond. I just hope we don't get another callout before this is resolved."

I exhaled the breath I held and relaxed a little, now that we had her cooperation. "Sounds like a plan." With a flash of inspiration, I formulated an excuse so that we could return to the trailer as needed. "And about the radios? I'd like to program them with the frequencies we've been using on searches. It'll make it easier if we're called out to get everyone communicating quickly. Cam said he'd help me, so we might come back to work on this in a day or two." I saw Cam compress his lips out of the corner of my eye, but after a moment, he nodded as if we'd discussed this earlier.

"What if the raccoon is still around when you come?" Peyton glanced from me to Cam and her brow creased.

Sticking his hands in his pockets, Cam jutted his

chin at Zackie. "We'll bring Zackie. She'll let us know if there's something in the trailer."

# # #

At Cam's insistence, I wiped my cheek with a napkin to remove the ketchup. He moistened another napkin in his water glass and handed it to me. "You missed a spot." The waitress artfully looked away as she passed us while we engaged in this social grooming behavior. Cam went back to sipping his third cup of coffee and looked thoughtful. "This one is going to be tricky. He's given us little enough to go on and the records for Native Americans are sparse, especially the earlier you go."

Cam worked as a genealogist, so I trusted his judgment about our ability to find information on this angry spirit. "Any idea why he's so pissed?"

Cam shook his head. "I didn't pick up on anything specific. No clues from his spirit body, other than maybe the red on his face." I thought back on what I had learned about the symbolism that spirits use to convey everything from their history to their emotional states. Body parts would go missing or they manifested in some way that provided visual cues to what they were feeling or what they experienced. It was similar to the way dreams try to convey information to the conscious mind, never coming out and saying something blatant or easy to interpret by the dreamer. This was a language of symbolism and metaphor and it was personal to the dreamer, or in this case, the spirit expressing these symbols.

"What do you think the red face means? Embarrassment?"

"No… It doesn't feel right. I don't think it fits the rest of his profile." Ticking off the list of emotions on his fingers, Cam continued. "Besides this incredible hostility, you said you got abandonment, fear, hopelessness and confusion. Am I right?"

"That about sums it up." I slumped down in my seat, the energy boost from the food already worn off. "You're right. Embarrassment is not something he's putting out there." I wadded the ketchup-stained napkin between my fingers and concentrated on what we could do to help this spirit. I did not want to fight this guy. I needed a peaceful solution. "We need to get him to talk to us."

"And how are we going to do that?" Cam squinted

at me and then raised an eyebrow.

"How do you get anyone to open up? We need to find common ground and somehow build trust with this guy."

The eyebrow stayed up. "We need something better than platitudes on how to win friends and influence people."

I took a deep breath, stared at the wet ball of napkin in my hands and dredged up a bad memory. "When I was seeing shrinks on a regular basis, I learned a lot about how they operate. Mostly, I learned for self-preservation, but some things may have application to the non-crazy world."

"Like what?" Cam sat up and leaned forward.

"Well, there's a school of thought that only like can counsel like. So, for instance, only an addict can truly reach another addict. You have to have that life experience if you're really going to make a connection."

"Wouldn't that drastically cut down on the number of available therapists?" Cam frowned and stared into his coffee, clearly not liking the idea. "I could see that approach leaving a lot of people in need out in the cold."

I twitched a shoulder. "From what I could tell, it was applied selectively. I remember this approach because I knew this guy who was Native American. He was adopted by a white family when he was a very little kid and he made trouble for them from the get-go. He was angry and violent all the time and it was only getting worse the older he got."

I took a deep breath, trying to de-stress and tossed the wadded napkin on the plate. The discussion roiled the contents of my stomach and queasiness reminded me that what goes down won't necessarily stay down. I hated talking about my past. "The shrinks worked with him, worked with the family, handed out pills like candy and nothing made a difference. The family ended up sending him for treatment out West. He lived with other tribal members and went for therapy with a Native American psychiatric counselor. He eventually got better, I think. We used to keep in touch, but things with me probably got too weird for him."

"So, what are you suggesting?" Cam spoke softly, careful not to make eye contact. He knows how touchy I am about this stuff. I never talk about it and he never pushes me.

I slid my coffee away and tucked my hands into my armpits, hunching over my uneasy belly. "I could try to get in contact with him. His name's Ron Falling-Leaf. He knows all about me, so I wouldn't have to pretend around him. Last time we spoke, he was big into learning about tribal spiritual beliefs and practices, but that was almost ten years ago when we were just kids. Maybe he's an accountant by now."

Cam's lips quirked and then he smiled a little. "I would hope that people don't change that much."

Grabbing the opportunity with both hands, I launched into a rapid change of topic. "Speaking of people not changing, I got a call from Lucas. It sounded like he might have a job for us. I would have thought after Hannah passed away, he'd quit doing the ghost show. He only did it to pay for her treatment after all."

"Maybe he still has bills to pay from the hospital and the funeral. Maybe he just wants stability after all the turmoil. Who knows?" Cam shrugged. "Did he say what he had in mind?"

"No, he left a message and it was pretty vague." I cocked my head as an idea presented on how to return

Lucas's call without having to engage in a risky one-on-one conversation. "I'm thinking we should call him from your truck and see what this is all about."

Cam looked at me for a moment without blinking, but refrained from making a direct comment. "Okay, let's both talk to him."

After settling the bill, we reconvened in Cam's truck. Zackie was unaccountably absent. "Huh, this is where I left her." Cam turned in the driver's seat and scanned the back seat and the truck bed. Lifting a shoulder, he faced forward again. "I guess she must have had pressing business elsewhere."

I put my phone on speaker and poked the screen to call Lucas. He picked up after a few rings, sounding tired and subdued. His voice was a rich baritone and he had an easy cadence when he spoke. The producers of his show loved both the voice and the way he looked on camera. Lucas had blond hair that he wore longer than was fashionable, but it gave the impression of someone who had no time for something so trivial, rather than vanity. Close-up shots emphasized intelligent gray eyes that conveyed honesty and sincerity to the viewers. Objectively speaking, Lucas was gorgeous and the camera loved him. But there were a lot of male models out there, primping and posing for the camera. What set Lucas apart was that he was unconcerned with his looks and completely unaware of his appeal.

"Hey, Lucas. I have you on speaker. Cam's here with me."

Cam leaned towards the phone. "How's it going, Lucas? I hear you have a job for us."

Lucas seemed to perk up and he sounded more animated. "Oh, yeah! What do you think of making a trip to Scotland?"

Cam's brow furrowed and he blew out a breath. "I don't know what Fia thinks, but I'd be delighted. There's a bit of a problem though… We have something local cooking right now."

Lucas did not speak for a moment. "I hadn't considered that." He sounded dejected and a little lost and my heart went out to him. The happiness from a moment ago had evaporated.

"Do you have a feel for when the Scotland thing might happen?" I bit my lip and held my breath. If we had to go right away, this would be a non-starter. We couldn't leave Peyton in the lurch, but I held out hope that we could make this work. Lucas's happiness meant a great deal to me. He wasn't in a good place and maybe a trip abroad would help turn things around.

Lucas blew out a breath. "Well, the producers want this done yesterday. I'm not sure I can stall them." He went silent again, but then tried for a Hail Mary. "Any chance I can jump on your local thing? If we had something to air in the near future, they might be persuaded to wait."

I exchanged a sad glance with Cam and my heart sank. "I don't think we can do it. The person involved is unaware of the underlying nature of the incidents and we're trying to resolve it without her being any the wiser."

Cam snorted. "She thinks it's a raccoon."

Lucas huffed out a rusty laugh. "Maybe it is. There are frequently rational, perfectly mundane explanations for what people experience."

I smiled at how he stubbornly held on to reasonable explanations, even after all we'd been through. "Yeah, Lucas, not this time."

Lucas groaned. “I have another call on the line. Hold on just a sec.” When he came back to our call, he sounded dull and listless again. “Can we maybe talk later? The producers just called and want to discuss sponsors.”

Cam’s brow furrowed at the sound of Lucas’s voice, but then he nudged me in the ribs. “How about we get together for dinner this week? I’ll give you a call later to pick a date.”

Promising to make contact soon, we said our goodbyes. Cam rubbed his face and then looked at me with bloodshot eyes. “Shall we go see if we can do something for Maggie?”

“Don’t we need Zackie for this?” Just as the words left my mouth, Zackie announced her return by poking me in the back of the head with her muzzle. “Never mind. I’ll meet you there.”

# # #

Gloaming, a Scottish word for twilight, seemed like the best description for the dying light. We stood in the forest as the sun began to set, infected by the melancholia from the clearing where Maggie had taken her life. The leaves, the trees and the sky were all in shades of gray, the air oppressive and still. She knelt in the leaves, arms wrapped around her torso, holding herself as she rocked. Maggie muttered something in a low voice that seemed to repeat, but the cadence of the refrain broke when she abruptly stopped and shook her head, spraying droplets of blood from her short, dark hair. Her hands reached up to her ruined head, but then dropped back before making contact, once again grasping at her torso.

Dropping to his knees, Cam placed his hands on her shoulders. “Maggie, it’s all right now. We’ll help you.” He sounded far away and his voice made a hollow echo in my ears.

Twisting away, Maggie rocked harder. “You’re not there, you’re not there, you’re not there…” The litany of denial went on and on as she refused to listen. Zackie crouched near her bowed head to reach Maggie’s face with tentative touches of her muzzle. Sobbing with naked grief, Maggie leaned in towards this comfort, but then wrenched herself away. “I can’t. I’m sorry… I’m sorry.” Her voice shrank to a thin, spidery whisper as her form faded and we were left alone in the clearing.

Cam looked at me with large, helpless eyes and Zackie circled the clearing, frantic to find the scent of that tortured soul. I closed my eyes and shook my head, swallowing hard on the funky, earthen taste in my mouth. “She’s in so much pain, Cam.” Wiping my mouth with the back of my good hand, I looked around the clearing for any signs of Maggie. “We can’t leave her like this.”

“She’s left us. I don’t know what we can do at this point.” Cam forced himself to his feet.

Unwilling to give up, I turned in a slow circle and called to her. “Maggie, come back. We can help you. You don’t have to stay like this.” I forced my senses to the extremes of their reach, desperate to make contact, and it took my breath away for a moment. I bent forward with my hands on my knees, recovering before I tried again. “Zackie can make the pain stop. You have to come back.” I gave it a moment, but felt nothing except the empty night.

Cam turned on his flashlight and walked in the direction of the trail. “Come on. She’s not going to come back.” Zackie followed him, making soft whining sounds. Both her head and tail were slung low and her pace dragged as she left the clearing. I wasn’t feeling much better, but staying here was futile. Reaching for the headlamp that gripped my baseball cap, I clicked on the light and followed Cam and Zackie back to the trail.

After a few minutes of silent thought, Cam ventured forth with a hesitant analysis. “She kept saying that we weren’t there.” He paused and stepped over a fallen log before continuing. “Do you think maybe she was not a believer in the afterlife? To discover existence was not over when the body dies would come as a terrible shock to someone who died by suicide.”

“It’s possible…” I let the thought trail and released my foot from a vine. “You think she’ll come around if we just give her time to adjust?”

Cam grunted a little as a rock tipped under his foot, turning his ankle a small ways before he adjusted his balance. “Probably, but that’s assuming we’re right about her.” He stopped and cast his flashlight in front of us, seeking the best way through the forest growth. Skirting a briar patch, he continued walking and talking through the difficult case that was Maggie. “She also said she was sorry. That statement combined with her method of suicide indicates she might feel guilty about something.”

“Maybe she was apologizing for not being able to

move on when Zackie offered." I tried to untangle a thorny branch from my shirt, but ended up cutting it with my multi-tool to get free. Ducking my head to avoid some branches, I stepped forward. "While we let Maggie simmer, we should try to understand her story. That might give us a clue if we're on the right path."

"How about asking Jill Creighton?"

Working through a thicket, a branch caught me in the face and I was happy to be wearing eye protection. I answered Cam as I untangled my hair from snagging branches. "She was at the search, so she might know something."

Cam caught himself as he stumbled over a decaying branch, but then picked up the conversation when he was steady on his feet again. "Cops talk to each other. I'll bet she knows something about what happened with Maggie. If nothing else, we could at least get confirmation that it really was suicide. Remember the search for Amy Turpin?"

My head snapped up and I almost tripped. "How am I supposed to forget that? Zackie almost killed a guy."

"Focus, Fia." Cam made an exasperated noise. "What you're not supposed to forget is that we made a wrong assumption. Amy was not a despondent. If we had been more critical at the start, we would not have ended up on the wrong end of a .38 special."

I nodded slowly and picked my way through the vines that tripped Cam. Thanks to Zackie, we survived and also thanks to Zackie, the explanation for our survival was considered an unbelievable stroke of luck. Jill Creighton was a New Jersey State Trooper on the search and we discussed this mad miracle over cold pizza as I waited for the police to finish questioning Cam. When Jill learned that in addition to almost being shot, I had also recently lost my job, she helped hook me up with my new gig at the crime scene cleanup company. A friend indeed…

Sighing with relief, we emerged from the woods and hit the trail back to the parking lot. "I'll give Jill a call tomorrow to see if she knows anything. But here's the thing, this feels like a suicide to me. I get all the telltale sensations that, for me, are linked to suicide."

"Look Fia, you might be right, you might be wrong. The best you can say is the sensations you experience are consistent with suicide. Don't disregard them, but don't completely buy into them. Untangling the emotional states involved in a death is a complex problem. It's possible to feel similar sensations for different reasons." He stopped on the trail, waiting until I nodded that I understood what he was telling me. "You can use your senses to rule something out, but it's impossible to make a definitive judgment based on your perceptions alone. The best advice I can give you is to get as much information from different lines of evidence as you can before drawing a conclusion."

"Nothing's ever simple, is it?" I shook my head and kicked at a small rock. My shoulders slumped a little as I followed Cam up the trail. Just when I thought I was mastering this stuff, I learned a little more and saw the limits of my understanding.

"If it were simple, no one would be earthbound. We could just point them to the portal and be done with it." We walked quietly for a while and I let the lesson sink in. Just before we reached the parking lot, Cam spoke again. "While you're chasing down Jill, don't forget about Ron Falling-Leaf. We need to know if he can help with our angry, trailer-thumping friend."

I made a check mark in the air to let him know I'd do it and continued to the parking lot.

CHAPTER 2

I had gone to bed feeling virtuous. Even though we had not been able to bring closure to any of the spirits under our care, it was at least a start. I had even been able to get in some grocery shopping after our interlude with Maggie. Everything was as under control as anyone could hope. But I awoke feeling crappy and unwilling to get my day started.

I sat on the edge of the bed and contemplated the heavy neoprene diving glove on my dead hand. I normally sleep with a light, cotton glove, but upon waking up and making my discovery, I leaped out of bed and put the heavy glove on over the sleeping glove. The dead hand had been active last night. In addition to a burnt piece of paper on my nightstand, one of the large kitchen knives also graced this surface. A sense of dread had shot me through me as I gazed at the staged display. Hoping against hope, I had probed my environment for the presence of a spirit, desperately wanting to find an alternate explanation. But the fact was, the dead hand had somehow persuaded the rest of my sleeping body to get up and do things. This knowledge left me feeling shaky and not in control.

This dead hand was violating my autonomy and the more I thought about it, the more outraged I became. Outrage was better than feeling weak and powerless, so I deliberately fed the anger and thought about all the dangerous and humiliating possibilities of not being in control when I slept. What if I woke up one morning in a back alley shooting heroin, or maybe peeling off the pasties as I left a strip club? The anger got my blood flowing and made me want to hit something. I have few possessions, all bought with hard-earned money and I didn't really want to sacrifice anything to this growing rage. I reined it in, stood up and stalked off to the shower to get ready for work. In a world frequently ruled by chaos, my first step was always self-control.

I was still seething as I shoved spoonfuls of cereal in my mouth and gulped coffee, but my mind churned, thinking it through and forming and rejecting ideas to deal with this new threat. I finally decided to tell Cam about this latest symptom and ask him to take me in if it got worse.

We could buy handcuffs and he could lock me down every night. Of course, this all might be an overreaction. The dead hand had never done anything remotely like this before, so it was possible this event was a one-off. We might never have to resort to a lockdown, but I wanted a plan, just in case. With a working solution to manage the situation, I forced myself to pretend everything was normal and got through the routine of washing the breakfast dishes and driving to work.

Cleanup work tended to be sporadic. While each job paid pretty well, the frequency of jobs was fairly random, ebbing and flowing according to local crime rates, suicides and random deaths. Happy to have been called in, I wasn't about to screw this up, issues with my dead hand or not.

Arriving at the job site, two white company vehicles stood in the driveway, so I parked in front of the house. Both the truck and the van bore discreet labels with the company name "BioSolutions" written in an unassuming font. People did not want to chat about crime scene cleanup with their neighbors, thus the non-descript company name and low-key presence. We were not the type of company that could leave a little sign on the front lawn to advertise our efforts when the job was done.

I walked to the truck and met Robert Gander, my on-site boss. Looking up to read the expression on his weathered face, I felt reassured that I wasn't late, and offered a greeting. In stark contrast to his mahogany skin, Gander wore a white hazmat suit that distinguished him as the consummate professional, on the scene and ready for action. This was my second job with Gander and I had so far learned just enough from him to get into trouble, if left to my own devices. The job was more than just cleaning, requiring a lot of technical know-how to prevent spreading biohazardous contamination. Coming around the truck and limping into view was the site safety specialist. JoJo Kennelly had a lot of metal in him from a motorcycle accident in his youth, so he couldn't do any of the heavy work. His job was to make sure we were properly suited up before entering any hazardous area. JoJo reminded me of an Old English Sheepdog, with a heavy fringe of gray hair flopping into his eyes and a sturdy build.

"Morning, Fia. Step in and suit up." Gander held the truck's door open for me and I made my way inside the vehicle. As soon as the door shut, I stripped down, placing everything I was wearing into a large, plastic container. Donning disposable underwear and socks, I stepped into the Tyvek hazmat suit and zipped up. Next came the boots, which I duct-taped around my ankles before pulling on disposable boot covers and duct-taping these securely to the boots. Grabbing a tight-fitting cotton hood, called a spray sock, I pulled it over my head and down my neck, and then enlarged the holes around my eyes and mouth so they could accommodate the goggles and the respirator. Corporate drilled into us the importance of universal precautions, which meant treating all bodily fluids as if they were infectious for bloodborne pathogens like HIV, hepatitis B and other stuff they don't even know to test for yet. We suited up for every job and everything we removed from a site was treated as a biohazard.

After running some tape down the zipper front to seal it, I grabbed goggles, a respirator, and then slipped on two pairs of nitrile gloves before hopping out of the truck. I guess I was still slow in suiting up, since a short line had formed outside the truck door. "Sorry, guys."

"No problemo, Fia." Goose favored me with a lazy smile and tucked a wild strand of white blond hair behind an ear. His real name was John Broker and he was a transplanted West Coast surfer dude. He adopted Goose as his handle after he started working for Gander and kept repeating that whatever was good for the Goose was good for the Gander, not realizing that since Gander was the boss, the order ought to have been reversed. Goose jabbed a thumb towards the new guy standing behind him. "Oh, hey, this grommet is Rory Craymore."

The new guy nodded my way. "Call me Roar." I honestly didn't think I could, so I just nodded back. He simply didn't look like someone with that name. His build wasn't fat or thin, just middling and kind of doughy. He was a little on the short side, with dull brown hair and a bland, non-descript face that would not stand out in a crowd. Rory Craymore would have made an excellent spy because no one would ever notice him. Apparently, an attention-grabbing name was a way to overcompensate for his physical limitations.

Gander propped the truck's door open and motioned for the guys to get in and suit up. Once the two men were sealed in, Gander leaned against the closed door and then cocked his head, looking to me for clarification. "What does grommet mean?"

"I think it means something like newbie." Oddly, my ability to interpret spirit meaning also seemed to work in translating surfer speak.

Nodding, Gander folded his arms across his chest and filled me in on the job. “What we have here is an unattended death.” He spoke with a gentle, Southern drawl and his tone was very matter-of-fact. “An elderly man passed away from natural causes and, unfortunately, his passing went unnoticed for several weeks.”

“And that’s where we come in?” I could only imagine what I’d be scrubbing today.

“Correct. The heirs wanted to sell the house, but they can’t put it on the market in its current condition. Remediation will include a mattress in the master bedroom, possibly the floor underneath it and we’ll have to neutralize the odor throughout the house.”

I turned to look at the house in question. It was ranch style and that was a big help when removing contaminated items. I was happy not to have to run up and down stairs to deal with the bedroom, but if anything leaked through the floorboards, I might end up going up and down the stairs to the basement. As I surveyed the house, I caught a glimpse of an old man with white, wispy hair gazing at us from a window. Glasses distorted his watery blue eyes and made them appear enormous. His mouth hung partially open in shock and he clutched at a gray cardigan around his thin chest, his fingers worrying the edges of the garment near his neck where a swarm of maggots crawled in decaying flesh. Just as our eyes met, Goose and the new guy piled out of the truck and my attention was drawn away. By the time I looked back, the man in the window had disappeared. Tensing, I bit my lip, but forced my attention back to the job.

The final touches of suiting up required JoJo's help. After taping the hood to the hazmat suit, he then snugged the sleeves around the wrists of our gloves with some more tape and we were at last ready to slip on the goggles and respirators. I was just starting to drip sweat when Gander directed us to the van where we loaded up on duct tape, zip ties, a large roll of heavy plastic and some biohazard bags. Burdened with the tools of our trade, we entered the house through the back door. The smell hit me immediately, but I did my best not to show it. Goose was a veteran of these jobs and was not so inhibited in front of Gander. "Bro, good thing they hired us. That's foul, totally buggery."

Gander led the way through the living room and then cut right to a hallway that took us past the open doors of an office and a guest room. Aside from the odor and a thin film of dust collecting on surfaces, the house seemed neat and orderly. The last room at the end was the master bedroom. On the bed lay a comforter and sheets, stiff and encrusted with a dried substance that proved to be the source of the house-penetrating odor. I set to work stripping the bed, first placing the pillows in a biohazard bag and sealing the twisted end closed with a zip tie. Next, I unhooked the corners of the fitted sheet from the mattress and wrapped the other sheets inside of this, keeping the contaminating material contained in the bundle. This too went into a biohazard bag. Grabbing a bag in each hand, I headed out of the bedroom while the others hoisted the mattress and began sealing it in heavy-duty plastic.

As I turned to enter the hallway, I encountered the old man as he peeked around the corner of the doorframe into the bedroom. Twisting his fingers in the opening of his cardigan, he spoke in a whisper. "I am so dreadfully sorry about the mess." He wouldn't meet my eyes as he apologized and his cheeks flushed a deep red. I had to jerk my head twice before he noticed that I was indicating that we needed to move away from the open door before we could speak. Once I had his attention, I moved farther up the hall and he followed.

Putting down the bags, I turned to him and felt

sweat trickling down my ribs. "It's not your fault. This is completely natural. We'll clean it up and it will look like nothing ever happened, okay?"

He nodded, but I could feel his misery and mortification that strangers saw his house in such a state. Was he a neatnik in life? The messiness of death must really offend his sensibilities. I did what I could to reassure him. "Why don't you keep watch for a while and make sure that everything is spick and span? If you see anything that still isn't right when we're done, you can let me know and I'll make sure we leave your house spotless."

The old man gave me a shy smile. "Thank you for doing this." Having a small measure of control over the mess seemed to put him more at ease. I smiled back the best I could through the respirator, picked up the bags and continued to the van. Depositing the bags in the back of the vehicle, I made sure there would be plenty of room for the mattress and box spring.

By the time I returned to the bedroom, the old man was stationed at the threshold watching the activity. The guys had wrapped and sealed the mattress, using duct tape to hold it all together and to add handles that would help us to carry it out. I grabbed a handle towards the front and the new guy took up the rear.

Rory Craymore did not look like he had much experience with malevolent odors. The respirators did little to filter out the stench, so I couldn't really blame him when he pushed his face into his arm and made a small retching noise. "Gaah! So, like, was that dead guy made out of shit, or something?"

Everyone paused what they were doing and looked at the new guy. The old man put his hands up to cover his face. He looked out from between his fingers, deeply ashamed, his eyes wide and his face coloring with embarrassment. Gander crossed his arms over his chest and stared at Rory. Without voicing any disapproval, his silence spoke volumes about being more respectful of the dead.

Goose looked at the floor and slowly shook his head. "Uncool, grommet."

I cleared my throat and spoke up, more for the old man's sake than to chastise the new guy. "Look, everyone's body will do this." Gazing at the new guy, I kept my voice low and gentle. "That will be you some day, so don't act all offended by it." I picked up my end of the mattress. The new guy stood rigid as he stared at me, his hands balled into fists. He was probably pissed by everyone's reaction and decided he wanted to take it out on me, since being female, I was the least likely to deck him. As much as I wanted to prove him wrong, I wanted to keep this job more. Ignoring his reaction, I tried to get the work back on track. "Come on, let's move this out." For a moment, nothing happened, but then the Rory unclenched his fists and yanked the mattress up from the floor. Goose and Gander exchanged a look as we moved out.

Reaching the van, we slid the mattress in on its edge, braced it against a wall and then returned to the bedroom. Experience showed as Goose and Gander repeated the duct taping process with the box spring. Before we really had a chance to rest, they had completed the job. As Goose maneuvered the wrapped box spring towards us, Gander stepped over the bed frame and examined the floor.

"Good news. Looks like everything was contained in the bed. The floor's okay." Sweeping his eyes along the headboard and the bed frame, Gander nodded. "Nothing on the bed frame either." Goose carefully checked the ceiling and the walls surrounding the bed and gave a thumbs up.

Goose and Gander squeezed past the box spring and

headed for the van, leaving the new guy and me to finish the carryout. By the time we reached the van, Gander had unloaded two heat-powered foggers and Goose was pulling out jugs of Thermo-55 disinfectant-deodorant.

Carrying two jugs, I went back in the house, ostensibly to watch how the fogger was set up. The old man stood in the bedroom with his hands clasped behind his back and a smile on his face as we set up the machine. As I asked my question, I watched the old guy listen in. "So, what's the point of running the fogger?"

Gander answered me as he poured the chemical into the machine. "The Thermo-55 will coat the entire interior of the house and make everything smell like cherries. It even has insecticide to kill insects, so after this double whammy, the house ought to be market-ready."

"So, afterwards everything will be done here and we can move on?" I said this last part looking the old man in the eye.

After turning on the device, Gander called over his shoulder to me as he picked up the machine and started fogging the room. "Yes, but I'm not sure what we'd move on to. There's no new job scheduled yet." The old man, meanwhile, nodded to me with a smile. Feeling secure that he was good to go, I trailed after Gander and helped to refill the machine as he fogged each room, moving from the master bedroom toward the backdoor exit. Goose and the grommet fogged everything from the basement to the opposite end of the house. Between both teams, the house was sanitized in no time. We locked the back door behind us and headed to the truck. Respirators, goggles and boots went to JoJo to sterilize. Everything else was disposed of in a biohazard bag before hitting the truck's shower to decontaminate. I washed off the sweat and who-knows-what-else from the house and was squeaky clean by the time I drove home.

###

"She was pregnant." Jill was about to start her shift and was talking fast, but I heard these three words loud and clear. After getting home and cooking a grilled cheese sandwich for lunch, I made several futile attempts to contact Ron Falling-Leaf. When none of my old contact information worked, I decided to call Jill Creighton to see if she had any new information on Maggie. State Troopers usually work a twelve hour tour from seven a.m. to seven p.m., or vice versa, so realistically, I had little hope of speaking to her and figured I'd just leave a message. To my surprise, Jill picked up on the third ring. She told me she was about to start a flex shift from three to three and she didn't have a lot of time to chat.

"Pregnant…" My lips were numb as I thought of the sad figure of Maggie, alone in the woods. "Is this from the autopsy?"

"No. Autopsy hasn't been performed yet. She was visibly pregnant when they stored her body and it was in her medical records from the accident." Something scraped against the receiver and Jill cursed. "Sorry, got caught on the earpiece. I'm trying to get my uniform on."

"What's the deal with the accident?"

"Car accident. The husband died. She was severely injured. Head trauma. That's all I've got."

"Will you let me know if anything funny turns up in the autopsy?"

"You want to know if this is another Amy Turpin? Suicide or homicide? Sure."

The question was unspoken, but I thought I owed

Jill some kind of explanation for why I was following up. "Thanks for helping. Just trying to fill in the gaps on lost person behavior. It'll help with future searches."

After we said our good-byes, I immediately dialed Cam to tell him what Jill said.

Cam let out a whooshing breath. "Really? Pregnant?" The soft clicking of a keyboard came over the phone. "I'm looking up the obituary for the husband. She was pregnant when the accident was reported, so the funeral must have been held in the last few months." Cam was a genealogist and had access to more databases than was healthy for normal folk.

Feeling like I ought to be doing something, I got up and started pacing around the little card table where I ate my meals. "How's the obituary going to help us? It seems obvious that she was depressed because she lost her husband."

"We don't know how anything can help until we take a look." After a few more clicks, Cam continued. "Here it is. Gregory Pierceson." I listened to him breathe while he read the article. "It says he leaves behind a wife named Maggie and they'd been married seven years."

"No other children?"

"No, this would have been their first."

I rubbed some dried cheese off the corner of my mouth and thought about that. "Either this was a whoops baby or they'd been trying for a while."

"Or they waited until things were right with their jobs or they'd saved enough money to buy a home. Who knows?" Cam sounded distracted as he typed some more. "I'm pulling up the accident. It must have happened a short time before the date of the funeral."

I was still stuck on the implications of a late pregnancy. "Well, whatever the reasons for waiting to have a baby, I think that this would be a reason to hang on – not to kill herself. The baby was the last thing she had left of her husband. You'd think she'd want to live and have it."

"Maybe… Is there such a thing as prepartum depression? I'll look that up next. Meanwhile, I've got the news report on the accident in front of me." There was a pause as he read the article. "It happened last spring. They were driving at night and there was a sudden downpour. He was at the wheel and lost control of the vehicle. Slammed into a tree. Based on the picture of the wreck, she was lucky to have survived."

"So, no other vehicle and no one to blame? No reason to stay earthbound for vengeance?"

Cam took a moment to skim the article. "Doesn't look that way. Just a single-car crash. No mention of alcohol or drugs. It must have just been an accident. Bad luck."

"Okay…Can you look up prepartum depression?" I did another lap around the table while he clicked.

"Huh. It does exist. Says here that doctors used to think that pregnancy was a 'honeymoon' away from depression risk, but that turned out to be a myth."

"So, maybe she was just depressed?" I went still and waited for his answer.

"And this was exacerbated by the loss of her husband? Maybe, but why the gun? I still think that says something about her state of mind."

"Maybe it was just convenient. The gun was there and she used it."

"There's nothing convenient about trekking a half

mile into wilderness and then blowing your brains out. I don't think so." Cam sighed into the phone. "The gun is meaningful."

I shrugged my shoulders. "You might be right." Forcing damp bangs out of my face, I took a deep breath and held it for a few seconds and then slowly blew it out. "What do you think we should do next?"

"We'll have to go back and talk to her. We need to see if anything we're coming up with strikes a chord."

I rubbed my face with my good hand. "Okay, fine. But let's go during daylight this time and put up some flagging tape along the easiest path to the clearing. I don't think this is going to be our last trip there."

Cam grumbled something affirming my thoughts and we made plans to meet the next day. With exaggerated casualness and alarming speed, he changed the subject. "By the way, tonight's our dinner with Lucas. Wear something nice. He's treating, so it won't be fast food."

I stopped my pacing and put a hand to my damp hair. "Dude, really? Tonight?"

"Oh, come on. As if you had any plans tonight." It

sounded like he was smirking, as he filled me in on where and when we would meet. Resigned, I just nodded and jotted down the time and the name of the restaurant. As I stared at the dead hand dutifully scribing my appointment, I decided I could not put off telling Cam about the events of the morning.

"One last thing before we hang up. I need to tell you about a new symptom." Pacing around the table in the opposite direction, I spoke rapidly in a monotone and gave Cam the facts as I knew them about the message from the dead hand. "So, if this gets worse, I'll need you to lock me down at night." I said this as matter-of-factly as I could manage and then tensed for his reply.

"Was this a threat or a warning?" Cam kept his voice all business.

"How the hell should I know?" I dragged my hand through my hair and started pacing again.

"It's your hand…" Cam was really forcing himself to sound reasonable and logical, but the strain came through.

"Is it?" I heard my voice crack as I spoke and immediately regretted this loss of control. Striving for a flippant tone, I continued. "So, what you're saying is that I need to get in touch with my dead side? Maybe go to couple's therapy? Cause, you know, it never really listens to me when I ask it to take out the trash."

Cam was silent for a moment. "You know I'll help you any way I can. You don't have to deal with this by yourself."

I took a breath and paused before answering. He really did have my back and I trusted him completely. "Yeah, I know. Thanks, Cam." I tried to sound as grateful as I felt.

After ending the call, I needed to get out. Grabbing a jacket, I walked down the driveway to Joel Armstrong's house. He was my landlord and as part of my rent, I walked his dogs while he was at work. Joel was a contractor and he was always out early and back late and the dogs' need to pee tended to fit my schedule better than his. Heckle and Jeckle were yellow and black labs, and it was a nice change of pace hanging around regular dogs sometimes. Unlike Zackie, they never gave me sarcastic looks or made me feel stupid with a conversationally well-timed, snarky huffing noise. Just as the dogs and I returned from my daily drag around the block, Joel's red pickup pulled into the driveway. I felt a prickly sense of déjà vu creep up my scalp and I unconsciously touched the scar on my temple, a reminder of a few months ago when Joel had also shown up unexpectedly early after a dog walk. He had let loose with a story about seeing a dead little girl and this led to the most horrific encounter with a spirit that I had ever faced.

Stepping out of the truck, Joel wore a sunny smile and I let out the breath I was holding. "How's it going, Fia?"

I took some involuntary steps forward as the dogs dragged me to Joel. "Oh, you know, same old, same old. What's up with you?"

Joel was as excited as I'd ever seen him. He was a big man and his gray hair gave him the air of respectability, but he was practically bouncing on his toes like a five year old. "We're working on this historic house over in Phillipsburg. It's called the Roseberry Homestead. I have a book somewhere about the old ways of construction and I wanted to bring it to the site."

"Cool. How old is the house?"

"Might have been built around the Revolutionary War by the looks of it." The dogs nudged his hands with their noses. "Aw, who's a good boy?" Joel reached down and rubbed the dogs' heads before continuing. "It's a stone house and we're gonna need to repair the masonry after we fix the roof and then think about installing windows and doors that are right for that era. We're working with an architectural historian to make sure we get things right."

I nodded, impressed by the need for historical accuracy in the project. "I have a friend who's studying to be a master stonemason. I think she'd be really interested in this kind of preservation work."

Joel grinned and spread his hands expansively. "The more the merrier. Bring her by. I'll let you know when the historian will be onsite."

###

I was under-dressed for an upscale restaurant like the Meridian, but my belly was growling, so I was determined to brazen my way through the meal. I wore a simple white top with dark slacks and flats. A little black dress with heels would have been more appropriate for this place, but due to an overwhelming need to pay the rent, that was not the type of outfit hanging in my wardrobe. At least my hair was dry. I had deliberately pulled it back in a loose ponytail to keep it out of my food. I figured this was one less thing that could go wrong during the meal. I even ate a little before I left, so that I wouldn't automatically start stuffing myself, but this was to no avail. My stomach made it clear that it wanted to be fed again.

When I arrived, both Cam and Lucas stood near the maitre d's podium waiting for me. Lucas opened his arms for a hug as I approached. "Fia, great seeing you."

"Good to see you, too." I hugged him back and I swear, my pupils dilated and my heart gave a hard squeeze in my chest. As I stepped back, I forced a smile and tried to act unaffected by the contact. Standing this close to him, I got a whiff of sandalwood cologne, but also a faint ammonia smell that I associated with hospitals. Hannah must be near. I raised an eyebrow at Cam and he returned the gesture with a slight nod. He sensed her too. As always, the only one unaware of a discarnate presence was Lucas. This must have been incredibly frustrating for Hannah.

Turning to the maitre d', Lucas smiled and gestured towards Cam and me. "This is all of us."

"Very good, Mr. Tremaine. Let me show you to

your table." The man turned smartly, tucked three menus under his arm and proceeded through the crowded dining room to a corner table near a window. I sat down in the seat he proffered and stared out at the great view of the fall foliage, all lit up by the setting sun.

Looking through the menu, I eliminated the onion soup, the lobster and any pasta dishes from consideration. My white blouse would not survive these. Just as our server appeared, I settled on the salmon and crossed my fingers.

"My name is Angela and I will be your server tonight. Can I start you off with something to drink?" Angela was a petite young woman. With her doe eyes and lustrous, long hair, she probably did okay with tips. To be fair, she also appeared to be calm and competent, as opposed to the irritated and put-upon demeanor that I radiated when I was waiting tables. Lucas and Cam both ordered glasses of red wine. Glancing down at my shirt again, I asked for a club soda. I could both quench my thirst and do any touch ups that might be necessary.

When Angela returned with the drinks, she asked if we were ready to order. I requested the salmon, Lucas ordered the seafood fra diavolo and Cam went with beef sirloin tips au jus. Once the waitress left with our orders, the conversation ambled along at a comfortable pace. We talked about the weather, sports and the radical departure from our normal diet that this meal presented, thanking Lucas for his generosity. He brushed it off and said his production company was footing the bill. Officially, this was a business dinner, so as long as we spoke about ghost hunting at some point during the meal, all was copacetic. The conversation reached a lull and Lucas turned to me and touched my hand.

"So, how have you been?" His eyes were shadowed from lack of sleep and he looked like he might have lost a little weight. I should have been asking him this question.

"I'm doing okay. The new job is interesting." I made no effort to move my hand as I continued to study his face, holding his eyes and trying to freeze this moment. In the past, I would have found some excuse to get up and move away, but things were different now that Hannah was dead. To lessen any residual guilt I felt about touching a deceased woman's husband, I reminded myself that he was the one who initiated contact. I was merely doing everything in my power to sustain it.

Trying to get our attention, Cam interrupted. "I am also doing well." At least, I think that's what he said. I confess that I wasn't paying much attention. Something else besides Cam was niggling at the edges of my conscious mind, but my full attention was on Lucas and nothing beyond his touch was really breaking through. Until it did. The scent of ammonia became overpowering and my eyes started to water. In that instant, Angela showed up with a large tray laden with our meals. As she used one hand to open a small support table to receive her burden, two bloodless, white hands grasped the edge of the tray and flipped it towards me. The entire contents of each dish poured over my chest and landed in my lap. I was coated in tomato sauce, au jus and lemony butter, as well as the more solid components of each meal. All conversation in the dining room ceased and I felt the hot glare of attention. Grinding my teeth, I thought that the club soda I ordered wasn't going to cut it.

Angela's eyes filled with tears and she began apologizing up and down for dumping the food on me. Conversation hummed back to life as the maitre d' rushed over and handed me several napkins to mop up the worst of it. I was certain Angela would be afraid of losing her job, so grinning, I tried to make light of the accident. "Okay, pressure's off. I don't have to worry about staining my shirt anymore." As I stood to make my way to the lady's room, I tried to do some damage control with the maitre d' to help poor Angela. "It wasn't her fault. Someone brushed by her as she was setting the tray down."

On the way to the ladies' room, I thought better of it and headed out to my car instead. Rummaging through the search and rescue equipment in my trunk, I came up with a bright orange tactical shirt. Back in the restaurant, I found the ladies' room, took a look at myself in the mirror and decided it was a good thing I was already in a mindset to brazen it out. Removing the shirt that used to be white, I chucked it in the garbage. It was never going to come clean. I did a quick wipe down of my arms and torso with some wet paper towels and then slipped on the tactical shirt. Surveying my slacks for damage, I found that they were better off than the shirt. The napkin had caught a good deal of the mess and the black fabric hid a lot of the stains. Still, I left the tails of the shirt out. As I ran my hands through my hair to make sure nothing needed cleaning there, I caught the odor of ammonia and then the image of Hannah in the mirror. She stood behind me, grinning like the Cheshire Cat. Hannah looked every inch the cancer fatality and I felt a surge of pity for her. Still dressed in a hospital gown, her head was denuded of hair, including eyebrows and eyelashes, and it made her face appear washed out and vaguely reptilian. Black streaks traced the veins in her arms where the chemo had been injected and she was painfully thin. Despite all this, her grin had more mischief than malice.

I met her eyes in the reflection and let her have her moment. "Ha, ha. Very funny." Doubling over with laughter, Hannah's guffaws echoed in the bathroom as she disappeared. Determined not to let her have her way completely, I marched to our table, resplendent in my ridiculous, high visibility orange shirt. If I thought that I was under-dressed before, this look sealed the deal.

As I made my way through the dining room, I felt countless eyes boring through me. I've been stared at many times in my life after experiencing worse episodes involving unruly spirits, so I was practiced at feigning nonchalance. Squaring my shoulders, I set my face into a neutral expression and began another Oscar-winning performance. I froze when the diners broke out in a spontaneous round of applause. Scanning the room, there was no sign of derision or mockery. The diners' faces were open and approving and some even smiled. Playing along, I forced a smile and acknowledged my new fans with an improvised curtsy before continuing my progress towards

Cam and Lucas. Both men stood as I reached the table and I resisted the urge to say something sarcastic to cut the formality.

Whether or not he intended to, Cam took the white hot spotlight of attention away by raising his wine glass in a toast and congratulating me. “Well done, Fia. They comped the meal.” He took a sip and then bowed his head in mock sadness. “I only wish now that I had been paying.”

Lucas rolled his eyes and held out my seat. “Are you all right? You didn’t get burned or anything?”

I sat down quickly to make myself a smaller target. “I’m fine. Just starving. Are they bringing the food out soon?”

Cam raised an eyebrow at Lucas. “Obviously, she’s not too traumatized to eat.”

Lucas nodded back solemnly. “We’ll know for sure something’s wrong if she doesn’t eat.”

I narrowed my eyes at Lucas. “That’s it, Tremaine. Just for that, I get your dessert.” There was no point in telling him Hannah was behind the spill. He wouldn’t believe it. Grabbing a freshly folded napkin from the new table setting, I unfurled it with a flourish and placed it on my lap as I considered conversational topics that would take the focus from me. "So, what's going on in Scotland that needs our attention?"

Folding his hands on the table, Lucas became serious. "Well, it's only hearsay at this point. I haven't gone to investigate the reports, so I can't vouch for their credibility."

Cam waved his hand, circumventing the coming lecture. "Yes, yes, rationale explanations and logical interpretations. Yada, yada, yada. We understand."

"You know me so well." Cracking a grin, Lucas accepted the conversational redirect.

I shook my head and had to ask. "So, you've never experienced anything that would lead you to a supernatural explanation?" Would he have something new to say now that Hannah was always near? He must have gotten a faint whiff of ammonia or felt a chill in an otherwise warm room, or maybe even seen something out of the corner of his eye.

Lucas didn't even blink. "I see what you're getting at." But he didn't see what I was getting at. He responded as if it were a philosophical question. "I admit that what happened to us at the Changewater house and in North Carolina are still open questions. Something very unusual happened in these places, but I'm still not convinced the events can't be explained by natural phenomena. It's just going to take someone smarter than me to come up with these explanations." Lucas shrugged his shoulders and sipped some wine before continuing. "Granted, the underlying reasons we get from experts might be weird and out of the ordinary, but I'll bet they would still conform to natural laws." He paused again and his eyes squinted as he thought for a moment and then shook his head. "Aside from the Changewater case, there's been nothing else in my experience before or since that couldn't be readily explained by either psychological predisposition or environmental conditions."

Hannah let loose with a distinctly frustrated sigh. Shaking his head, Cam gave me a look of bemusement. The depths of psychic insensitivity that one person could display took my breath away. Like Cam and me, Lucas was definitely out on the farthest reach of the bell curve for this trait. The difference was that we were on one end of the curve and he was on the other.

Cam brought us back on topic. “So, what was the nature of the reports out of Scotland?”

Leaning forward, Lucas continued his update, unaware that something tugged on the tablecloth next to him. “The gist of it is that a man was savaged by an unseen force while jogging along a country lane. A passing cyclist used his phone to record the attack. At first blush, it appears to be legitimate.”

Ignoring Hannah’s antics, I turned my thoughts to the story emerging from Scotland. “No history of attacks at this site or on the individual?” As my mind began to draw the inevitable connections, I took a sip of my club soda and started wishing I had ordered something stronger. What had tipped the balance into violence in Scotland? Did this foreshadow future behavior for our angry Native American?

Lucas shrugged. “I don’t have any background about the site or the individual, so I can’t answer these questions. We’re too early in this investigation to have interviews or even any research done.” Lucas raised an eyebrow and leaned forward. “But I can give you details on the location if you want to get a jump on this and start looking into the case.”

Cam shook his head. “Much as I’d like to give it a go, you’ve got people for that and we’ve got our hands full at the moment.”

“So you’ve mentioned.” Lucas sat back and sipped his wine. “Can you tell me anything about it? Maybe it would make a few good episodes for the show.”

Cam and I filled Lucas in, describing Maggie’s case, but being careful not to make this sound like an invitation to film. We did not bring up Peyton’s problem, since it was still possible that we could resolve the situation without anyone, especially Peyton, being the wiser. Bringing in a film crew just might tip her off.

Lucas cast his eyes down and fiddled with his silverware. “Yeah, no. I can’t and won’t do anything with Maggie’s case. It’s too fresh and it’s a suicide. We’d only do a story like this if the family called us in or if the event were years old. We don’t want to compound the tragedy for the family.”

I nodded my approval. Say what you want about how Lucas reconciled his staunch disbelief in the supernatural with being the front man on a ghost show – he was unwilling to engage in exploitation of others just to earn a buck or get attention. That was all right in my book.

My thoughts must have been too plain on my face. The scent of ammonia was again violating my airspace. Whispering in my ear, Hannah let me know her thoughts on the matter. “And that’s why I fell for him.” In the next breath, the smell was gone and I was left pondering the implications of a relationship with someone still in a relationship, despite the fulfillment of the ‘until death do us part’ vow.

The food arrived just in time to spare me any deeper thinking. Instead of a tray, several of the wait staff carried out each of the dishes and presented them to us. Better safe than sorry, I guess. Angela blushed and fussed with the place settings and would not make eye contact with anyone at the table.

I tried to get her attention. “Psst…” When Angela finally looked up, I attempted to reassure her. “I’ve also waited tables. I know what it’s like. No harm done, okay?”

Angela flashed me a shy smile and whispered back. “Thanks. I’m still really sorry.” Busy with her other tables, she dashed off after making sure everyone was content with their food and drink. All was well in my corner and I tucked into my food with gusto, no longer inhibited by a white shirt, and convinced that it would be impossible for my normal eating habits to bring me to a state as bad as the initial food avalanche.

I came out looking okay by the time dessert rolled around, aided by the properties of the tactical shirt. Aside from being made of rip-stop material, the tactical shirt was like Teflon, leaving no trace of water and food stains after a quick wipe. Surprising myself, I did not order dessert. Between the complimentary appetizers, the fresh baked bread, soup, salad, the main course, and my meal before coming to the restaurant, I was feeling uncomfortably full. This did not stop Lucas from requesting two dessert forks and offering to share his death-by-chocolate cake.

"You don't get my dessert without a fight, but I am willing to share." His eyes twinkled with amusement when he saw my dilemma. My eyes bulged from the pressure of all the food in my belly, but he held up the fork, daring me to eat more. And sharing food seemed like such an intimate gesture. Maybe this was just playfulness and I was reading more into it than was warranted, but I couldn't pass up this chance to get closer to Lucas. Besides, the sweet decadence of the cake's dark chocolate mousse filling called to me. In the immortal words of Oscar Wilde, ‘the only way to get rid of temptation is to yield to it.’

Cam pulled his strawberry cheesecake closer. “Do what you want, this is mine.”

When the meal was finally done, I resisted the urge to put my head down on the table. A food coma was coming for me and I needed to end the evening. Lucas left a substantial tip and we thanked the maitre d’ for a wonderful evening, assuring him that we would return. He looked relieved and offered to pay for my dry cleaning, which I declined. The white shirt was no longer my problem.

We parted ways in the parking lot, thanking Lucas for the night out and wishing each other a good night. As Lucas walked off to his car with a light step and a smile on his face, Cam murmured, “Mission accomplished. This is what the lad needed - a decent meal and some time away from his work and grief.”

###

Typical of flagging tape, a lot went a little way. My

roll was nearing depletion as we flagged a path to Maggie's clearing. Zackie was in high spirits, running ahead and then waiting, twitching with impatience for us to catch up. She appeared eager to make contact with Maggie again, perhaps optimistic this would be the encounter that convinces Maggie to go with her to the afterlife. I wondered why she didn't try harder with Hannah. Success with Hannah would have a huge impact on my life, but I wasn't sure how to broach the subject with Zackie. The last time I attempted two-way communication with her, I think it made my brain bleed. Conversations with an immortal required more synapses than I currently possessed. I was almost sure there was something different about Cam that made it easier for him to endure the information overload. He and Zackie seemed to be in constant casual conversation and never once had I seen evidence of even so much as a headache.

Maggie lay on her side in the bed of decaying leaves, her shaking fingers moving lightly through her hair, occasionally touching her skull where the bullet entered and then skittering away to feel her distended belly. As before, she murmured to herself, repeating the same words over and over. Zackie lay down near Maggie's head and urged the fingers away with her muzzle.

Kneeling on the leaves next to Zackie, Cam whispered to the suffering woman. “We’ve come back, Maggie. We still want to help.”

Maggie curled into a fetal position. Shutting her eyes, she put her hands over her ears. “You’re not there… not there…not there.”

I took a long look at Cam and shook my head. She was still locking us out. How could we even begin to speak to her when she refused to listen? I wasn’t sure what to do. If I grabbed her hands away from her ears and forced her to listen, would she disappear on us? As I stood there paralyzed with indecision, Zackie jumped up and planted her front paws on Maggie’s shoulders, forcing her on to her back and exposing her distended belly. Pinning her to the ground with her face inches from Maggie’s, Zackie issued one loud bark that echoed through the woods. Nothing was as loud as a Plott Hound and Maggie’s eyes sprung open, round with fear and surprise. Placing herself between Maggie’s outstretched arm and her torso, Zackie clamped her jaws around Maggie’s shoulder and lay down next to the spirit, keeping her pinned to the ground. Maggie was going nowhere and she knew it. The pain from the psychopomp’s bite made the spirit pant and grit her teeth. I felt sick for adding to her suffering, but she would flee and be lost to us if we freed her. This was a necessary evil if we were ever going to help her. Swallowing down the nausea, I knew we could not be soft, so I steeled myself to do what was necessary.

"I'm glad we finally have your attention." Cam spoke quickly and rotated on his knees to face her. "We need to talk to you about your husband, Gregory."

Maggie swallowed hard, her eyes darting from Cam to me and then finally resting on Zackie. When she did not respond, Zackie released her hold long enough to nudged Maggie under the jaw with her muzzle. Maggie whimpered, but then spoke in a thin, broken voice. "I loved him."

Kneeling on her other side, I planted my palms on the ground and leaned towards her. "Don't you want to be with him? Zackie can take you to Gregory."

Maggie wailed and shook her head, struggling to get up and away from us. "I can't! I can't go! Why won't you understand?"

Cam took her hand and held it. "Why can't you go? Can you help us understand?"

"The baby…I can't leave the baby." She thrashed and struggled, but was making no headway against Zackie.

Cam tightened his grip on her hand and reached out with his other hand to turn her face towards him. "Maggie…Maggie, look at me. The baby is dead too."

Maggie stared glassy-eyed at Cam and stopped struggling. She went limp and whispered to herself. "It's my fault. I wasn't strong enough." She sobbed and then threw her head back and screamed at the sky. "It's my fault!"

Crawling forward, I touched her cheek and tried to calm her. "It's not your fault, Maggie. Were you depressed because your husband died?" She wouldn't look at me, but I persisted. "Is that why you took the gun?"

"Nooooooo! You don't understand. I have to save the baby from them." She began howling in agony, her eyes rolling in her head and arms rigid at her sides, fingers clawing at the earth.

Cam gripped her other shoulder and was about to speak when Zackie erupted in a low, warning growl. Her message was clear. We needed to stop. Now. This was torturing Maggie. Cam and I clambered to our feet and backed away to give them space. Licking the tears from Maggie's face, Zackie made soft sounds until gradually, the howling gave way to low moans and Maggie threw her arms around the psychopomp, desperately seeking comfort. Laying her chest on Maggie's upper body, Zackie continued to sooth her until she was quiet. In slow motion, she placed first one paw and then another on the ground, finally releasing Maggie. Within seconds, Maggie disappeared, leaving us with a feeling of complete desolation.

"I don't understand what just happened." I hung my head and a tear flowed down my cheek. Maggie was in a wretched condition and I was useless. I'd done nothing to help and I might have made things worse. Her grief and despair washed over me again and again, like waves pounding a body until the breath is gone.

Cam buried his face in his hands, hunching and trying to purge the emotions that trapped Maggie in this place. He took one shuddering breath after another and I realized that even though he was stronger than me, he was drowning too. Maggie's death state was powerful and bleak and it was dragging us both under.

Before my knees could buckle, a warm, firm

presence pushed at the back of my legs. It turned my body, making me move into the grasping brush that edged the clearing. As I moved deeper into the woods, I glanced over my shoulder and saw Zackie do the same thing with Cam, pushing him along behind me. It wasn't instant relief, but it did feel better to remove ourselves from Maggie's domain. I don't know if taking on some part of her pain relieved her in any way, or if all of this was just a useless by-product of interacting with tormented spirits. Whatever, we walked it off, or at least tried to.

When we reached the parking lot, I popped my trunk and grabbed two bottles of coconut water. After a run-in with a violent spirit that landed me in the hospital, I found out that our electrolytes can become screwed up in a radical way after an encounter with the dead. A doctor at the hospital recommended coconut water to restore balance and to help fight the debilitating fatigue. I've followed his advice ever since.

Cam pulled down his tailgate to give us a seat and we drank companionably for a spell, unspeaking and still recovering from our time with Maggie. Zackie lay a few yards from the truck, watching the woods and occasionally glancing at us, as if she were making sure we were okay. I thought this must be what sheep felt like.

Gathering our empties, I threw them in my trunk and took two new bottles before returning to the tailgate. "What do you think she meant when she said she needed to save the baby?"

Cam accepted the coconut water and focused on twisting the cap before answering. "I'm not sure. She also said she needed to save the baby from 'them.' Who would want to harm the baby?"

I shook my head, unable to answer. Taking a long pull from the bottle, I wiped my mouth on my shirt sleeve. "How does that work, anyway? How can you be dead and pregnant?"

Cam sipped some of his drink and stared into the woods. "This is an unusual case, for sure. If you think about folktales and ghost stories, you hear about the spirits of mothers who lost their children through accidents or their own misdeeds." He paused and took a drink before continuing. "They can't rest because of the trauma and the guilt. You never hear about pregnant ghosts."

"Maybe it's a pseudo-pregnancy? She only thinks she's still pregnant?"

Cam shrugged. "Maybe, but if she is pregnant, that makes two spirits that we need to convince to move on."

I paused and thought about what this would mean. "Have you ever done a baby before?"

"Lots of little kids and even a few toddlers, but so far, only one baby." Cam's mouth turned down and he sighed softly. "The kids are usually easy. You just let them know they need to find their mum and you send them off with Zackie. They're generally very trusting."

I sensed that he didn't want to talk about the baby, so he chose to focus on the little kids. Because it might help with Maggie's case, I needed to understand his experience with the spirit of the infant, even if it was uncomfortable for him. Keeping my voice low and gentle, I brought him back on topic. "Can you tell me about the baby?"

Cam lifted a shoulder and then stared at the bottle in his hands. "Not much to tell, really. It was 1975 and I was working a job in Kings Worthy." Glancing at me, he elaborated. "That's in England. It's a very old place. It was listed in the Domesday Book – you know, the survey taken in 1066?"

I bristled a little. "By William the Conqueror after

the Norman Conquest. I know. I was a history major, remember?"

Nodding, Cam took up the story again. "Anyway, I was busy trying to lay the ghost of a Victorian clergyman who had taken up residence in the old church. At the same time, there was an archaeological dig taking place in the churchyard. They were interested in the old Anglo-Saxon burials and they eventually unearthed the skeletal remains of a young woman." He took another drink and affected nonchalance as he continued the story. "Lying between the long bones of her legs, they found the skull of a full-term infant, but the fetal leg bones were still clearly within her pelvic cavity."

"A coffin birth?" My eyes went wide at this thought.

Cam nodded again. "It happens. A pregnant woman dies and is buried and because of pressure from the gases that build up during decomposition, the dead fetus is expelled from the equally dead mother." Looking down at his hands again, Cam picked at the label on the bottle. "Anyway, shortly after this find, the cries of a baby could be heard coming from the graveyard. It so disturbed the archaeological team that no one wanted to dig anymore and the work came to a grinding halt."

"And did it also disturb you? Cam, I can tell this is difficult to talk about."

Cam rolled his eyes and exhaled deeply, his words were clipped. "Yes, right. It bothered me a great deal. The baby was an innocent and completely blameless, yet she was left to suffer horribly for centuries."

"But wasn't the mother with the baby? How did you finally help her to move on?"

"I went into the churchyard with Zackie late one night to find the baby. The mother was nowhere to be found, so I assume she crossed over shortly after her death."

"She left the baby?" My mouth hung open, aghast at the thought of just taking off and leaving an infant.

"She probably didn't know the baby remained. In her time, the belief was that unbaptized infants went to Limbo, so in all likelihood, she died assuming that the baby would find its way and be taken care of." Cam shrugged again. "Who knows? All I know is that earthbound souls of infants are a rarity, so most of the time, they move on with no difficulties. Something went wrong for this one." Cam frowned as he stared into the middle distance for a beat. "But, you know, as soon as she saw Zackie, she quieted and stopped crying. Getting her to go through the portal was a breeze compared to the clergyman. I had to work another two weeks before the clergyman moved on."

I closed my slack jaw with an audible clack. "That's really counterintuitive. I would have thought that it would be harder persuading a baby to move on because you can't reason with it." I took this information as good news. Maggie by herself was proving to be a nearly intractable problem. Adding a reluctant baby to the mix would lower the probability of success even further, but a cooperative baby might help induce the mother to move on. I said as much to Cam.

Cam nodded as he considered this, but then his eyes drifted and he rubbed the stubble on his jaw. "I hate to burst your bubble, but it might play out in the opposite direction. Maggie might prevent the baby from crossing over due to her belief that she needs to protect it." Tilting his head back, he closed his eyes and expelled air through his nose. "We still don't have enough to go on to figure out how to work with Maggie. I feel like we're missing something vital."

I had to agree, but I felt as stuck as Maggie with this. Swinging my feet, I thought out loud to try to pinpoint the gap in our knowledge. "Whatever is holding her back is so strong that even the promise of seeing her husband again didn't turn her from her obsession. Talking about the husband and the accident didn't seem to reach her." I chugged the last of my coconut water and then held the bottle between my knees with both hands, crunching the plastic a little. "The only fact we're sure about is the accident. We don't know if this trauma led to depression and suicide or if she had mental health issues all along. If she had a preexisting problem, this could be why they waited to have a kid."

Cam grabbed the bottle from me to stop the crunching noise. "We don't know the results of the autopsy either. What if this is a murder and that's why she feels compelled to protect the baby? She could be constantly churning through her last thoughts before she was murdered."

I slanted my eyes toward Cam. "It could happen that we'll never get at the truth of the matter. What if we picked one of the scenarios and tried to work it out with

Maggie based on that assumption?"

Cam grimaced. "It would be better to take a little time and try harder to understand what happened. Moving forward with Maggie based on the most probable scenarios is like a doctor treating a patient without doing any diagnostics. It's not likely the patient will be cured and a very real possibility that harm could be done."

I flinched as he said this, having a sudden and vivid flashback of Maggie's suffering on our last effort. We were coming at this all wrong and our actions were harming her. I grunted my agreement with Cam's assessment, took my bottle back and went back to crunching the plastic. "I guess we wait on Jill. She said she'd let me know what happened with the autopsy."

It was Cam's turn to grunt agreement. "We need some downtime from Maggie, in any event. The coconut water only goes so far. We have to recharge what she's taken from us or we're no good to her."

I sighed and nodded. My battery felt drained and another encounter with Maggie too soon could cause me real damage. Neither of us was satisfied with moving so slowly and allowing Maggie's suffering to continue, but things would only get worse if our intervention was not up to the job. We didn't have much of a choice here.

###

Ron Falling-Leaf's grandmother was like a kitten. She looked soft and cuddly, but in reality, she was all claws and teeth. She wasn't his biological grandmother, but when his white family sent him to Oklahoma for psychiatric treatment, Lenora Ottertooth took Ron into her home and under her wing.

"You still chasing my grandson, little girl?" Lenora's voice sounded raspy over the phone, but the years had not diminished the force of her personality. She was still imperious, drawing a line in the sand and daring me to step over it. If she weren't my last resort to reach Ron, I would never have subjected myself to this conversation.

I was sweating and nauseous as I paced around the apartment, one hand gripping the phone, the other holding my belly. "Lenora, it's not like that. It's never been like that." She had high hopes that Ron would marry within the tribe and in her mind, my very existence threatened this possibility. I started to wonder if she might have been the reason Ron and I lost touch. My stomach curdled at the thought of speaking to Ron again. All my memories of him were bound up with bad memories of the drugs and the psychiatrists.

"Then what's it like, little girl? Why're you bothering me?"

I stopped in my tracks and my words only shook a little as I struggled to keep my voice even. "I need to get in touch with Ron. I need his help. Would you please just tell him that I called?"

"You find someone else to help you. Ron don't need none of your interference in his life. When you around, *kpëchehòsu*."

"He acts crazy? What's that supposed to mean? I had nothing to do with the problems he had with his family."

Lenora inhaled sharply. "How you know our language, little girl?"

Oh crap. I should have been more careful, but that old woman drove me to distraction. Shoving my bangs out of my face, I started pacing again, holding the phone in a death grip. I needed to divert her attention. “That’s not important. What is important is that a tribal man needs his help.”

There was a short silence and I could almost hear Lenora’s brain clicking as she balanced her dislike for me against the needs of a tribal member. “Well, that’s different. You say you need his help and I don’t care. You say a tribal man’s in trouble, I do care. I go get Ron.” With that, the phone clattered on a surface and I was left to wait. I put my back to a wall and let my feet slide out in front of me. After a few minutes, I transferred the phone to my other hand and shook out the tightness from gripping it so hard.

“Fia, is that you?” Ron was breathing hard, sounding like he had run a mile to get to the phone.

I hunched forward and closed my eyes. “Yeah, it’s me. Is Lenora with you, listening in?”

“Nah, I left her in the pasture with the herd. She can’t keep up with me when I run.”

Swallowing hard, I tried for small talk. “How are you doing, Ron?”

"Good…I'm good." There was a pause and I could hear him breathing. "You still crazy?"

I was sure that he was only half joking, but I cracked a grin and opened my eyes. "Maybe a little. How about you? Still sucker punching everyone in sight?"

A rumbling chuckle made its way over the connection. "Once in a while, just for old times' sake." We suffered a moment of uncomfortable silence and then Ron got to the point. "So, why'd you call? *Uma* said something about a tribal man in trouble."

"Yeah, something like that." I pinched the bridge of my nose with my free hand. The explanation was not going to be easy, despite the fact that Ron and I had history. A lot of time had gone by and maybe he had stopped believing that my experiences had any foundation in reality. Clearing my throat, I forged on. "Remember how I used to get the crap beaten out of me on a regular basis?"

Ron was quiet for a moment. When he responded, his voice was softer. "Yeah, I remember." He didn't automatically launch into something revisionist to explain the beatings and I took this as a good sign, a sign of still accepting the existence of the unseen world. Ron expelled a breath into the phone and then spoke louder, almost angry. "That still happening?"

"Not so much anymore. I met this older guy, Cam, and he sees them too." My voice brightened as I went on. "Ron, he knows how to make them move on and he's been teaching me."

"I'm glad to hear that, Fia. There were times I wasn't sure you were going to make it."

"You and me both." I gave a shaky laugh. "So, this tribal man…He's one of them. He's mad as hell and he's refusing to communicate with us."

Ron sighed. "I'm not sure how I can help. You know I can't sense them that well."

"You might be able to understand his rage. I think he threatened us when we first met him."

"What makes you say that?"

"Well, I'm not a hundred percent sure, but he was straight-up scary. He spoke in some native dialect and I couldn't force the meaning out of his words, but he was kind of yelling at us. I heard…" Pausing, I closed my eyes and tapped my forehead with my fingertips as I tried to recall exactly the sounds of his words. With my eyes still closed, I repeated the words phonetically as best as I could. "I heard him say 'Oh wen hech key' and then he said 'Aah poo hech awen kay skaerl ah niche sheet.'"

Ron mumbled the phrases to himself. "Huh, that's the Southern Unami Dialect. Your dude is Lenape. Fia, where are you calling from? Where did this happen?"

"I'm in New Jersey, why?"

"Oh, okay. It makes sense then." Ron chuckled. "Look at me, saying any of this makes sense… Anyway, the Lenape people are from New Jersey."

"I thought you were Lenape." My brow knit as I tried to puzzle out what happened to Ron. "Why'd they send you all the way to Oklahoma if your tribe is in New Jersey?"

"It's a long, long story, but some of the tribe ended up in Oklahoma in the 1860's. And let me tell you, my people did not take the direct route." Ron's voice grew louder and angrier as he explained, but then he blew out a breath. "Sorry, old wounds." After a pause, he continued. "At any rate, this guy did not threaten you. *Awèn hèch ki* means 'Who are you?' and *Ahpu hèch awèn kèski alënixsit* means 'Does anyone here speak Lenape?'"

"Good to know." I let his words sink in for a moment. Maybe this Lenape spirit would not try to kill us. "Ron, when can you come to New Jersey?" He started hemming and hawing, so before he could develop any real conviction, I interrupted. "Before you say you can't, you need to understand that this guy is going to stay stuck if you don't come. He's suffering, Ron, and it's been going on for a really long time. Cam and I can't even talk to him and that's half the battle in helping the dead to move on."

Ron blew out an exasperated breath and started grumbling. "You know, some things just never change - you're still really bossy." When he began thinking out loud, I thought I had him. "Let's see…I can get a friend to help *Uma* with the cattle and goats. If I do laundry tonight… Two days? Maybe three? But that's only if all the stars align. I can't promise you anything."

Something was better than nothing. At least he was willing. Rather than keep pushing and possibly turn him off with my demands, my mind skittered to another topic and I started babbling, trying to keep the conversation going. "You have goats?" My hand began crushing the phone again as I remembered a previous case where we needed help and called in reinforcements who also kept goats. I now had a bad association with goats thanks to that case.

"Yeah, we're trying this new thing where we graze them on the same pasture with the cattle. It's been working out really well. The goats don't go MIA so much, since the cattle don't want to go anywhere and the goats want to stick with the herd – but, why do you care?"

"Nevermind. Sorry. Just getting distracted." I shook my head a little to clear the goat thoughts and I tried for some gentle pressure. "Two or three days would be great, if you can do it. Just let me know when you know. And thank you so much for trying. I know this is a huge imposition." Before I forgot, I made a final request. "And Ron? Can you give me your cell number? I really don't want to have to run Lenora's gauntlet again."

Ron laughed and I wrote down the number he gave me. After we hung up, I took a breather to give my stomach acid a chance to subside. Sitting on the floor, I took four deep breaths and tried to relax. I hadn't exactly achieved a clear victory – maybe he'd come – and revisiting my past was like going through an emotional meat grinder. Those were the bad old days and if it were solely up to me, I would put a tight lid on that box of memories and cast it into the sea.

I had a narrow escape from that life and I was pretty sure I was on a better path now. But was it maybe a case of escaping the frying pan and willingly walking into the fire? Just because I now chose to interact with the dead didn't mean that this was how I should live my life. Rubbing the scar on my temple, I thought it also didn't mean that I was any safer than before. Maybe my life wasn't heading in the direction I had hoped. There was still nothing on the horizon resembling a house with a white picket fence and two point five kids playing in the yard.

I pulled off the cotton glove and stared at the dead hand to remind myself where things stood. Had I merely redefined normal and just went with the flow when Cam and Zackie presented an alternative? I remember being desperate enough at the time to be open to any alternative. I couldn't help but wonder if there was something out there that would make it possible for me to get out completely and never have to deal with the dead. I cast my eyes down, knowing I should be grateful for what I had and not go around wasting my energy wishing for a pipe dream. But sometimes, just sometimes, I longed for a peaceful place and a little time where I wouldn't always have to be on my guard.

Shaking my head, I put the glove back on, hauled myself to my feet and put an end to the pity party. We had two spirits who weren't any closer to crossing over and they were suffering in ways I couldn't even imagine. I grabbed my phone and dialed Cam to let him know that Ron was on board, more or less. Possibly less.

Cam was ever the optimist. "He'll come."

"What makes you so certain? I think the situation will obey Murphy's Quantum Law."

"Murphy's Law, I've heard of. What the devil are you talking about?"

"Anything that can, could have, or will go wrong, is going wrong, all at once."

"Okay, that I buy into –"

"Wait, I'm not done. There's a corollary. If there are two or more ways to do something, and one of those ways can result in a catastrophe or pregnancy, then someone will do it."

Chuckling, Cam tried to refute my unassailable

logic. “Look, Ron is someone who has suffered, right?” He continued without waiting for my reply. “Because of this, he understands what it means to endure suffering and it will not sit well on his conscience to allow our Lenape friend to remain in this unenviable state of limbo for the rest of eternity. He’ll come.”

As I was about to argue some more, Cam asked me to hang on, that he had another call coming through. While I waited, I grabbed plates and a mug from the dish drain in an attempt to at least restore full order to my domain.

“Fia?”

Balancing the phone against my ear with my shoulder, I returned first the plates and then the mug to their respective cabinets. “I’m here and I decided I’m not a big fan of call waiting.”

“Nevermind that. A friend from the *Express Times* just called. He said they’re holding a wake for Maggie in a few hours at Saint John’s Methodist Church. They must have released the body.”

“Huh. I didn’t hear anything from Jill about – Wait…Isn’t that the church in Hope Township near the Moravian Cemetery?”

“The very one. You should have pleasant memories of your first success in laying a spirit when we return there tonight.”

The memory brought back the feeling of nausea rising up against a swollen tongue and I rubbed my forearms, feeling again the raised postules from smallpox erupting on my healthy skin. There were a lot of events related to helping lost souls pass over that I didn’t need to remember.

Shuddering, I forced John Lewis Luckenbach out of my mind and focused on Maggie. “So, we’re going to the wake to meet friends or family who can tell us about Maggie, right? What are the odds that we learn something that will help us to free her? It’s a wake. All they’ll tell us is what a wonderful person she was.”

“Well, there is a zero percent probability of learning anything if we don’t go. What do you think of those odds?”

“You don’t have to get snippy. I’m just managing expectations –”

“I’ll let you know when I find your tail, Eeyore.” Cam drawled out the words.

"All right, all right. Just tell me when I have to be there and I'll be there."

###

Before entering the church, I stole a glance towards the deepening shadows at the back of the churchyard. Mr. Luckenbach's grave was marked by a worn flat stone, not visible from where I stood. I knew its approximate location and, without meaning to, I probed to sense his presence. The space was empty, he had moved on. It gave me a lift to know we'd succeeded with him.

Satisfied, I pulled open the bright red church door and stepped inside. The church smelled of lemon oil, and the woodwork on the pews and walls glowed in the warm light. Scanning the room, Maggie's closed casket sat on a dais at the front of the church, but there was no sign of Maggie's spirit. About thirty people milled about in somber circles, heads bent and voices low. I drifted among the circles and listened to the friends and family talk about Maggie.

"She was so sweet. I worked with her for five years and she never forgot my birthday…"

"I'm going to miss seeing her on Sundays. She was such a big part of this church. I'm glad they decided to do the wake here."

"She wanted that baby more than anything in the world. Such a tragedy!"

"Maybe now she and Greg can be together again…"

It was everything I expected and it was also so much worse. These people really loved Maggie and of course they said nice things about her, but they were suffering deeply with their loss. The suicide had stripped them emotionally raw and I could feel the aching wounds in their hearts made by the woman who left them so violently and so suddenly. I almost headed for the exit to escape their anguish, but I forced myself to stay and learn what I could to help Maggie.

An open door to the right provided access to a gathering room where a long table held bottled drinks, finger sandwiches, cookies and cake for those who came to pay their respects. Balancing a piece of cake on a paper plate, Cam stood near the table, deep in conversation with a woman. She had a Mona Lisa quality about her. Her eyes were gentle and she had a generous mouth, but her features were drawn down by the weight of grief, making it impossible to judge her age. Her shoulders stooped and her gestures were slow and tired. She was barely holding it together.

When he noticed me at his elbow, Cam brought me into the conversation. "This is Fia. She was also on the search." As I shook her hand, Cam introduced the grieving woman as Maggie's sister, Katherine.

"I'm very sorry for your loss." Katherine thanked me and then appeared distracted for a moment, her eyes darting aimlessly around the room. How many times had she responded to similar words of condolence? Still, I had nothing better to offer.

Coming back from her reverie, Katherine focused on my eyes and then searched Cam's face for something. She appeared to find what she was looking for and her posture relaxed. "I want to thank you both for finding my sister. Please tell the other searchers that I am grateful for their help." I shifted uneasily, unsure how to respond. To my relief, she continued speaking and spared me from saying something inadequate. "I wish I could say that all of this was unexpected, but she was never the same after the accident. I should have seen the signs and done something."

Cam urged her on, his voice quiet and gentle. "It must have been terrible for her, losing her husband."

"It was…it was just awful." Katherine wiped away a tear. "Everything was so happy one moment – they were finally going to have a baby…they'd been trying for so long. Maggie and Greg were decorating the nursery and buying baby things…and then it all got taken away." The tears began falling in earnest and she grabbed a napkin from the table. "But Maggie was strong. I think she could have survived Greg's loss eventually." Katherine blotted her face with the napkin and took a deep breath.

I touched her arm, uncertain how to ease her. "Then why? Why would she take her own life?"

"She had a head injury, did you know that?" Katherine looked from me to Cam before continuing. "She was different after that. It was the voices…she couldn't make them stop. They gave her brain scans, antipsychotics, the whole nine yards. She tried, she really, really tried. Nothing helped."

Cam slanted his eyes at me at this revelation, but then turned his full attention back to Katherine. "There was nothing you could have done." He gave her a penetrating look as she shook her head. "She was getting help. What happened was not your fault." Katherine stopped shaking her head and then bit her lip as she stared into the distance. This was a start. At least she appeared to be thinking about it.

Katherine sighed. "She was my sister. I should have taken better care of her."

I pulled her into a gentle embrace. "You did the best you could. That's all anyone can do." As I said the words, a little bit of weight dropped from my shoulders. It felt like dandruff, but I had to be honest with myself and admit that Maggie was a tough case. We had also done the best we could under the circumstances. I just wished we could do this faster for Maggie. With new information, maybe we could move closer to freeing her in the next round.

###

"I told you so." Cam's eyes glinted with triumph.

I moved toward the next bright pink length of flagging tape en route to Maggie and struggled to come up with a witty response. “Shut up.”

I hadn’t slept well the night before because my dreams were full of blood, disembodied voices, and Maggie. I was suffering from a wicked headache and my temples were throbbing. We had done this trip so many times that I felt like I was on a first name basis with every briar patch along the way. I was in no mood to play, but this made little difference to Cam and Zackie. Spying the next piece of flapping pink tape, I advanced towards it with Zackie gamboling about my heels like a puppy. She was doing this on purpose to irritate me, so I ignored her and trudged on. Bored with me, Zackie drifted towards Cam.

“I will not shut up. I have quite a low success rate of being right in this world and I will not squander the opportunity to crow when I am right.” Cam swore as he tripped over Zackie and almost went sprawling. “Bloody hound! I’m having my moment. Don’t interrupt me.”

I stopped trudging and closed my eyes. “All right. You were right. We learned something worth knowing at the wake.” I rubbed my throbbing temples. “How are we going to use this information to help Maggie?”

“Take a break.” My eyes flew open as Cam gripped

my elbow and guided me to a fallen tree. "Here, sit." I slipped off my pack and perched on the tree trunk. Cam rummaged through his pack and handed me a bottle of coconut water and some aspirin. "Take some prophylactically. It's not going to get better after we meet with Maggie."

The wisdom of his words penetrated my painful brain. "Thanks."

I chugged down the bottle of coconut water and after a few more moments to let me recover, Cam took up the topic of Maggie again. "We can fit together two pieces of the puzzle at this point. When we first spoke to Maggie, she kept telling us that we weren't there, right?" I nodded. "We were just two more voices in the cacophony. Whether she continues to hear other voices or if this is part of her perimortem suffering, and now she's just remembering the voices, I don't know."

"You think the voices were real?"

"I do. A head injury can re-wire the neural circuitry in odd ways. It's probably a one in a billion event that certain synapses form links between just the right neurons to make neurotypical brains more like our brains, but it does happen."

"Holy crap…" I rubbed my temples with renewed vigor. "Now you're telling me I have to be a neuroscientist to understand this stuff?"

Cam grinned. "I learned this stuff from my sister. She's the one I told you about who counsels people with past life trauma."

"I remember you telling me about your family. You also have a brother who does spirit attachment work, right?"

"Yes, and there are other, more distant family with other callings. Anyway, Essex –"

"Really? Essex? Her name is Essex? That name must have been a real joy to her when she was an adolescent."

"Anyway…" Cam let the word draw out, waiting to see if I'd interrupt again. "Essex is trained in biological psychiatry. When we first met, you mentioned that people like us must spend a lot of time trying to self-diagnose. Well, Essex took that to a whole other level."

"So, as your sister Essex would see it, Maggie's

head trauma changed her brain and made her suddenly able to hear the dead?" Cam nodded. My eyes widened and I put my hand to my mouth. "That must have been horrifying for her. I was born to it and I never really adjusted."

Cam raised an eyebrow. "I think that's what put her over the edge."

Jumping to my feet, I pulled on my pack with a new sense of urgency. "We need to find Maggie." I left Cam in the dust as I set out, headache and fatigue forgotten. Zackie seemed pleased with my faster pace and ran ahead to each marker, leading the way. With his longer stride, Cam caught up with me just as I reached the clearing and we both stopped short when Maggie stepped towards us, bloody hands raised. For a moment, I thought she would claw my face, but the psychopomp moved forward with animal grace and softly planted her front paws on Maggie's chest. The spirit sobbed and held her in an embrace. What Maggie wanted, what she was reaching for, was Zackie and the comfort she offered.

The two separated and Zackie led Maggie to the center of the clearing. The hound circled and then lay down as the natural colors of the woods seeped out of my vision. Maggie sat, hip against flank, wrapping her arms around

Zackie. As painful and devastating as our last visit had been for Maggie, she had learned the psychopomp was the only thing in this world that could give her relief. She would not run from us again.

I sat on the ground facing Maggie, my legs crossed under me. Cam grunted as he lowered himself nearby. "Can't we ever have a conversation standing up?"

"Maggie? Katherine told us that you started hearing voices after the accident. Do you still hear them?" I leaned forward, willing her to interact with me.

She looked at me through filmy eyes and whispered. "Less now."

"What did the voices say?" Cam asked.

Her face broke and the tears started again. "He said they'd come and take the baby from me."

"He? Who is he?" Cam frowned and leaned forward.

"I don't know… I don't know…" She took a shuddering breath and paused, squinting her eyes as she concentrated. "He said I shouldn't do it."

"Shouldn't do what?" I clasped my hands around my elbows and tried to keep my frustration in check. Between the blunted sound of everything ringing in my ears and her vague attributions, I was having trouble focusing and my irritation was rising. Closing my eyes, I forced myself to concentrate on what she said.

"Use the gun. I shouldn't have used the gun. I should have listened… *Apëwi këlukahëla.*" Her hands flew to her head and she began rocking and weeping.

My eyes shot open and my gut dropped as if I were on a carnival ride. I knew the rhythm of those words and through Maggie, I understood the meaning. "He said you give up too easily?"

"I needed it to stop… I needed them to stop talking to me." Maggie shuddered and began pulling at her hair, a thin wail escaping her lips.

Cam crept to a kneeling position and touched her arm. "It's okay, Maggie. We understand how frightening it was for you."

"I couldn't take it, but I knew if I made it stop, I'd harm the baby." Maggie wrapped her arms around her torso and rocked. "It was my fault that the baby got hurt. I deserved the pain. I should be punished." She was rocking harder and gasping. Her pain was a terrible thing to watch and I launched to my feet to do something, but I had no idea what. Zackie jumped up as well and ran a tight circle around Maggie, keeping me back. When Maggie reached out blindly, the psychopomp dove into her arms and yielded to her embrace. Groaning as the pain passed through her, Maggie held on until the tendons nearly broke through the papery skin of her arms. "I'm so sorry. It's my fault." Maggie's agitation escalated and her image began flickering, like tiny lightning strikes. We had to let her phase out or she would continue to suffer.

Cam kept contact with her, touching her arm. "Maggie, we're going to let you go, okay? It's all right to go now. We'll come back later."

Maggie nodded, jerking her head as if she were having a seizure. When she released Zackie, the edges of her silhouette blurred and she faded from our view as the waves of despair crashed down on us.

I stumbled out of the clearing and threw up in a bush. Spitting and wiping my mouth on the back of my hand, I ran forward blindly, the only clear thought being that I needed to put distance between Maggie and me. I could hear Cam crashing through the woods on my left, in similar distress, and urgently trying to get away. Zackie ran in front of me and forced me to veer left, closer to Cam. She circled us and then pushed us left again. We reached the fallen tree, a familiar landmark, thanks to her herding, and at last staggered to a halt.

Breathing heavily, Cam slumped to the ground with his back against the trunk and put his head between his knees. "Crikey, it gets worse every time."

I tasted sour stomach acid and the funky mushroomy residue in my mouth and was in no shape to respond without retching. Walking a few paces away, I spat and tried to clear my mouth.

"Didn't your mother ever tell you it wasn't ladylike to spit?" Cam's eyes were shut and his head was bowed, so it was useless to flip him the bird.

"That Lenape bastard did this to her." I spat again.

Cam looked up and his eyes were bloodshot. "She did use a Lenape phrase. That would seem to implicate him."

"You think?" I rolled my eyes and that made me

feel a little dizzy. Hobbling over, I sat down next to Cam. "What are we going to do about it?"

Cam snorted. "We do what we always do and try to get him to move on. How exactly that happens and what happens afterward, that's Zackie's department."

I stared at the psychopomp. She was facing us, lying on the forest floor like a sphinx, relaxed and unperturbed. After who knows how many millennia, it was impossible that this situation was a first for her. I was ready to trust the process, but I was still pissed.

"Why would this guy be such a major league asshat? What did Maggie ever do to him?"

"Remember your early lessons. 'As in life, so in death.'"

"So, he was a major league asshat in life and never lost the habit when he died?" I blew out a breath. "Somehow, that's completely unsatisfying. I'm thinking I should maybe kick his ass a little the next time we see him."

"Hey, none of this is meant to satisfy you. Do not go around picking fights." Cam raised his eyebrows and nodded sharply at me, holding my gaze until I acquiesced.

"All right. Whatever." I crossed my arms over my chest and slumped down. The posture made my stomach feel better, so I stayed in the slouch after my moment of petulance had passed. When the adrenaline wore off, I checked on Cam. "Are you okay?"

"I've been better."

"Should we try to make it back to the parking lot?"

"Are you going to throw up again?"

"Probably not." I sat up straighter to test this hypothesis. "Are you?"

"Probably not."

I got to my feet and extended a hand to pull Cam up. We made it back to the parking lot, guzzled some coconut water and headed home. Our systems were drained and we needed some time to recover before we could do any more spirit work.

###

After waking up groggy and a little disoriented, I ate a tuna sandwich and felt better about my world. I checked my phone while I munched and found five messages. The first was from Jill. She had called me while we were dealing with Maggie and I probably missed her because of the sound distortion Maggie produces. Hearing a ringtone while under water was not something I was good at. As expected, Maggie's autopsy revealed nothing unusual. The death was declared a suicide. I forwarded the message to Cam.

The next two messages were from Peyton asking for a call back. She didn't give any details, so I figured it was just Peyton being herself, high-drive and unrelenting. It probably wasn't life-or-death urgent and I made a mental note to get back to her later. Next up was Lucas and my heart beat an irregular tattoo. He must have been driving somewhere because the message was garbled, like he was drifting in and out of reception areas. As far as I could tell, he had a local job where he thought we could collaborate. He probably left a message with Cam too, so I decided to let him deal with it. The last call was from my boss and my heart dropped back to an all-business, money-to-pay-my-rent pace. Gander had another job for me and I needed to call back to confirm availability. I hit redial and let him know I would do it and he let me know I had to be onsite in two hours. And so began the first of many showers that day.

When I arrived at the scene, I was delighted to learn that this was one of the few cases where no fatalities were involved. I was not delighted to learn that this job involved a sewage backup in a residential property. But luckily for me, after having a lifetime of experience with the various stages of post mortem decay, I was already accustomed to the sights and smells that greeted me on this job.

The plumbers had come and gone, first removing the tree roots responsible for wrapping around and crushing the sewer line and then installing a new pipe. All that remained was for us to cleanse the house of human waste and sanitize or dispose of everything that the waste had touched.

Gander pointed to a pile of heavy duty plastic bags labeled with biohazard symbols and a collection of shovels in an adjacent pile. "Lady and gentlemen, the first order of business is to remove the solids. There is absorbent material in the truck that you will then use to sop up any liquid. Tear up and dispose of all carpeting, if you please." Patting the side of one of the wet/dry vac units, Gander continued. "Any remaining liquid will be suctioned using this device."

After several long hours spent eliminating the foul contamination, we piled the waste into a van that JoJo would take to our decon facility. The family, respecting the unstoppable force of the sewage overflow, had managed to remove all the furniture to safety. Thanks to their quick action, the only thing ruined was the flooring. While we were busy shoveling and tearing up carpet, JoJo had filled buckets with a mixed solution of TR-32 deodorizer and Thermo-55 disinfectant and then added bundles of clean, commercial grade, white terry-cloth rags to let them soak.

Gander surveyed the crew and then gave his next set of instructions. "We will now start decontaminating the home. Please fish out a rag from the bucket and clean the surfaces. Do not put used rags back in the bucket. Dispose of them in biohazard bags."

Following his instructions, I bent down on hands and knees near one of the toilets and began wiping the tiles. The only solace in the job was that at this point, I felt like I was making progress. I could hear Goose singing to himself as he scrubbed the hallway. "…and the toilet blew up later on the next day…"

"What are you singing, Goose?" I called from the bathroom.

"Just a little Zappa tune I thought was appropriate."

I shook my head and kept scrubbing, eventually leaving the bathroom and heading up the hall from Goose to start scrubbing one of the rooms. As I was finishing the room and backing up into the hallway, I sensed someone behind me. I figured it was Goose and didn't pay it any mind. While I was scrubbing the threshold and crawling backwards into the hall, the someone I sensed grabbed my butt. Before I could even react, the dead hand reached back, grabbed the man by an ankle and, with a strength I did not possess, yanked both his feet out from under him. There was a resounding crash as he hit the floor and both Goose and Gander came running to see what had happened.

Gander eyed my flushed face under the respirator and goggles and then directed his comments to Rory Craymore, lying on the floor and looking stunned. "Everything all right over here? What happened?"

I was still on my knees as I answered. Biting down

hard on my growing fury, I forced my voice to a normal volume and it only shook a little when I spoke. “He must have tripped over me.” I didn’t want to start a major incident. Gander would have a ton of paperwork to file if I screamed sexual harassment and my boss didn’t deserve that. Beyond these mundane problems, I had to get a tight grip on my emotions or I risked inciting the dead hand into doing something violent in front of witnesses. I had a mental image of it suddenly snaking out and disemboweling that little shit. My imagination painted a vivid picture of the horrified look on Rory’s face as his intestines spilled onto the floor and I briefly closed my eyes to dispel these bloody thoughts.

Goose narrowed his eyes, stared at the back of my hazmat suit and then glared at Rory. “Is that what happened, grommet?” Glancing behind me as Gander also took a look, I noticed an incriminating, dirty hand print on my posterior.

Rory swallowed and then responded in a small voice. “Yeah, I tripped over her.”

“Get up.” Gander did not extend a hand to help him. Once he was on his feet, Gander inspected his suit for any damage that would compromise its function. A small tear was visible near the ankle that the dead hand had grabbed. "You're done for the day. Get out."

Without saying a word, Rory turned on his heel and left. Gander reached out to me and helped me to stand. "Are you all right, Fia?"

Goose checked my suit for tears and found none. "He didn't hurt you when he 'fell,' did he?" Goose didn't bother to hide his sarcasm.

I could feel my cheeks burning as my anger seethed and I gritted my teeth. "I'm all right. Let's just get the job done and forget about this." I hadn't been on the job long enough for them to really know me and this was not how I wanted them to think about me. I wanted them to forget about it, but that guy humiliated me and I was not going to be able to just let it go.

Gander and Goose exchanged a look, but then decided to do things my way. When they turned their attention back to the work, I cleaned my suit with a towel and then, breathing hard as I exorcised the anger, began wiping down the floor again. We finished the initial scrubbing and then did a final pass with Spray &Wipe. As the last step, Gander set up an ozone machine that he was going to let run overnight to finally kill the odor. Once we were out of the house, there was no sign of Rory. JoJo helped us to remove the duct tape on the suits and then gathered up the items slated for either decontamination or disposal. I stepped into the truck, stripped down and threw my fouled gear as hard as I could against the wall. I stood with hands on hips and my head bowed as I again fought down the rage, now tinged with resentment that I always had to be the one with controlled emotions. Just once, I wanted to cut loose and let someone have it, say what I really thought and smack people silly if they deserved it. After a few moments, I regained my composure, slipped a nitrile glove on the dead hand and entered the shower. Between the sewage and Rory, I had never felt as filthy as I did right then. The shower was a real blessing.

I thought about what the dead hand did as I got wet, turned the water off and then soaped up and scrubbed vigorously. Maybe this thing helped me at a moment of vulnerability, but my stomach soured when I thought about its intrusion and my lack of autonomy. Turning the water back on for a final rinse, I decided to go to Cam and tell him about this latest fiasco. What if the dead hand hadn't stopped with slamming Rory to the ground? What if it had grabbed him by the throat and choked the life out of him?

With my history of psychiatric problems, I'd be charged with his death and locked up for good. I dried off, put on my street clothes and left the truck open for the guys. Telling them I'd see them next time, I headed for my car, dialing Cam as I walked.

###

Cam handed me a mug of coffee as I came through the door. "Tell it to me from the beginning." I told Cam exactly what happened and did not spare him the swearing, the fury over being pawed and my fears of what the dead hand might do next.

Grabbing my mug for a refill, Cam slid from his stool at the breakfast island and poured us both another cup. "I think he got a little bit of what he deserved."

"But what if this escalates? I can't stop the dead hand from doing things. I have absolutely no forewarning that something is going to happen, so it's not like I can walk away to stop it from reacting to a situation."

"It appears to me that it could very well have done anything to this Rory person as he lay helpless on the floor.

It didn't."

"So, you're saying I shouldn't worry?"

"Oh, no, go ahead and worry. And try to keep yourself out of situations where the hand could react."

I looked at him bleary eyed and then rubbed at my face in frustration. "I have no idea what its triggers are."

"You know that it doesn't like Rory, so stay clear of him. At the very least, do that for your own sake."

I rolled my eyes, but then nodded agreement at this bit of common sense and took the mug he offered. Relaxing my shoulders, I took a sip and then took a cleansing breath. "I'll just have to be really careful on the next job. I can't have that guy near me, but it's easier said than done, depending on what we're working on." Maybe I would have to file a complaint after all. That would force the company to keep that guy away from me until they did an investigation. The prospect of having to talk to management about that little shit made my belly curdle.

My thoughts were interrupted by my *In the Mood* ringtone. Peyton was calling. Crap. I was supposed to have called her back. "Cam, it's Peyton."

"Answer it and put her on speaker. Maybe we're lucky and the Lenape spirit found peace and left on his own."

I slit my eyes at Cam and shook my head, that he would harbor such fantasies. Tapping the phone, I let Peyton's call through. "Peyton, what's up?"

"The booming is getting worse."

Cam sat forward and his eyes narrowed. "Worse how?"

"Is that you, Cam?" Cam let her know that we were on speaker and she continued. "Well, it's not just loud anymore. The booming is starting to get rhythmic. How can a raccoon do that?"

Cam's eyes shifted in my direction as he began to confabulate a rationale. "Well, it's later in the day and the surface of the roof is metal. The sun could have caused it to heat up and now we're getting intermittent heat and the surface is expanding and contracting. That could cause a rhythmic booming, couldn't it?" Cam silently mouthed to me, 'Do you think she's buying it?'

I started to shake my head as Peyton responded.

"No."

Cam's eyes went wide. "What do you mean 'No?' I just gave you a perfectly reasonable explanation."

"No. I'm not stupid. I know how metal materials react to temperature shifts. This explanation is not the slightest bit plausible. The trailer's hide is too thick."

"Bollocks…" Cam folded his arms across his chest and he pursed his lips in a sour expression. He'd given up trying to be persuasive.

"Well, what do you think is happening?" I asked her. Sometimes it helped to try to get people to think rationally and insert their own perfectly reasonable explanation.

"I can't explain it and I don't like it." Peyton huffed out a frustrated breath. "If I had some answers, maybe I could find a way to deal with it. As things stand, there's no good way to resolve the situation. Pisses me off, Fia. This is bullshit."

The little hairs on the back of my neck stood at attention. On some level, Peyton recognized that we knew more than we were telling her and subconsciously, it was coming through in how she expressed herself. She was just sensitive enough to feel something wasn't right, but not sensitive enough to put her finger on it. This had loose cannon written all over it.

"What are you going to do?" My eyes slid to Cam, who leaned forward, listening attentively with furrowed brows.

Peyton's voice was shrill when she answered. "I'm going to do what everyone does. I'll search on the internet to see if anyone else had this happen and see what they did about it."

Cam pulled out his phone and placed it on the counter, so I could see as he put in the search term 'trailer making banging noises.' I kept Peyton talking. "Sounds like a plan. Let us know if you find anything useful." Reading the search results, there were over three million hits, the first page of which showed all manner of mechanical failure leading to thumping sounds. This should keep her busy while we waited for Ron Falling-Leaf to arrive.

"Yeah, I'll let you know if I need any help." Peyton's voice was barbed with sarcasm and she hung up without saying good-bye. She was frustrated with us, but probably unable to understand why. My stomach felt like I had swallowed shards of glass and I knew exactly why. I was a big-ass failure for hanging a friend out to dry.

"Stop looking like that." Cam stared at me, narrowing his eyes.

"Like what? What am I looking like?"

"Like the world uses you for a punching bag and it all makes sense now."

"What am I supposed to look like?" I forced the bangs from my eyes and stood up. "We're not helping Peyton or any of the spirits under our care and I have a dead hand that does whatever it wants. I've gotta be doing something wrong here, Cam."

"You're assuming things are under your control. That's a thinking error."

His words stopped me in mid expletive. "Are you telling me that nothing I do matters?"

"No, I'm saying that there are too many variables for outcomes to be predictable. You can avoid some problems by making smart decisions, but there's always going to be unintended consequences, even with the smart decisions."

I sat back down and mulled this over. "So, all I can do is the best I can under the circumstances and no one will blame me?"

"No, where'd you ever get that idea?" Cam chuckled without mirth. "There will be plenty of finger pointing when things go wrong. The best you can hope for is a clear conscience."

I stared at Cam wide-eyed and then my lips quirked. "Are you speaking from personal experience?"

"Always."

"Then how do I know this isn't just anecdotal? Results may vary, right?" Maybe this was the way the world operated, but it was a sucky way to do business.

Cam paused and gave me a careful assessment before answering. Every wrinkle on his face showed in stark relief and each gray hair had a story to tell. "Try it your way and let me know how it goes for you."

I grunted a noncommittal reply and then exercised my right to remain silent.

###

The callout came as I was about to eat lunch. I crammed the peanut butter and jelly sandwich into my mouth and gummed it viciously as I ran to my bedroom to change into a high visibility orange shirt, tactical pants and hiking boots. Everything else I needed was in my car trunk. With a quick swig of milk to wash down my lunch, I ran out the door with my cheeks bulging and slid in behind the steering wheel. Catching a glimpse of myself in the rearview mirror, I hastened to wipe away the milk mustache and stray bits of peanut butter before I started the car.

Staging was in the main parking lot of Kittatinny Valley State Park and a quick look around told me that only a handful of searchers had been able to make it during working hours. In contrast, the place was lousy with little girls dressed in Brownie uniforms. There were close to twenty girls, all around seven to eight years old, milling around the parking lot in various states of excitement. Three ashen-faced adults, presumably the troop leaders, faced Peyton as she fired off questions and then leaned forward, cupping a hand to one ear as the little girls chimed in energetically, offering their take on the situation. Two park rangers stood by, a study in stoicism, while the cacophony enveloped them.

"But you're going to find her, right?" The little girl tugged at Peyton's sleeve. Her face was white with fear and she was close to crying.

"We're going to work really, really hard to find her. Okay, honey?" Returning her attention to the questionnaire, Peyton asked the adults another question. She stood with slumped shoulders and an untucked shirt tail. Dark circles formed half moons under bloodshot eyes and she yawned as she jotted down responses. There were smudges on her glasses from her near constant eye rubbing.

I put out my hand for the clipboard and Peyton sighed with relief. "Take a break. I'll finish filling this out."

"Thanks. I gotta lie down a moment. Come get me when you're done." She nodded to the park rangers and moved away with a plodding step, head down and hands in her pockets.

Peyton had managed to fill in all the relevant subject information in the missing person questionnaire. The missing little girl was Chelsea Butcher from Harmony. She had freckles, brown hair and brown eyes, stood four foot two and weighed about sixty pounds. No medical disabilities, recent illnesses, allergies or phobias. I smiled as I read in the form that she was a non-smoker and had no criminal history. My faith in humanity restored, I forged on with the questionnaire.

"Let me guess, Chelsea was wearing a Brownie uniform?" The troop leaders nodded and I filled this in. "Have her parents been notified?"

The troop leader with short, dark hair nodded at me. "I called her father and he's driving here right now. Chelsea's mother abandoned the family last month. Just up and left them."

I flipped the comments box to take some free-hand notes. "How has that affected her?"

"Well, she used to be very outgoing and she had a really sunny personality. Lately, she's been withdrawn and just really fragile, crying easily and very sensitive." The dark haired woman shrugged helplessly. "But Chelsea was really looking forward to this trip. It was the first time in a long time that she seemed like her old self."

I nodded and scribbled down that Chelsea was likely depressed due to abandonment by her mother.

Flipping the form back to the standard questions, I found my place and poised my pen for the next answer. "How about footwear? Do you know what she's wearing or what her shoe size is?" The troop leaders looked blankly at each other and shook their heads.

"Chelsea has flashy light sneakers," a little girl called from my elbow.

I filled this in and asked, "So, if we look for the blinking lights, we should find her?"

"I dunno. She mighta left them home."

I pinched the bridge of my nose. "Was she wearing the flashy light sneakers today?"

"I dunno, but she has flashy light sneakers." The little girl nodded at me, her eyes wide.

"Okay, good to know." I crossed out this information and wrote 'unknown' in the footwear section. "Did she maybe leave a sweater or a bag?" These would make great scent articles for the search dogs and I crossed my fingers.

The adults conferred and the one with blonde hair answered. "No, the weather was supposed to be warm today, so we didn't tell them to bring sweaters. Bags would get lost, so they don't bring those either."

"How about the last place people saw Chelsea?"

"She was at the bathroom with me," squeaked a voice from behind.

A tall dark haired girl standing to the side crossed her arms over her chest. "No she wasn't. That was Jessica."

"Oh yeah," the squeaking voice agreed and then tried again. "On the bus?"

This might be important. I turned around to try to find the squeaking girl. "Did Chelsea sit with you on the bus?"

"Not with me, but she came on the bus with us." The squeaker was joined by a number of other voices, all agreeing that she came on the bus with them.

I turned back to the adults. "Do you know where she sat on the bus?" If we had this information, we could scent a dog off of the seat. Kittatinny would be a bitch to search using air scent dogs because of its size. I was holding out hope that we could use a trailing dog to find her fast.

The troop leaders whispered to each other and the blonde answered for them again, her eyes filled with unshed tears. "We don't know."

"That's okay. You've all done your best and been very helpful." As I stepped away to find Peyton and give her the dismal update, the blonde troop leader stumbled to the brush to throw up. On my way to the team trailer, I ran into Cam and Zackie.

"What's the good news?" Cam pointed with his chin towards the clipboard.

"I got nothin' and I need to tell Peyton." I trudged on and found Peyton behind the trailer talking to Sandra, an elfin brunette sporting a pixie cut. Peyton towered over the other woman and I entertained the thought that their conversation might involve yelling to each other because of the dramatic difference in height.

Peyton interrupted herself when she saw me. "What did you find out?"

"Other than the fact that she's dressed in a Brownie uniform, they don't know anything about what's on her feet, so we can't look for tracks. We have no scent articles from the girl and they have no idea where she was last seen, so we can't even begin a dog from a general start area."

"Aren't you a little ray of sunshine?" Peyton frowned at me and then turned her gaze back to Sandra. "I had to help run the search, so Simber's home. You got Baby Jax with you?" Baby Jax was a Dutch Shepherd renowned as much for his drive as his oddly asymmetric ears, one standing and the other floppy. Because his tail would wag furiously when he worked a trail, he was sometimes called Helicopter Butt by the team.

"He's in my truck. What do you need?" Sandra half turned, ready to get her dog.

Peyton shrugged. "There are five searchers on site and no one aside from the rangers and me and Fia has gone to where the Brownies set up for the day. How about we try a missing member search?"

Sandra nodded. "We can try. You and Fia go over and stand with the Brownies and I'll go get Jax."

Before we walked back to the Brownies, Peyton poked her head into the trailer and asked for operations to document this as task one and to radio any searchers on scene to stay back and away from the Brownie horde, so they wouldn't scent contaminate the area. I was relieved to find that the trailer held no special vibe. The Lenape man was either not around or keeping his distance. Either way, it worked for me, since it made for one less distraction during a search.

Upon reaching the troop of Brownies, we organized the girls, the troop leaders and the park rangers into a circle that we joined. When Sandra showed up with Baby Jax, he was already in harness and she led him around the circle at a distance to let him get familiar with whatever scents were around. She then brought him to the circle of people and had him take a whiff of everyone, all the while telling the dog 'No.' Passing me, the dog took a whiff of my outstretched hands and then lay down in front of me, executing three quick barks.

"What the…" Sandra looked confused for a moment and then nodded her head. Taking me aside, she asked, "Fia, have you been handling source? That's Baby Jax's human remains detection alert."

Crap. Baby Jax had sniffed out the dead hand. I nodded and said, "Yeah, I've been helping to train some new HRD dogs."

"Maybe double glove next time." Sandra shook her head, disgusted and went back to getting her dog to negative on everyone.

When the last person had been sniffed, Sandra looped the long lead behind her back, braced herself and then told Baby Jax to go find. The dog's head snapped to the left and he took off, nearly pulling Sandra off her feet as she leaned back hard into the loop of leash. Baby Jax followed the only scent that wasn't accounted for among the humans he had checked. By process of elimination, we hoped he had found Chelsea's trail.

"That dog will drag you on your belly when he's on scent." Peyton chuckled and shook her head. "Come on, let's flank her." We jogged after Sandra as she was dragged by the dog towards the trail marked with red blazes. After following this trail for about five minutes, the dog pulled Sandra into the woods. Another few minutes of walking brought us to the little girl. She was sitting on a fallen tree, red-faced and sobbing, clutching her belly. Baby Jax immediately gentled, sitting in front of the terrified child and touching her with his paw. This indication was Jax's way of telling us that this was the kid we were looking for.

"Chelsea?" Peyton called to her. The little girl

looked up from the dog and nodded, her lower lip trembling. Sandra praised the dog, who rolled over to present his belly for rubbing. While Sandra made a fuss over Baby Jax, Peyton checked Chelsea for injuries and I radioed to base that we had a find.

"Can I pet him?" Chelsea hiccupped as her sobs subsided and then sniffed, wiping her nose on her sleeve.

Sandra grinned. "Sure, go ahead. He loves getting pets."

Chelsea reached out a tentative hand and Baby Jax shoved his head under it, making it clear that he wanted his ears rubbed next. When the little girl giggled, I figured it was okay to ask her some questions. "So, how'd you get here, Chelsea?"

"Loren was mean to me. She said my hair was the color of poo, so I left."

I nodded. "Oh, yeah. I can understand not wanting to stay and be called a poopy head."

"But then I had to pee, so I went into the woods and I got lost." In a small voice, she continued. "I was so scared."

Peyton ruffled the little girl's hair. "You did really good staying put, you know that?"

"I know," she sighed, relaxing as she stroked Jax's head. "We learned from Hug-A-Tree when you get lost, you hug a tree and stay where you are."

We grinned at each other and Peyton gave Sandra a high five. The Hug-A-Tree program had done some good. Members of different SAR teams gave the program to little kids during school events to teach them what to do if they got lost. The most important thing was to stay put and stop moving and this little girl had put that lesson to good use.

Sandra smiled at the child and cocked her head. "You ready to head back, honey?"

"Okay. I'm not in trouble, am I?"

"No, you're not in trouble." I put my hand out and she slipped her small hand in mine.

The Brownie troop cheered when Chelsea ran into her father's open arms. Returning to the fold, she accepted their praise like a returning hero. That girl will run for office some day, I thought. After a quick head count, the troop leaders decided to quit before anything else happened. Chelsea left with her father and the rest of the girls were herded on to the bus, where they were repeatedly told to sit down and calm down for the trip home. Waving good-bye as the Brownies drove away, the park rangers and searchers congratulated each other on a successful search.

"A perfect outcome." Cam whistled as he loaded his pack into the truck. Zackie jumped in and circled a few times to make herself comfortable, kicking slightly at the pack with her hind legs to get it out of her way.

I leaned against his tailgate. "You're not disappointed that you and Zackie didn't get a task?"

Peyton walked by carrying the clipboard. "Course not. They're professionals."

"In all but pay," Cam agreed. "Peyton, how goes it?"

"It's going painfully slow at the moment." She rubbed the back of her neck and then rocked her head left and right to stretch the muscles. "I'm just glad we found her fast. I gotta get some sleep."

I risked a quick glance at Cam. "The internet research been keeping you up?"

"No, that's not the problem." She put her hands overhead to stretch her back and then rubbed her neck again. "There's more stuff on broken trailers than I care to get into, but I think I'm making progress." She yawned, covering her mouth. "It's that god-awful booming."

Cam winced. "Has it gotten much worse?"

"I can't say it's gotten louder, but it just won't quit. I was a little afraid to bring the trailer today, but we couldn't do without it."

It was a rat bastard thing to do, but I kept playing dumb. "Seems all right now. I didn't hear any booming."

"Yeah, I can't explain it. Like I said, at home it won't quit." Peyton cast a bleary eye around the parking area. "You know what? I'm going to ask the park rangers if it's okay to leave the trailer here tonight. I just want one decent night's sleep, that's all." She stalked off in search of a ranger, leaving Cam and me to wallow in guilt.

Cam leaned against the tailgate with me, drawing his shoulders up and tucking his elbows into his sides. "Any word from Ron on when he's coming?"

I shook my head, compressing my lips. "I haven't

heard from him. He said two or three days when I spoke to him and that was three days ago. He ought to be here by now."

"Call him."

"What, right now?"

"No time like the present. At least we'll know where we stand."

I pulled out my phone, found Ron's number and hit dial. I seriously hoped this wasn't going to sound like a nag. Irritating him when he was being charitable was not a good way to ensure high quality help. The phone rang and then rang some more until I was sent to his voicemail.

"Uh, hi Ron? This is Fia?" My cheeks flushed and I cleared my throat. "Sorry to bug you, but do you know about when you'll be coming here to help with the Lenape guy? I don't want to be a pain, but…" I let the thought trail off and bit my lip. "Okay, so thanks for getting back to me." I hung up before it got really awkward.

Cam tilted his head and regarded me like I was a laboratory specimen. "So, what is it about Ron that makes you so uncomfortable? Does Lucas have competition?"

I executed a world class eye roll. "It's not like that."

"What's it like, then?"

"I swear I just had this conversation…" I threw my hands up in resignation. "Look, Ron is someone who knows me from the really dark days. Memories of Ron come with a whole lot of baggage." I folded my arms around my torso and ducked my head as I struggled to come up with a way to articulate my feelings. When I spoke again, my lungs just didn't have enough air in them for a normal volume and my voice came out sounding small. "I guess I'm afraid of relapsing. He'll bring back all those memories and maybe it'll be like before."

"Like before? Like when you were a helpless child?" Cam drew his fingers through his mop of hair and set his gaze at some distant point. "Fia, you've come too far to end up overwhelmed and incapacitated. You're too strong for that now."

I nodded, but didn't trust myself to speak. I hoped he was right.

Cam turned his gaze to take a careful look at me. "Look, a big part of this effort is self-preservation. You're on the right track if you worry for your own safety. Don't let them drain you empty and always do a proper rehab between events and you'll do okay."

"Listen to the man, Fia. That's SAR wisdom, right there." Sandra performed a mock salute as she walked by, fiddling with her GPS. She must have heard the tail end of the conversation and drew her own conclusions.

Straightening up from the tailgate, I forced a smile and gave my own mock salute. "Thanks Cam. I better go help break down and pack up."

###

Dinner was history and I stooped over the sink, washing the dishes and wishing I had something for dessert. When my phone sounded with an incoming text, I finished my task before answering it and congratulated myself on not being a slave to an electronic device. A quick glance at the screen showed that Ron had finally responded. His text was short and vague, but I was still glad to hear from him. Everything was taking longer than expected due to unforeseen circumstances, but he would arrive the next day at the Greyhound station in Bethlehem. I forwarded the message to Cam to keep him in the loop and then texted

Ron to let him know I'd be there to pick him up. Mission not quite accomplished, since Ron wasn't here yet, we still had an unquiet spirit in our future and we had a marked absence of a realistic plan to move him along. But it was still a small victory and I decided to celebrate by going to bed.

CHAPTER 3

Gander's text had come in the middle of the night and I had slept through the alert. I might have missed the job all together, except the dead hand gripped the phone on the pillow right in front of my face. Some might have construed this act as something helpful, but I couldn't ignore the fact that the dead hand seemed awfully eager to go on this job. If I had more compassion for Rory or was less strapped for cash, I might have turned down the work. As things stood, warm and fuzzy feelings were starkly absent where Rory was concerned and I needed the paycheck. I'd just have to be vigilant about keeping my distance from that grommet.

Arriving at the job site, I was surprised to find myself back at the Meridian, the upscale restaurant where Cam and I had enjoyed a night out with Lucas. Gander's briefing revealed that the restaurant had recently suffered a norovirus-related incident, but not an outbreak. To prevent an outbreak and a black mark on the establishment's stellar reputation, management decided to briefly close the restaurant for 'renovations.'

"Patient zero had recently returned from an affected cruise to the Bahamas and had waited until visiting this restaurant to become symptomatic." Gander's cheek twitched as he related the story. Since most of our work either involved human tragedy or was deeply disgusting by anyone's standards, demonstrating amusement over the current situation was excusable. "Restaurant management was understandably perturbed by the possible repercussions of an infected guest and rather than take any chances, they called us in." Gander next split us into two teams. Goose and I would tackle the dining room, while he and Rory took care of the kitchen.

"Pretty swanky food hut." Goose surveyed the dining area and although it was stripped of all its finery, the room still had an ambience.

"You should see it when they're serving. A friend invited me to dinner here once." I related the story of the food avalanche to Goose while we prepped the bleach solution for surface decontamination.

"Cheah, that's the only other way we make it into places like this. A friend's gotta break out the corpo card." Goose ripped open a bag of clean towels and set to work swabbing the table tops. "At least you didn't end up dropping a depth charge on your ride home."

I giggled and grabbed a towel. "No, I didn't have to pull over once driving back. Never got sick. I think we were here long before patient zero."

I dipped my towel in the bleach solution and hummed as I wiped down table after table. Next, we tackled the chairs and while Gander and Rory worked on the bathrooms, Goose and I finished up by treating the carpets with some Thermo-55 disinfectant. Rory was kept well away from me during the entire job. It appeared that whatever plans the dead hand might have had for him were thwarted by Gander's skills as a manager.

After we completed the final touches, treating all door knobs and any other area that might be touched by a human hand with the bleach solution, we assembled outside and began stripping duct tape from the hazmat suits before showering off. Angela, the doe-eyed waitress from that fateful night out, found us in the parking area as we returned our equipment to JoJo Kennelly. I waved to her and her eyes lit up with recognition.

"Looks like you're dressed for another meal with me." Angela grinned as she looked me up and down. "I thought you waited tables like me."

"Former life. I kind of sucked at it, so this is what I do now." I felt a nudge in my ribs from Goose, who was looking at Angela with deep interest, so I introduced the crew.

"Nice meeting you folks." Angela gave a little wave in lieu of shaking anyone's gloved hand. "My manager sent me out to invite everyone back for some free drinks when we do the grand re-opening. The place is sparkling and they wanted to show their appreciation for a job well done." The crew thanked her for the invitation and she gave another little wave as she went back into the restaurant.

I looked at Gander for confirmation. "Wow, that's pretty generous of them. Are we allowed to take them up on this invitation?"

Goose followed Angela with his eyes as she retreated. "I'd like to creedle into some sectors…"

Gander raised his eyebrows at this comment, so I

translated for him. “I think Goose has taken a shine to Angela.” What he really said was that he wanted to hang out with this hot chick, but I thought Gander needed to hear a more sanitized version of this sentiment.

Nodding, Gander answered my question. “There’s no company policy against it. But just so you know, this is their little way of making sure that the job really is well done. If we’re willing to return and partake of their offerings, then we have confidence that we have eradicated the norovirus from their premises.”

I shrugged. “Free is free and we do a really thorough job. I have no problem coming back.” There was general agreement with this statement from everyone except Rory, who remained silent and avoided eye contact with me. Just as well, since I had no use for him either and I had no desire to incite the dead hand. Aside from his silence, Rory appeared sullen and withdrawn, and I wondered how much his work time with Gander had to do with it. Maybe he would decide against socializing with the team when the restaurant reopened and either quit on his own or get reassigned. Aside from the morning antics, the dead hand was quiescent and did not appear to be threatening violence, at least for the moment. The grommet made my skin crawl and his presence violated my sense of justice, but I did not believe he deserved the death penalty for being an asshat. Slowly and casually, I maneuvered myself farther away, placing JoJo and Gander between the grommet and me.

I finished my work day with a cleansing shower and headed home. I had just enough time to walk Heckle and Jeckle before picking Ron up at the bus station. The plan was to bring him to Cam's house, since a real guest room made for a more comfortable stay. I didn't even have a couch for him to crash on, so staying with me was out of the question. And if I were honest with myself, I needed some space from Ron. I was still a little freaked out by my past making its way into my present. We would eat dinner and fill Ron in on the Lenape spirit and then make our way over to Peyton's house the following day. After that, it was improvisation time.

I arrived early and stood waiting at the bus stop, chewing my cuticles and pacing. The bus pulled in five minutes late and I had managed to restrain my chewing so that only a small drop of blood appeared near my thumb nail. Weary passengers stepped off the bus and cast suspicious eyes on their new location. The eighth person to emerge from the bus was Ron. I fixed my face into an expression of welcome and took a deep breath to calm my nerves. His hair was still long and black, trailing over his shoulders in a freefall. He was no longer the skinny kid I remembered. His frame was bulked with muscle to the point where he must resemble the bulls on his ranch.

Ron flashed me a grin and waved briefly before turning to help the next passenger to disembark. An elderly woman with a cane and an enormous purse climbed slowly down the steps of the bus. Lenora Ottertooth. Clasping an elbow to steady her descent, Ron turned back towards me with a sheepish grin. My heart kicked up a beat and my gut clenched, but I kept my face frozen in a determined expression of greeting and forced one foot in front of the other to meet them.

Stepping around a scowling Lenora, Ron gave me a quick hug. "Yeah, so now you know why it took a while to get here. *Uma* wanted to come and she gets stiff if she sits too long. We needed to take some travel breaks."

Impossibly, the scowl deepened on Lenora's face as Ron stepped away, but I nodded and kept the stiff smile plastered on my face. "I'm very glad you both could come." I recited the words and then decided that I better blink and risk some genuine tears at this turn of events.

"You go get the bags." Lenora pushed Ron in the direction of the accumulating pile of luggage that was being extricated from the bowels of the bus. When I stood there uncertainly with half formed phrases of small talk rolling around in my mouth, she scowled and made a shooing motion at me. "You go get your car."

Doing as I was bidden, I found my car and pulled it up to the curb just in time to watch Ron's determined progress, hidden in a moving pile of blue and yellow luggage that slowly made its way towards the pickup zone. Lenora walked in front, guiding Ron as he kicked two bags with casters in front of him, dragged another two behind him with the aid of straps looped around his wrists, which were otherwise occupied with balancing two additional bags under each arm. He gripped the final two bags by their handles in meaty fists. I took a look at this mountain of stuff and worried that they would never leave.

I jumped out of the car and popped the trunk. "Here, let me help you with that." I reached for one of the kicked bags as it flew towards me and loaded it into the trunk. Ron was smiling cheerfully and not at all out of breath as he wrangled the remaining luggage to the gaping trunk.

Setting his burden down, Ron put his hands on his hips and surveyed the trunk. “Um, you’ve got a lot of equipment back here. We can maybe fit another two bags if we rearrange.” He moved and stacked until some promising holes opened up in the collection of SAR equipment and he was able to squeeze in the prophesied bags. “I can fit some of it in the backseat and still have room for me, but…” He scratched his head and then made a hopeful exclamation. “Ah! Just what the doctor ordered.” Yanking out a duffel bag with a broken zipper from the trunk, Ron revealed my stash of webbing, old, expired cord and carabiners.

Working together, we lashed several bags to the roof of my vehicle and crammed the remainder into the backseat. Ron crawled in behind the luggage, contorting arms and legs into a conformation that was compatible with the front seat distance and getting a seatbelt to secure. Closing the door on Ron, I stood waiting for a beat until I realized that Lenora expected me to open her door. Standing stock still with her hands grasping her enormous purse, her eyes darted to the door and then to me, back to the door and then to me. I helped her into the car.

We pulled out and after a few minutes on local roads, made it to route 33 and then the slow lane of Route

78 East. I imagined that the TV addicts among the commuters whizzing by us may have had flashbacks to the *Beverly Hillbillies*, complete with Granny and Jethro. If Zackie had been with us, we would have a hound to complete the picture, but my gut feeling was that she would have escaped through her special portal to avoid the crowding.

Items shifted in the back seat as Ron readjusted his space. "So, how've you been, Fia?"

"Don't you bother her when she's driving, boy." Lenora half turned in her seat and for a moment, I thought she'd smack him one. After a pregnant pause, satisfied that he was done bothering me, she turned to face front and crossed her arms over her chest.

"It's really okay, Lenora. I can carry on a conversation while I drive."

"You drive. Don't talk." Her eyes stared rigidly ahead and Ron shrugged in the rearview mirror.

My eyes widened and I gave a small shake of my head. "Right, I drive and don't talk. What was I thinking."

When we arrived at Cam's house, he and Zackie

met us in the driveway and I went ahead with the introductions, feeling confident in my ability to speak now that I was no longer driving.

"*Mwekane, màxksit,*" Lenora mumbled as Zackie approached her. *Dog, the red one* touched my mind. Glancing at Cam, he gave a slight nod in acknowledgment of her words.

"She said red dog," Ron offered unnecessarily.

"Zackie is indeed that." Cam helped Lenora from the car and then extended a hand to Ron. "So glad you both could come." Cam sounded sincere, but a frown creased his brow as the magnitude of the luggage we carried became evident. "It's, er, nice that you could clear your schedules to make this *short* visit." When he received no direct response regarding the length of their stay, he tried again. "Are you planning on vacationing in the area after we have completed our task?"

Ron wore a sunny smile. "No, no plans for a vacation in the area."

Lenora took in Cam's measure as he gripped her elbow to steady her. "Big man. That's good. You can help with the luggage." Removing her elbow from his grasp, she ambled towards his house and let herself in.

Blushing, but still grinning, Ron shook his head. "*Uma* must be tired after the trip. She probably needs to rest." He hoisted four of the blue bags, leaving the remaining mix of four blue and yellow bags to Cam and me to wrangle into the house.

Upon entering the house, the sound of clanging pots and running water met our ears. We left the luggage in the front room and found Lenora in the kitchen, standing at the counter and extracting a bag of flour from her purse. Without turning around, she called out directions. "Bring me the yellow bag with the food and then fix up the rooms and put the rest of the luggage there. I'm cooking dinner."

Cam looked at me with raised eyebrows and I looked at Ron. He shrugged his shoulders in reply. "Best do as she says and no one gets hurt." Turning on his heel, he made for the front room and grabbed a few bags. "Which room is *Uma's*?"

Cam sighed and ran a hand through his hair. "Right this way."

I wavered for a moment, wondering if I should offer to help cook or if I should go back to being a porter. The thought of all that alone time with Lenora decided it for me, and I returned to the front room and picked up some bags.

###

Dinner was served. I stuffed my face with a savory stew and hot fried bread that melted in my mouth. Dessert was a baked pudding packed with brown sugar, molasses, cinnamon and maple syrup. I was in heaven. Any thought of conversation during the meal was inconceivable after the first bite and Cam gave up trying to include me until I came up for air.

"Oh, God. I'm stuffed. I can't feel my legs…" I pushed back from the table and both Ron and Cam handed me napkins.

Lenora stared at me wide-eyed, one hand on her cheek. "How'd you eat like that, little girl?"

I dabbed at my face with the napkins. "Er, I get a lot of practice?"

Cam cleared his throat. "Thank you for that delicious meal, Lenora."

“You’re welcome.” For a moment, Lenora looked pleased, but then she crossed her arms over her chest, tilting her head as she challenged Cam. “Why’d you not invite the tribal man? If he’s got trouble, a full belly’s the best thing for him.”

Cam cocked an eyebrow and shifted his eyes towards Ron. “I take it you didn’t tell her anything?”

“Naw, I thought I’d leave that to you.” Ron mumbled and stared at the napkin he crumpled between his fingers.

“Right…” Cam cleared his throat again. “Lenora, we invited Ron here to help us translate what your tribal man says.”

Ducking my head, I muttered softly under my breath. “So, that accounts for Ron. I’m not exactly sure why she’s here.”

Lenora swiveled her dark eyes to meet mine and her brows came down as she spoke. “I’m here to keep this youngin’ out of trouble. And you, you’re trouble.”

Cam grinned and his eyes shone with amusement. “She is most certainly that.” His face became serious again as he returned to the topic of the Lenape spirit. "Back to the tribal man…I did not invite him here tonight to meet you because he's dead."

"The tribal man died? Oh, that's terrible. What happened?" Lenora uncrossed her arms and leaned forward, concern etched in her face.

I shook my head. "He didn't die recently."

Lenora's face creased in confusion and Cam picked up the conversational ball. "We think he died several hundred years ago. I don't know what your views are on –"

"Are you talking ancestor spirit?"

Cam looked at me and then back to Lenora. "Yes, ancestor spirit."

"Crap."

"Why 'crap,' *Uma*?" Ron looked up from his twisted napkin and cocked his head.

"Crap because the souls of evil people remain on earth, to visit all the places where they committed bad deeds and to be punished there. Bad news for us if this spirit's evil."

Ron looked at me, his eyes wide and his face a shade paler. “Is he evil?”

“Maybe.” I fidgeted and had trouble meeting his eyes. “Look, I don’t know for sure. Another spirit said some things that make me wonder about him, but I would not knowingly bring you in to do something dangerous. I -”

“More possibilities.” Lenora raised a finger to interrupt me. “What soul we dealing with here?”

“I beg your pardon?” Cam scrunched his eyebrows and leaned forward with his elbows on the table.

“The lenapeokan is the true soul, and then there’s the blood soul. The true soul is in the heart and body and looks like a person. You die when this soul leaves the body. The blood soul also leaves the body at death, but it looks like a bright ball.”

“Are you kidding me? An orb?” I was stunned by this information. Ghost hunters like Lucas were forever taking pictures of orbs in haunted places. People always said that the images were caused by dust reflecting the camera flash and were just meaningless artifacts of photography.

Lenora turned her gaze to me. "That's right. The blood soul can wander the earth forever. They're bad. They cause paralysis, strokes, lameness…Don't ever eat in the dark or leave a sick person in a dark room because the blood souls wander." She rapped on the table top once with her knuckles for emphasis, to make sure I got the point.

Ron nodded. "*Uma's* grandfather was a shaman. She learned from him."

"Are you also a shaman?" Cam leaned towards Lenora. "Can you do something for the Lenape man?"

Lenora shook her head. "I'm a…how do you say?" She looked at Ron quizzically.

"A midwife."

"Yeah, I'm a midwife. I learned enough from Grandfather about the herbs and spirits to do this for my people."

"Okay, back to the spirits." I put my hands on my bloated stomach and forced myself to concentrate. The food coma was starting to shut me down. "What would a Lenape spirit need to find rest?"

"Maybe he's not buried right and that's what makes

him walk." Lenora shrugged. "You seen him? What's he look like?"

"He's wearing buckskin and a breech-cloth."

"Was it worn or patched?"

"No, nothing repaired on his clothes, no stains." I shook my head and then motioned with my hands. "The sides and front of his head are bald, but he has this clump of black hair at the crown with two feathers."

"Was it shiny with grease or normal looking?"

I thought for a moment. "Normal hair, no grease. And his face is all red."

Lenora shook her head. "No, that ain't it then."

"Based on what, exactly? How do you know if he was buried properly? Why ain't that it?" Cam threw his hands in the air in exasperation.

Lenora returned his exasperation and looked at Cam as if he were an idiot. "Because, Kemosabe, he's dressed in new clothes."

"Seriously, *Uma*? Kemosabe?" Ron's eyes squinted with merriment as a grin erupted on his face and he let out a deep chuckle. "You're quoting the *Lone Ranger* now?"

Ignoring him, she went on. "We wash the body of our dead and dress them in new clothing." She began holding up a finger for each point she made. "We comb the hair, but we don't give it grease. That's only for the living. And we paint the face with olaman before we put them in the ground. That makes it red." Crossing her arms over her chest, she sat back, daring Cam to contradict her.

Cam blew air from his puffed cheeks and also sat back. "All right, I guess I buy it."

"And that spirit's not confused. He knows he's dead. He comes with his face painted red." Lenora circled her own face with a finger.

For a few long minutes, no one said anything as we pondered the plight of the Lenape spirit. I slumped in my seat and my limbs grew heavy. The images of the people seated at the table swam and distorted as I fought to keep my eyes open. I was nearly out when Lenora came up with something that made me bolt upright.

"Bring your dog to him."

"Wha- what?" I looked straight at Cam. Did she

know?

Cam had a much better poker face than me and his voice was level when he spoke. “Why should we do that, Lenora?”

“Once the lenapeokan departs from the body, it travels along the Milky Way, and eventually joins the Creator in the twelfth heaven. Deceased dogs stand guard at the bridges connecting the Milky Way to the abode of the Creator. Souls of people who mistreated a dog or done other evil will not be allowed to cross these bridges. If this spirit is evil, he will be afraid of the dog.”

A wave of relief washed over me. Zackie’s secret was safe. If people knew about the psychopomp, there would be no end of trouble with folks wanting to send messages to their dearly departed or making special requests for escort to the other side. “Oh, well that makes sense. I guess we-”

“Also, the old Lenape used to bury the dead with dogs. Dogs served as guides for the departed souls on their way to the next world.” She said this so matter-of-factly that I actually nodded in agreement before my head snapped around to look at Cam again.

Cam's features froze in that bland look he does when he needs to feel something out. "I see… So, you think Zackie might be able to help this spirit go on to the afterlife?"

"Maybe. The dog will do what she wants to do. We can't force her to help him."

Ron leaned forward, planting his elbows on his knees and looked at us earnestly. "See, we don't believe that man has dominion over the earth and animals. We're just a part of things and all things of creation are equal and necessary, worthy of respect and honor."

Intuitively, Lenora and Ron understood the fundamental truth about Zackie. The best thing about their worldview was that if Zackie were able to bring the Lenape man through the portal, there would be nothing surprising in this. It would just be accepted. As far as I was concerned, the fewer explanations required, the better.

Cam nodded and his face cleared. "We'll do just that. Zackie will come with us when we talk to the Lenape spirit."

"Good." Lenora stood up. "You all clean up. I'm going to bed."

# # #

"I exhausted all natural explanations, so I needed to look into unnatural explanations." Peyton arched an eyebrow in silent accusation as she told me this. I thought I'd be the first to arrive at Peyton's home, beating Cam and his sleepy houseguests by a good fifteen minutes. Ron and Lenora were only an hour off from their regular waking time in Oklahoma, but travel had taken its toll and they were slow to rise that morning. Meanwhile, Lucas and his film crew had been devastatingly efficient and were already busy filming background footage for the story.

I stuck my hands in the pockets of my fleece as I watched the activity. "So, you thought you'd call in some ghost busters?"

"That's right. You got a problem with that?"

I sighed and scraped my fingers through my bangs. Out loud, I said, "No, no problem with that." Internally, I thought that this was going to royally complicate everything.

Lucas finished directing the crew on what images to

capture and his eyes widened in recognition and surprise as he approached. His arms extended and he grabbed me in a bear hug, lifting me off my feet. "Fia! Wonderful to see you again."

I returned the hug, because, well… Lucas. "Good to see you, too." He smelled of sandal wood and coconut shampoo and I got a rush of memories from our last spirit encounter. As he returned me to solid ground, I thought that maybe between us we could make things work and release the Lenape spirit.

Lucas took the opportunity to murmur into my ear. "This is the case where she thought it was a raccoon?" I gave enough of a nod for him to feel and he gave me a squeeze to let me know he understood.

Peyton took in the scene of fond familiarity and narrowed her eyes at me. "Why do I get the feeling that this isn't your first rodeo?" Crossing her arms over her chest, she turned her gaze to Lucas. "I take it no introductions are necessary?"

Grinning, Lucas dropped an arm over my shoulders. "Definitely not. We've worked together before."

"Oh, have you now?" Peyton directed this question

to me, but I was spared from answering as Cam's truck pulled up. The warmth of his embrace left me as Lucas strode towards the truck to greet Cam.

"Cam! How the hell are you?"

"Good, good." Cam exited the cab and engaged Lucas in a back-slapping hug before opening the tailgate for Zackie. Meanwhile, Ron emerged and trotted around the truck to help Lenora. Armed with her capacious handbag, she gingerly stepped down from the cab. Moving forward to wish them a good morning, I caught a whiff of ammonia before Hannah shoved me and I stumbled.

"Fleet of foot is our Fia." Ron chuckled as he caught me one-handed before I hit the dirt.

Blushing heavily, I struggled to get my feet under me and caught the look of uncertainty in Lucas's eyes as I righted myself. His grin faltered as he gazed at Ron. At that moment, Lenora stared hard at Lucas and then squealed and burst into a smile liked an excited little kid. Having never seen her smile before, I froze, immobile as an ice sculpture, not knowing what to expect. "Hey, I know you. You're that ghost hunter guy. I watch your show all the time."

The grin returned and Lucas stepped forward to

shake her hand. "I'm Lucas Tremaine. Very pleased to meet you."

Ron spun around to see the celebrity, abruptly releasing me to wobble in place a moment before regaining my balance. "Oh my God! It's Lucas Tremaine." Ron stuck out his hand and pumped Lucas's hand vigorously. "I'm Ron and this is Lenora. We watch you all the time back in Oklahoma."

"Great to meet you, Ron. How do you know Fia?"

Before Ron could speak, I interjected. "We met when we were little kids." I did not want Lucas to know anything about my psychotic past, how Ron and I were institutionalized when we were kids. He thought I was pretty normal except for the spirit detecting thing, and I wanted it to stay that way. Maybe Ron would show some discretion, but I couldn't be sure.

"Oh, childhood sweethearts?" Lucas's voice was teasing, but his eyes were still shadowed by uncertainty.

Ron laughed. "We shared more than Valentines growing up. We lived—" Catching the look of near panic in my eyes, he stopped speaking and changed course. "We were close."

Lucas bit his lip and nodded. "Well, I guess I better get back to work and go take a few readings…" He let his voice trail off and he shot a furtive glance at me before walking back to the crew. I almost called out to him to stop, to let me explain, but then the moment passed.

"You might have been better off with the truth." Cam muttered the words, but Peyton's sharp ears picked up his comment.

"Speaking of truth, how about I get a little of that?" Peyton looked from me to Cam. She shifted her weight to take on a casual stance, but I could tell she was pissed.

Lenora sensed the tension and decided to take the opportunity to pile on. "You been lying to this lady, little girl?"

I blew out a breath. "Not exactly. It's more like we offer up logical explanations and let her draw her own conclusions."

Ron nodded. "That's why I like Lucas's show. He does that. I never saw him make a claim that something weird was going on. He just gives you the evidence and you figure it out."

"Well, we got something really weird going on right here." Peyton's eyes widened as she spoke and color rose in her cheeks as she struggled to keep her temper. "I want you to tell me straight up what you think is going on. Is it that dead woman from the search? Did she follow me home?"

Cam took a step forward and laid a gentle hand on her arm. "Easy there. It's not Maggie Pierceson." He slanted his eyes towards me and gave an imperceptible shrug. "It is a spirit, so you're right on that front."

Peyton whirled on him. "Well, why didn't you just tell me this from the get-go?"

"Would you have believed us from the get-go?" Cam kept his voice level and did not react to Peyton's escalating anger.

She inhaled deeply, bunched her fists and was about to launch into a diatribe, but then she clamped her lips shut and breathed heavily through her nose. Briefly closing her eyes, Peyton shook her head as if to clear it. Throwing her hands in the air as the universal sign of 'I give up,' she took another moment to think before she spoke. "No. You're right. I would not have believed you. I needed time to come to my own conclusions."

"Look, I'm really sorry we have to do things this way, but sometimes we can just clear things up and no one has to be traumatized by anything." I sighed. "Things didn't work out that easily for you, unfortunately."

Peyton nodded in resignation. "Yeah, but things aren't really worked out yet, right? I heard booming from the trailer just this morning. If it's not the dead woman, who is it?"

"He's a tribal man from a long time back. That's what they told us." Lenora jutted her chin towards Cam and me.

Peyton's mouth fell open. "For real? But why? What did I do to bring this on?"

"Why you? Don't know, but we'll ask." Lenora shrugged eloquently.

"All of this just makes no sense to me." Peyton's shoulders slumped and she shook her head morosely.

"Welcome to the club." Cam turned on his heel and began walking towards the trailer. Zackie had preceded him and was circling it, nose to the ground. There was no sign of our Lenape friend and I worried that Ron and Lenora had made that long trip for nothing. If the spirit didn't want to show himself, we had little recourse. We gathered around the trailer and soon, our small group was joined by Lucas and his film crew.

"Is he here?" Peyton's eyes shifted nervously.

I shook my head. "I don't see anything, but-" A spray of gravel flew past me and bounced off the side of the trailer with a sound like a hail storm. Awesome. Just what we needed. The spirit had gone poltergeist. I spun around, shielding my face with upraised arms, while trying to pinpoint where the gravel came from. From the corner of my eye, I spotted Lucas with a handheld camera aimed towards the woods. The second round of gravel formed an arc around him and was then directed back into the woods as Hannah returned fire. She was having none of it. Flying gravel from the woods stung my arms and I felt a moment's irritation as the lack of cover for the rest of us registered. Hannah cared only for Lucas.

A voice growled from the woods. "*Alëmskakw, wèmi, yukwe!*"

I shook my head, struggling for comprehension.

With nothing making sense, I yelled out, repeating what I heard. “Ron! He said ‘Alem skok wemi yuk way.’”

Lenora spat an invective as Ron shielded her from the worst of it with his broad back. “*Mahtënu!*” The word formed meaning in my brain - Bad man!

The rain of gravel ceased as suddenly as it had started. Ron shifted slightly, minutely relaxing his defense of Lenora. “He said ‘Leave, all of you, now!’” Twitching wide, frightened eyes toward me, his voice sounded strained. “Maybe we should –”

Before I could respond, the voice from the woods came again, but this time he was sobbing. “*Ktalënixsi... ktalënixsi!*” And this time, I understood. *You speak Lenape!*

Ron began to repeat what he’d heard. “He said – ”

“He said, ‘You speak Lenape.’ I can understand him now.” I grinned back at him.

“We have our breakthrough at last.” Cam wiped a trickle of blood from his face and closed his eyes briefly.

The voice from the woods cried out again and it was pitiful. “Where have you been? All these long years…I searched and I searched for you…” The voice broke and a wailing sob echoed through the woods. But this was heard only by Cam and me.

Peyton cocked her head and squinted. “What was that? It didn’t sound like a screech owl or a coyote. It was really faint, but the hair on my arms is standing up.” The camera crew dutifully filmed the hair on Peyton’s arms and I rolled my eyes.

The voice had faded to a croaking rasp. “Is she with you?”

I sidled over to Cam and lowered my voice. “Who is the ‘she’ he’s talking about? Maggie? Zackie? Someone else?”

“How the hell should I know?” Cam glowered at me as he whispered back. “We should just ask for clarification.”

I hissed my response, yanking my bangs back in frustration. “What if we piss him off because we don’t know who ‘she’ is? He might go back to throwing gravel or just take off on us.”

“Zackie can go and hold him in place while we try to figure this out.” Turning his gaze to Zackie, she cocked her ears and tilted her head and then shook herself. It seemed like the canine version of shrugging her shoulders and saying 'whatever,' since she subsequently trotted off into the woods.

"Aiiiiaaa! Let go!" The brush rustled vigorously, accompanied by the sound of breaking branches. "I am not ready. You cannot force me, red dog." A short, low growl thundered from the woods and the tumult ceased.

"Should we go in?" I took a step forward, but Cam held me back and shook his head.

"Let Zackie handle him. He can hear us fine from where we are."

Lenora breathed a sigh of relief. "Oh, that's good. I'm too old for that shit."

Cheek twitching as he suppressed a smile at this remark, Lucas motioned to the camera crew to reposition on the periphery of the woods in order to capture the action from several angles. The woods were deathly still – no birdsong, no skittering of small animals in the brush. Even the breeze had died. The sky was blue with a bright sun, but the stillness felt ominous and I chewed on a cuticle.

Cam cleared his throat and began. “Who is she? The woman you asked about?”

The spirit’s voice cracked. “She-Who-Ate-Audachienrra.” The branches started rustling again, at first gently, but then with increasing violence. The scent of ozone filled the air and I feared that we would lose him.

Turning to Ron and Lenora, I relayed what the spirit said. “What is Audachienrra?”

Lenora answered me, her eyes watching the branches as thick pieces began to fly despite the lack of wind. “The root of the may-apple. It’s very poisonous. Kills you in two hours.”

“Back off, Cam, or we’re going to lose him. Whoever ‘she’ is died because someone poisoned her and this event is too emotional to start with. Ask him something else and quick.” I forced the bangs out of my face and nervously shifted my weight.

Cam fired off a new question to divert the spirit’s attention. “What is your name?”

Lenora spun towards him, her face livid. “Don’t ask him that!”

“Why the hell not?” Cam threw his hands in the air and his brow furrowed.

“The name dies with the man,” Ron explained. “It is an abuse to say the name again after someone dies. Ask him who he was instead.”

“You can ask him yourself.” Cam folded his arms, obviously nonplussed by all the unknown rules in dealing with this spirit.

Ron repeated the question in Lenape and the voice from the woods replied with pride. “I was the one who counseled the chief.” The force behind the swaying branches diminished with the scent of ozone and I smelled tobacco wafting in the air.

Lenora nodded when I shared what the spirit said. “He-Who-Counseled-the-Chief, how did you die?” Cocking her head as if she could hear him, she waited for a reply.

“I hunted bear with my family. Brother bear grabbed me by the jaw and crushed my head. He was quick and I did not suffer.” I winced as he said this and heard in my mind a sharp crack as his skull gave way. “Brother bear had a good hunt that day.”

I translated for the hearing impaired and then asked a question of my own. "What did you do to Maggie?"

The spirit roared and my eyes widened as I took an involuntary step back, almost tripping over Cam. "Fia, he'd just calmed down! Now look what you've done!" In an effort to mitigate my inflammatory question, Cam tried to soothe the spirit. "What she means is, do you know what happened to Maggie?"

"She died, just like She-Who-Ate-Audachienrra!" The spirit screamed the words, setting my ears ringing as heat from an inferno blasted against my skin. Thick branches broke from the trees and brush, going airborne in all directions and knocking one of Lucas's crew to the ground. Lucas ran to the man and helped him up. His scalp was bleeding and he looked dazed as Lucas hurried him away to the safety of Peyton's front porch. Calling over his shoulder, Lucas told the rest of his crew to abandon their equipment and get out of there. After a flash of lightning split the clear, blue sky, Cam cried out to Zackie to release the spirit. The sky lit up a final time, silhouetting the form of He-Who-Counseled-the-Chief on the roof of the trailer as he smashed his fist down with a resounding crash that left us hunching and protecting our ears. With one last whooshing sound, the world was still again for a moment and ozone filled my sinuses, burning my throat and making me cough. Just when we thought it was over, the brush parted and Zackie emerged from the woods, licking her chops.

Peyton stared at me, the whites of her eyes exposed. “What the hell did you people just do?”

Lenora made a disparaging grunt. “It’s not what they did, it’s what they didn’t do. He-Who-Counseled-the-Chief is still out there.” She grimaced and patted her chest over her heart. I hoped we wouldn’t have to perform CPR.

“And more riled up than when we started.” Peyton shook her head, definitely freaked out by what she’d experienced. “He’s gonna pound on that trailer night and day until I die of sleep deprivation.” Staring at the cameraman in the distance, she watched as he blotted blood from his head on to a wad of tissues. “Or maybe he’ll do something worse.”

“Look, these things can take time to resolve.” I wanted to offer comfort, to give her some hope. “We didn’t know what his triggers were and we managed to hit a bunch of them right off the bat. That was just bad luck. But now we know." I looked to Cam for help.

"He's already given us some information that will help us next time." Cam raised a finger as he made his point. "The way he died did not disturb him –"

"It disturbed me!" I shook off a chill as I remembered the cracking sound.

"As I was saying, his manner of death is not the cause for why he walks. He was deeply disturbed when we mentioned Maggie and the other woman. Something extremely traumatic connects these two. I think we need to think harder about this and try to understand the connection."

I started thinking harder about it before Cam finished speaking, but my thoughts were interrupted by Peyton. "I'm going to check on the camera guy, see if he wants to sue me." Squaring her shoulders, she shook off her unease and marched out. The rest of us followed her example and trailed after her.

While the head wound oozed and dripped, the cameraman insisted that it wasn't serious and Lucas assured Peyton that the company's workmans' comp insurance would take care of any expenses related to the accident. Relieved that she bore no financial responsibility for the wounded cameraman, Peyton remembered her manners and offered her guests hot beverages. Hoping to put as much physical distance between themselves and the distressing incident as soon as possible, everyone except Lenora declined. After gathering up the discarded equipment, Lucas sent his crew off and then joined Cam, Ron and me in Peyton's cheerful yellow kitchen, where we kept Lenora company as she sipped her coffee. Feeling a bit peaked, I took the opportunity to visit my car, so I could right my teetering electrolyte balance with some coconut water. No one else except Cam accepted my offer for a bottle. Their loss. When I returned, Peyton tried to carry on with polite conversation, but she sat rigid on the edge of her seat. It seemed like she was exerting all of her military discipline to not look at her watch or beat out a tattoo with an impatient foot. She probably needed time alone to process current events.

Unbidden, my brain obsessed on the random bits of information I'd accumulated. I no longer thought that the Lenape spirit somehow killed Maggie because of the anguish he displayed when we brought it up. But he was there when she died, there was no disputing that fact. He told her *Apëwi këlukahëla* – you give up easily. I repeated the words to myself, trying to puzzle it out.

"Who gives up easily?" Ron asked, overhearing me as I mumbled to myself. Unlike the others, Ron appeared calm and capable of taking on the next thing. Maybe because of his difficult childhood, he was like me, schooled in the art of quick recovery. You never knew when the next blow would land, so it did not serve your purposes to freeze up or panic.

"What? Oh, yeah, that was the other spirit, Maggie, the one we asked him about. She said he spoke to her either before she died or while she was dying. I can't be sure. Her mind is kind of messed up, so it's hard to make sense of what she says." I gave my head a slight shake to clear Maggie's scrambled thought processes. "Anyway, he told her that she gives up too easily."

"Why would he taunt her when she was so vulnerable?" Ron's eyes were a molten chocolate, soft with concern for a dead woman he didn't know. It made me think about why we became friends.

"I don't know that it was a taunt. It really upset him when I asked him about Maggie. Her death bothered him." My mouth formed a grim line while I pondered the contradictions.

"Do you hear that?" Peyton pointed vaguely in the direction of the trailer, her eyes wide.

Lenora shook her head. "Hear what? I don't hear nothing and my ears still work good."

"Exactly. It's been about a half hour now and I haven't heard any booming. Maybe something good came out of today after all." A smile lit up her face and her posture relaxed. Watching this change, it occurred to me that she hadn't been impatient for us all to leave. She was waiting for the situation to relapse and for the booming to start up again.

"You thought it would be worse after confronting him?" Cam ventured.

Peyton nodded. "I was pretty sure he'd start in again with a vengeance and you'd all go to your nice quiet homes and leave me to deal with it." Her smile trembled and she had a sickly pallor that made the dark circles under eyes dominate her face. Peyton was the classic image of a haunted woman. That same face looked back at me in the mirror for years and I knew better than most how the stress of living like this could eat you like a cancer. Because

Peyton had a low degree of sensitivity to the unseen world, I thought she would have some protection. I was wrong. My cheeks burned and I hung my head, unable to look Peyton or anyone else in the eye. I had been so concerned with freeing the dead that I neglected to protect the living.

A cold, wet nose nudged my hand. Looking up from my guilt-induced stoop, the tawny silver face of Simber stared back at me, a somber look in her eyes. In addition to searching for the missing, Simber was also a certified therapy dog and my morose attitude had activated her instinct to comfort. She put a paw on my knee and I tousled her ears, immediately feeling better for it. Some people saw wolf when they looked at her, but to me, she had the appearance of a teddy bear. After a few more minutes spent stroking her, Simber determined that I was sufficiently revived and with a final lick to my hand, she sauntered off to rest beneath the table. Zackie had stationed herself in front of the door and dozed with one eye now fixed on me. I sensed a slight disapproval and the words '*Suck it up, buttercup*' echoed softly on the edges of my awareness.

Always tuned in to Zackie, Cam caught the exchange. "Remember, the best you can hope for is a clear conscience." He murmured just loud enough for me to hear and I nodded in response, silently resolving to do better for Peyton and others like her down the road.

I was startled out of my reverie when Lenora stood up and took her mug to the sink. "Okay, I'm done now. Let's go." With a nod towards Peyton, she opened the door. "Thank you for the coffee."

Shrugging, the rest of also got up to leave and Peyton followed us to the door to say good-bye. Taking her by the elbow, I steered her to the side as the others exited. "If the Lenape man does anything weird, give me a call. Even if it's just thumping on the trailer again, let me know."

"Count on it." Peyton took off her glasses and rubbed her bloodshot eyes. "I'm going to get some shut-eye while the peace lasts."

I patted her arm and stepped through the door, shutting it behind me. Walking quickly, I caught up with the group near the parked cars. Cam was opening the tailgate of his truck for Zackie when she froze and put her nose in the air. Re-orienting her body towards the woods behind the trailer, she continued to sample the scents. With a bay worthy of a pack of hounds, she shot across Peyton's property at full speed. All I saw was a red streak and brush swaying as she entered the woods.

"Your dog's gone," Ron said unnecessarily. He shielded his eyes as he tracked her progress and then shook his head.

Cam sat heavily on the tailgate. "I guess we wait. She'll come back here when she's done." I sighed deeply. Cam was playing out the charade for the sake of our companions. Zackie could materialize in the truck, at home, on a plane in mid flight, heck, pretty much anywhere she felt like it, and at the time of her choosing. She wasn't some lost dog that we needed to wait for.

I opened my trunk to deposit the empty coconut water bottles and then pulled out a folded camp chair for Lenora. She sat down without commenting, drew a multi-colored knitting project from her voluminous handbag and set to work. I wondered if she was still carrying a supply of flour with her.

"How long does she usually disappear for when she runs off?" Lucas fingered the knitted yarn and murmured something appreciative to Lenora, who smiled in response.

Cam shrugged. "It varies. I guess it depends on

whatever it is she was chasing." Looking at his watch, Cam then glanced toward Peyton's house. "I suppose we could ask Peyton to keep an eye out for Zackie if she's not back soon."

Ron clucked his tongue in disapproval. "Maybe you should go into the woods and yell for her. She ought to come when you call."

I snorted, but then decided to play along. "Yeah, well, hounds are not a pliant breed. They're kind of independent-minded. But it might not hurt to go yell for her, Cam." I kept a straight face as I thought about Cam fruitlessly crawling through the brambles, calling for Zackie.

"Er, right… Zackie is not the best trained dog. I doubt it would do any good." Cam left it at that, his eyes straying towards the prickly flora lining the perimeter of the woods. There were limits to how far he was willing to go to maintain the pretense that Zackie was a normal dog. There were no limits to how much amusement I might derive from continuing to test his limits.

"But she might be lost and scared, Cam. I think the least you could do – "

My entertainment was interrupted by a loud rustling as Zackie pushed through the vegetation near the trailer. She gazed at Cam and then turned and glanced over her shoulder as if she expected him to follow.

"Oh, no you don't." Cam jumped off the tailgate and reached into the truck bed for a box of assorted junk. Pulling out a handheld device and a dog collar with an antenna, he turned back towards Zackie and motioned for her to come to the truck. Chuffing and grumbling, Zackie approached the vehicle and leaped onto the tailgate.

"What's that thingie?" Lenora stopped knitting and stared at the devices.

Cam turned on both pieces of equipment, clicked a button on the handheld device and held the collar up against it. "These thingies are an Astro collar and GPS – I am linking the two at the moment. They will allow me to see where Zackie is when she goes back into the woods." Cam fitted the collar around Zackie's neck and told her to be off.

As Zackie sped off through the brush, Lenora pulled a face. "Damn it, I thought we wouldn't have to bushwhack. I told you I'm too old for that shit."

Cam raised an eyebrow and tilted his head. "Exactly why I tagged Zackie with the collar. We'll try to find an easier way to reach her destination."

# # #

I rode shotgun, calling out directions to Cam as he drove and I studied the GPS. Lucas, Ron and Lenora sat in cozy proximity in the back seat. The blip that was Zackie had stopped moving and the GPS told me that she had treed something. Right, because she was really out hunting raccoon.

"She's stopped moving." I glanced back down at the GPS and then checked the road in front of us. "Turn right up ahead. I think there's a trail head we can use to get to her."

Cam swung the truck in the direction I indicated and parked it on the side of the road near an opening in the dense foliage. "How far in do we need to go?"

"Hold on a sec." I fiddled with the GPS and got it to set a course for Zackie. "Looks like it's only a few hundred yards. And we're in luck – we can stay on the trail most of the way." If we had cut through the woods, we would have had to hike about five miles from Peyton's house to make it to Zackie. Luck was with us because Zackie could have stopped somewhere inconvenient in the middle of the expanse of forest, and it would have been a few miles in no matter how we tried to get to her.

Cam dug around in his truck bed and came out with two hiking sticks that he handed to Lenora. "The trail is fairly gentle, but use these. They'll do you better than the cane." Lenora stared dubiously at the sticks, but then put her cane in the truck and started down the trail with the rest of us following her. Just as well that she was in the lead, since we could not go faster than our slowest hiker and I'd rather have her where I could see her. The trail was flat and covered with soft mulch, so the going was easy.

When we reached a point where we were parallel to Zackie's location, I told the crew that we needed to cut into the woods. Ron held the brush back to allow Lenora to enter, and to her credit, she didn't swear once. But keeping her balance was tricky as every step forward caused her to become snagged on brush and there were now rocks and other forest debris to make her lose her footing.

Ron caught her arm as she wobbled. "*Uma*, stop.

This isn't safe for you."

"We can't leave her here alone. That's not safe either." Cam frowned and then looked my way. "Maybe you should stay with her."

I bit my lip. "I'm okay with that, but what if you need me? You don't know what Zackie has going on."

Cam expelled a noisy breath and rubbed his face. "And I might need Ron to translate."

"I'll be fine. You people go on. I can wait here." Lenora thrust her chin out defiantly and dug the sticks into the ground to steady herself.

"No, *Uma*. We are not leaving you here. There could be bear or coyote in these woods." Ron pointed to the GPS in my hand. "How much farther does it say?"

"About another two, three hundred yards."

Ron stepped in front of Lenora and faced away from her. "Come on. Get on my back. I can carry you the rest of the way."

Grumbling, Lenora handed me her purse and then the sticks. "Making me look like a useless old woman, Ron

Falling-Leaf."

Ron bent his knees and she clambered on top of him. He clasped her knees in the crook of his arm and straightened. "Okay, lead on."

I stepped forward and oriented myself by the GPS before striking out. Ron followed me, while Cam and Lucas took up the rear guard, keeping a watchful eye in case Ron slipped in the uneven terrain. I shifted the purse to my other shoulder and decided that yes, Lenora was carrying a supply of flour. We made slow progress and I'd occasionally risk a backward glance to see how Ron was doing. That dude was not even breathing hard and somehow managed not to stumble. I wondered if they did this often, since Ron and Lenora seemed so practiced at it. This was not something you saw every day. Watching an old lady being carried piggyback through the woods was definitely worth the price of admission.

My feelings of amusement bled out of me as we got closer to Zackie. The sound of flowing water and feelings of dread flooded my senses. "Cam…" I left the alert hanging as I concentrated on fleshing out the details of what we approached.

"Go slow, Fia. This isn't good." Cam's voice was level, but there was tension when he spoke. I swallowed and put one foot in front of the other, sweeping my eyes and other faculties in a deep arc before taking another step.

The ground became spongy as we neared the water and blood seeped up from the earth fouling my boots. I shot a quick look behind me, but neither Lucas nor Ron reacted in any way to this horror. Casting my eyes forward, I took another hesitant step, whimpering a little as the stench of blood grew stronger. Fog condensed around me, obscuring my vision and the metallic smell of blood now left me close to gagging. I came to a full stop and everything in me said not to move forward, to go back to the truck and get the hell out of here. Zackie appeared out of the heavy mist and walked at heel beside me, guiding me closer to the water. I dug my fingers into the red fur on her back and was calmed, despite feeling the raised hackles erupting at her shoulders and along her spine. Her feet were mired in thick, bloody clots and it gave me pause to think that she was leading me to the source of this gore.

By the time we reached the water's edge, I was ankle deep in blood and something rubbery slithered beneath my feet making it hard to step normally. Bits of skull with long strands of black hair floated in the muck and my hand flew to my mouth, whether to stifle a moan or control the reflex to vomit, I didn't know. I dropped the purse and the GPS, gasping and forcing air in and out of my lungs as shock and raw terror tore through me. The emotions shattered me and my knees buckled.

"Oh my God…what happened here?" Cam appeared at my side and his eyes were filled with unshed tears. He wrapped an arm around me and told me to breathe normally and let the emotions wash through me. I hunched and closed my eyes, trying not to see the butchered remains that floated around us. My breathing slowed as I focused on trying to get my control back. I wasn't even close when I heard splashing and a cry of deep anguish.

"*Nènhìlëwèt!*" The word was laced with torment and grief. I couldn't understand. My mind would not translate and I stood shaking my head, trapped in the fog and desperately trying to comprehend. I repeated the word as I heard it – nen-hill-u-wet, nen-hill-u-wet – struggling to force meaning from the sound.

"Ron, Lenora – what does it mean?" Cam turned and I felt my body turn with him as his arm wrapped around me and kept me on my feet. Lenora stood next to

Ron, his hand on her arm keeping her steady.

"It means murderer." Ron spoke at a normal volume, but his voice had a dangerous edge.

Lenora heard it too and she turned sharply to look at him. She lunged for her fallen purse and kneeled next to it, pawing through the contents. "Boy, you help me here." She pulled two things out of the bag and held one up to Ron. "Light a fire. Do it now." Ron had a wild look in his eyes and his fists were clenched. Lenora grabbed one of his hands and forced him to take the lighter she held and to look at her. "Now, boy. Light a fire."

Ron shook his head slightly and briefly closed his eyes. He took a deep breath and helped Lenora stand. "Yes, *Uma*."

"Right," Lucas said. "We'll need tinder and kindling." He looked rapidly from Lenora and Ron to Cam and me. His face was creased with concern and he had a look of bewilderment, but he didn't stop to ask questions. He foraged for small, dry items and built a pile near Lenora. After a moment, Ron joined him, finding larger pieces of wood that would burn. In two minutes, they had enough for Ron to use Lenora's lighter to get a flame going. Ron knelt next to the small fire, cupping his hand around it and using the lighter to spread the flame to the bits of twig and bark they had gathered.

When the fire had caught, Lenora brought the second item she pulled from her purse close to the dancing flame. The bundle of sage lit and began to smoke. Chanting, she waved the burning sage around Ron and then handed him the bundle. As Ron trailed the smoke around us, Lenora went back to her purse and pulled out a small, zip-lock bag full of green-gray matter.

"Dried herbs," Lenora muttered. Taking a small amount between her fingers, she sang a discordant melody under her breath and threw the herbs into the fire. The flame brightened and then burned blue for a few seconds.

My head cleared and I was able to focus. Cam let out a breath and I told him it was okay to let me go now. Nothing else had changed. I was still standing in what looked like the bloody discharge of an abattoir, fog danced on the water and settled on the land, so that it was impossible to see very far from where I stood. But I could think again and I was not overwhelmed with the emotions that poisoned the soil, trees and water around us.

The splashing sound came again and I looked towards the stream. Many hands rose from the water and through the fog, grasping and desperate. I could not get an accurate count with the fog shifting in and out and hands bobbing up from the water and then sinking below. As the fog broke, I caught a glimpse of He-Who-Counseled-the-Chief splashing in the deep water, his face etched with grief as he tried again and again to grasp the hands and pull them above the surface.

He turned to look at us in pleading desperation before the fog closed in again. "*Wichëmi...*" *Help me...* This time I understood and heard him clearly. Without a second thought, I pulled the laces and kicked off my hiking boots just before plunging into the water. It was freezing and I gasped in shock, but refused to let my body give in to the cold. Two other splashes sounded behind me and Cam, Zackie and I swam towards the Lenape man as if he were drowning. One by one, the hands disappeared below the surface and our urgency grew as the Lenape spirit howled with frustration and distress. Reaching the point where we had last seen the hands, I took a deep breath and dove down under the water, heedless of the depth. Searching as I swam, trying to hold my own against the current, the silt in the water obscured my vision and my lungs began to burn with the need for air. Just as I thought I had lost my position and would have to surface and reorient, I saw them. They were shadows lying at the bottom of the stream, but I could see something wrapped around their torsos that tangled with large rocks, restraining them and holding them down. With the last of my breath, I kicked towards them and pulled at the restraints on one of the bodies, trying to break it and release at least one of them. Try as I might, I could not sever the bonds and I wanted to cry out in frustration.

Something bumped my hands out of the way and I recognized Zackie swimming next to me, moving my hands away with her muzzle. Biting down on the restraint, she broke the rope with her teeth and I grabbed the body under the arms, kicked off from the bottom and shot to the surface with the body in tow. Once I broke the surface, I took a huge, gasping breath and treaded water as I held on to the limp spirit of a woman. In the next second, Cam came up clutching a man. As soon as he was ready, we began to swim to the shore, grasping the spirits and dragging them with us. Zackie swam behind us, her teeth gripping the clout of the baby she had pulled from the streambed. The Lenape man held two small children in one arm as he swam towards land.

The current had pushed us downstream and we emerged from the water a short distance from where we left Ron, Lenora and Lucas. I started thinking about hypothermia. The water was freezing and it was not much better on the land. My scalp prickled and it felt like my hair was stiffening in the cold as I forced myself to move. The spirits we rescued followed us numbly, still in shock and unable to speak. My teeth chattered and I was shivering as we walked back to where we started. Cam was no better off and he urged me to move faster.

The others met us, holding dry clothes and blankets, after we had only gone a few paces into the woods. We stripped out of our wet clothes, unmindful of modesty or fashion in the face of survival. Lenora stood by with a drawn blanket to shield me from the men and maybe when I was warm, I would appreciate her efforts, but just at that moment, all I cared about was putting on the dry clothes and huddling into the blankets. My hands were clumsy because my fingers were numb and I had a hard time gripping the clothes that were several sizes too large for me. The shivering was intense, but that only meant I was really, really cold, but not yet severely hypothermic. I'd start worrying if I stopped shivering. Finally dressed, I managed not to fall over as I shoved my unfeeling feet into my hiking boots. Lenora folded the pants legs up and then wrapped the blanket around my shoulders before walking me the rest of the way to our impromptu camp. She sat me next to the fire, which was thankfully significantly larger than when I'd left. While I shook and hunched, I thought about how nice it would be to have a hot drink to really warm me up, but that wasn't going to happen. I felt grateful for the dry clothes and the big fire, and that I could be moderately sure that I wasn't going to die right then.

Zackie set the baby down next to the dead woman, shook off and then lay by the fire, unperturbed by the cold or the company. The Astro collar was water-logged and would probably never work again, but that kind of thing happened with equipment during any mission. As my brain thawed and I was finally certain that I wouldn't freeze to death, I took a look around at what could have been a cozy scene. The fog had lifted and the ground was no longer saturated with grisly reminders of mortality and the frailty of the human form. Our living friends and the dead gathered around the fire and all were careful not to speak until Cam and I were ready.

We were still shivering when Cam broke the silence. "That was going well beyond our training and I'm quite sure we did not do that safely."

"Clue me in. Just what in the hell was that all about?" Lucas's face flushed as he yelled at us and he gestured wildly with his hands, ultimately pointing at the stream. "Are you trying to die?"

I looked at him for understanding. "It was reflex. There were spirits in the water who were in trouble. They asked for our help."

"Did it maybe occur to you that they were already dead? Lives were not at risk here." Lucas spoke loudly, but at least the shouting had stopped. He stared at Cam and me, his expression hard. Pacing back and forth to soothe his agitation, he paused only to rub his face, shaking his head and mumbling into his hands.

Trying to lighten the mood, I asked him, "Did you manage to get it on film?"

He looked at me like I was crazy. "Oh, for the love of…" He started pacing again. "No, no I did not get it on film. When I saw you dive into the stream, I ran back to the truck to get whatever I could to keep you from dying if – and it was a big if – you managed to get out of the water." Pausing for a moment, he gestured towards Ron and

Lenora. "They built up the fire and picked up your hiking boots. Ron knew about where the current would take you when you surfaced, so we got a head start in meeting you there."

"It takes a village…" Cam murmured.

"…to save my sorry ass." I finished the thought less eloquently than he probably intended, but the crass words could not mask the warm wave of gratitude I felt for their caring and quick thinking.

"You're welcome." Ron added another branch to the fire and then turned solemn eyes on Cam and me. "Was it worth it? Did you help them?"

Cam shifted and snugged the blanket over his head. "I think we made progress, but they're not free yet. They're with us right now, sitting around the fire."

Ron's eyes grew large and he swallowed visibly. "Something evil happened here. Even I could feel it. It shouldn't have happened and I wanted to beat something into a bloody heap because of it." He shook his head, suddenly morose. "What can we do to help them?"

"Start at the beginning. Who are 'they' and what

happened out there?" Lucas stopped pacing and pulled a small, spiral bound pad and a pen from his jacket pocket. He gripped the pen tightly and slashed some notes in the small book, his mouth a grim line. He was still worked up about the risk we took and maybe falling back on his role as documentarian would calm him.

Cam described everything, from the bloody, sodden mess of the ground near the water to pulling the bodies up from the streambed. Staring through the flames at our new companions, Cam concluded his report. "They appear to be Native American. There is a man, a woman, two small children and a baby."

"Modern or historic?" Lucas's pen poised over the pad.

"They're wearing buckskin, so historic," Cam reported.

"He-Who-Counseled-the-Chief is also still with us." I shifted my head towards where he sat and all eyes turned to look, whether they could see him or not.

Cam examined our guests again and was about to say something when he stopped and looked appraisingly at Ron. I caught his eye and he gave a barely perceptible shake of his head.

I shook my head back. “No, go ahead. Tell them. He’ll be all right.”

Sighing, Cam continued with his description. “The man has a gunshot wound to his chest. The woman and all the children appear to have been bludgeoned about the head and shoulders.”

Lenora inhaled sharply and drew back, her arms wrapping protectively around her chest. “Even the baby? Who would do that to a baby?” My mind shot back to little Maria Matilda Castner. There had been no mercy for her either, but I said nothing rather than pollute Lenora’s mind with yet another story of cruelty and evil.

Ron’s face was ashen and the skin was stretched tightly around his eyes. He looked like he was either about to cry or murder someone. His voice was quiet, but deadly. “What happened? Who did this to my people?”

“Easy there. Whoever did this is long dead.” Lucas kept his eyes on the pad and continued to jot notes, but gave a quick glance up to Ron before going back to scribbling. It was Ron’s turn to pace as he tried to work off the rage at learning that a whole family of Delaware

Indians had been massacred.

"I would have liked to go to war shoulder to shoulder with this one." He-Who-Counseled-the-Chief pointed to Ron and gave an approving nod.

When I relayed the spirit's comment to Ron, he stood stock still for a moment. Looking in the direction of where he knew the spirit to be, Ron replied in Lenape. "I am honored. I would have taken great pleasure in finding justice for this family."

Lucas kept his voice low and asked for a translation, so he could record the exchange. Writing quickly to catch up, he raised his eyebrows as Cam repeated what we had heard. "Violent much?" Lucas murmured.

Lenora's sharp ears caught this comment. "He used to be. I fixed that." Gesturing towards the fire and our unseen guests, she frowned. "But going after the ones who did this…this is not violence. This is justice." Shaking her head in disgust, she continued. "Can you imagine? A baby?"

I did not want to imagine, but the worst part was that in my experience, the truth could easily outstrip my imagination. But we had to get to the bottom of this if these spirits were going to find peace. It must have been more than a hundred years that they were trapped here, so I was just going to have to deal with whatever brutal tale emerged. It wasn't about me. Sighing, I directed my question to He-Who-Counseled-the-Chief, the least damaged of the spirits. "What happened? Did you survive this attack, only to be killed by a bear later?"

He-Who-Counseled-the-Chief laughed, but the merriment didn't reach his eyes. "I was dead and wandering before this man's grandfather's grandfather was a baby." The Lenape spirit pointed to the man with the gunshot wound.

Cam repeated the answer for Ron and Lenora and then counted on his fingers. "At twenty years for each generation… let's see… that's almost a hundred years before this family met their end." Cocking his head, Cam stared at He-Who-Counseled-the-Chief. "You're going to have to explain. We don't understand."

He-Who-Counseled-the-Chief exhaled deeply and hung his head. "I died and I wandered. My story will not help these people." Raising his head, he spread his hands to indicate the family.

The man with the gunshot wound croaked out some words and air leaked from the hole in his chest as he spoke. "I saw this one just before I charged the one with the gun. He had the red olaman on his face and I knew him for an ancestor. I knew then I would die, but I thought I could save my family." He shook his head slowly and tears leaked from his eyes.

The woman raised her head and she held the baby to her breast. Both had gaping head wounds that bled and dripped as she rocked the baby. "You were brave, but you could not stop what happened." The tears flowed and mingled with the blood. She wiped at her face absently and then continued. "We were in the canoe and traveling down the river. We were ambushed."

The two small children clambered onto the lap of the man and he held them, gently cupping their faces and their ruined skulls. "My poor boys…" The man sobbed and hugged his children. Taking a deep breath, he continued the story. "He pointed the gun at us and told us to get out of the canoe. If we went farther, he would shoot us down. We had no choice. Our only chance was to do as he said."

"Who did this?" Ron demanded after Cam conveyed what was said. His eyes were dark, like an avenging angel.

"It was Tom Quick." Lenora gasped as I relayed the woman's whispered words. Ron bared his teeth and pounded his fist into the trunk of a tree.

The mother's body shook and she hunched defensively over the baby. Rocking the infant, she shushed and crooned to it as it cried weakly. Looking up, her face was streaked with bloody tears. "I was breastfeeding this one. My husband got out of the canoe and went on shore." She rocked her body, the baby clinging to her, and gave in to weeping, taking deep, shuddering breaths. Zackie stood up and went to them, leaning her flank against the woman, softly touching the mother and child with her muzzle while making quiet whimpering noises. The woman wrapped an arm around Zackie and released a long breath. "I thought he would not kill the children and when he shot my husband, I tried to protect the baby. But he had a tomahawk and he started swinging, striking me until he broke my head…" The woman made a choking sound and pressed her face into Zackie's flank.

He-Who-Counseled-the-Chief took up the story. "I saw everything and could do nothing. When this one who was the mother was dead, he crushed the baby's skull with the tomahawk and then went after the little boys." He closed his eyes and shook his head. "I wish my mind could forget what my eyes have seen…" Gathering himself, He-Who-Counseled-the-Chief finished the story. "He collected the bodies and was afraid this atrocity would be discovered, so he tried to conceal his crime. He gathered heavy rocks and made ropes from the bark of a basswood tree. He tied the stones to the bodies and then dumped them in the deepest part of the water." He-Who-Counseled-the-Chief wiped hard at his eyes and pressed his lips together until they formed a grim line. "Then he destroyed the canoe and the few things the family had with them. And no one but me knew what he had done."

Silence reigned when the tale was finished. Looking around, I surveyed our friends. I was sure this would hit them hard. I can't say that I was used to these stories – I hope to never be that hardened – but I was at least not surprised by the violence. Lenora pressed her knuckles to her mouth, her eyes were wide and tears trailed down her weathered face. Ron was on his knees in the dirt, his hands in the earth and clenching, his head bowed. He was breathing hard. Lucas was frozen with a look of horror and he stared back at me. "How can you stand it?" he asked.

I wiped my eyes to clear the tears that I hadn't noticed a moment ago. "I stand it because I have to."

Cam cleared his throat, but his voice was weak. "Who was this Tom Quick person?"

Wanting to let go of the raw emotion that threatened to overwhelm me, I let the history major in me take over and I rattled off what little I knew. My mind floated in a sort of auto-pilot as I spoke. "He was an Indian slayer. Celebrated in his time." I thought for a moment. "That was around the mid to late 1700's." I shuddered, trying to shake off the cold and relieve the ache that the story left in my core. I stood with effort and my legs trembled, but I managed to stay upright.

Zackie made her rounds to each of the family members, nuzzling and licking, wiping away the tears. She approached the Lenape spirit and he stood and backed away from her, melting into the forest. He was not ready, but the family was bone-weary from centuries of enduring the cold waters, forgotten and tormented by the brutal end to their lives. But the worst was over for them now. We knew what happened to them. They were no longer lost to history and the pain of their deaths was shared among the living who heard their tale. Someone mourned them now and that was enough.

It was growing dark and the light from the fire left the surrounding woods shadowy and ill-defined. Our friends could not see Zackie as she gathered the family on the far side of the flames and opened the portal. I closed my eyes and bowed my head, but I could sense the intense light and turned away to avoid being blinded through my closed lids. "We should go. They're leaving."

"The family and Lenape man will be at rest?" Lenora's lips quivered and her eyes pleaded that this be true.

Cam stood and walked to Ron, putting a comforting hand on his back, but keeping his face averted from the light of the portal. "The family will find peace. The Lenape man is not ready."

Ron stood, chanting softly as he rose. Lenora joined him after a moment and from somewhere in the woods, a deep male voice connected with the rhythm of the chant. The melody was sad and slow, like the wind wailing through trees, music for a funeral. I kept my head bowed to show respect. The silvery sound of the flowing stream complemented the lament and a crisp breeze filled with the perfume of autumn's fallen leaves wafted through the forest, leaving the air clean and fresh. I felt the change in the texture of the growing night when the family stepped through the portal with Zackie. The sweet scent of spring flowers washed over me and for a moment, I was warmed by the rays of a gentle sun.

###

I don't remember exactly how I got home. I think I staggered up the trail and then Ron and Lucas took over the driving to get Cam and me home. Between fighting off hypothermia and having the spirits of the family and the Lenape man drain our batteries, Cam and I were spent. It was all we could do to remain upright. After a few bottles of coconut water and a short, overnight coma, by morning I felt intellectually challenged and physically unfit.

I sat at the card table-cum-dining table and rubbed hard at my face. While the Lenape family had been freed, our two original spirits were still at large. On the bright side, I hadn't received any messages from Peyton telling me that He-Who-Counseled-the-Chief was making a pest of himself. Flipping through the messages on my phone, I did have a text from Lucas asking me to check in, so he'd know if I was okay after yesterday's festivities. Gander had left a group message letting everyone on the crew know that the grand reopening of the upscale restaurant was that evening. Because the restaurant management wanted to draw a huge crowd to the event, we were encouraged to bring guests who would each be entitled to one free drink sample, which I took to mean some kind of mini-drink. Maybe this was what we needed, a night off to just have fun. I had no reserves left for dealing with spiritual matters, so it's not like we could make any progress on that front. So, what the hell? Why not?

I called Cam to invite him and his house guests. "Sure, but what's a drink sample?" Cam's voice sounded rough, like he just woke up.

"I predict fancy Dixie cups with minimal alcohol. My guess is that it's a way to promote a craving to make you buy more."

"Are you inviting Lucas? Maybe we can talk ghosts with him and get him to put it on his expense account."

I confirmed that I would call Lucas next, but offered

the opinion that the presence of the work crew would make it hard to talk shop and then ended the call with Cam. Bringing up Lucas's text, I poked at the call back option and then felt a surge of nervousness as the phone rang.

"Lucas? Consider this call my proof of life. Do you need me to send a picture of me holding up today's newspaper?"

"No, don't bother. Anyone could photoshop that. I'm going to need something more definitive."

"How about meeting me at the Meridian tonight?" I explained how the clean up job led to the opportunity for free drink samples.

"Hmmm… Norovirus. If it were anyone else asking, I think I might pass. But okay, let's – wait, can you hold on? I have another call." I held on as he asked, but Lord, I hated call waiting. He came back almost immediately, speaking fast. "Sorry, Fia. Producers breathing down my neck again. I have to call them right back. So, it's a date. I'll meet you there." And with that, we hung up.

Chewing on the cuticles of my good hand, I stressed about what he meant by that last bit. Maybe I had date, except that it wasn't really a date. But maybe Lucas was just using a colloquialism and all he meant was that it was penciled into his calendar. Holy crapping crap. Now what? I couldn't call him back to clarify, that would be really awkward. I decided I'd just show up and act natural, pretend that there was no confusion and that it was always a group thing. Because it was. But I'd find something nice to wear, just in case.

# # #

I ended up paying a visit to Sandra and Baby Jax. She was about my size, she knew how to dress and she worked at the Lilith Salon. When she and Jax weren't on a search, I'd see her in clothes that had that designer look and her hair and makeup were perfect. I wanted that look. Maybe I could even pull it off for just one night.

Sandra stood with her hands on hips and looked appraisingly at me before giving a salacious wink. "Hot date tonight?"

Bending down, I ruffled Baby Jax's ears. "Nah, the work crew is going out for free drinks at a restaurant where we did a job." I decided to keep it simple. I didn't want to get into the whole Lucas story, not that I could even begin to tell Sandra about the Hannah complication in all of this.

"Uh-huh. So, there's some guy on the crew you have your eye on?"

I rolled my eyes. "Okay, you got me. Now, can you help me look good tonight?"

Sandra crossed her arms and tilted her head, narrowing her eyes as she envisioned the future me. "Something sexy, but not slutty. We'll do your hair down and play up your eyes. And just a soft pink for your lips." She unwound her arms and straightened, nodding approval of her fashion choices. "Let me see your hands."

I froze and then tucked my gloved hands behind my back. I still had my coat on, so it seemed normal that I also still had gloves on. "I kind of bashed my hand on something. It looks pretty bad. Do you think we can do something to hide it?"

"Let me see." She made 'give me' motions with her hands.

Sighing, I brought my hands forward and peeled back just enough of the glove on my dead hand so that I could show her a hint of the purplish black marbling. "It's pretty gross."

"Ugh! Cover that up. That is disgusting." Turning away, Sandra walked toward her bedroom, Baby Jax at her heels. I followed mutely, feeling self-conscious about my deformities and nursing my growing unease about going out that night. Before the unease could blossom into full-blown anxiety, Sandra flew into action. "Fortunately for you, I have just the thing." She flung open a door in her bedroom and we entered into a cavernous walk-in closet, clothing hung like a rainbow along each of the walls. "I've only got the fall/winter apparel stocked right now and I've arranged everything by color, so it should be easy to find." She made a beeline to the cluster of black clothing at the back of the closet, clicking hangers aside until she pulled out an outfit with a small triumphant cry. A long top and leggings floated on the hanger, the fabric shimmering coolly with dark, delicate beadwork sewn in intricate patterns along the bodice and sleeves. Holding up a sleeve, she explained the outfit to me. "See the sleeves? They're made extra long with attached fingerless gloves that covers the hands to the last finger knuckle. It's designed to draw attention to the artwork on your nails."

"I've never seen anything like it. Where'd you get it?" I was sincerely curious. This must be some kind of high fashion piece and I wondered how Sandra could afford it.

"I made it." She grinned proudly, holding the clothing up for inspection. "It's nylon-spandex and tight and low on your upper body, so be prepared to show off some cleavage. I cut it so it drapes around the leggings tunic-style." Turning the hanger, she admired her work. "See, classy, sexy clothes are all about balance. If you're going to bring attention to your boobs, you should cover up your legs. If you go around with both showing, you're going to end up looking slutty."

I nodded my head, as if I understood anything about fashion philosophy and took the clothes from her. She next selected a pair of black boots with a low heel to go with the outfit and handed these to me. "Okay, you put these on while I set up my makeup kit." After Sandra left, I did as she said and then quickly used some mortuary makeup to touch up the dead hand.

"Reporting for makeup, ma'am." I gave Sandra a quick salute and she turned from her table of bottles, brushes and palettes of eye shadow to look me over.

"Nice. I like your black polish, it goes with the outfit. Let's leave your nails that way. Here, sit." Sandra brushed the bangs out of my face. "You been working nights? What's up with these dark circles under your eyes? And you need to take better care of your skin. You don't look healthy."

"Yeah, I've been working a lot lately." I felt another pang of self-consciousness and wondered if all this effort was going to do any good, if I would be able to pull off the appearance of being young and carefree and normal. I just wanted one night…

After what seemed like hours of fussing, Sandra finally said she was done. "And just like that, you're Cinderella before the ball." I stood up and she marched me in front of a full-length mirror.

"Oh wow." She really did know what she was doing. The look was dramatic without being ostentatious and it had a refined sophistication that I wasn't sure I could do justice. I bit my lip, wallowing in uncertainty, but then made my decision and swung around to grasp her hand. "I can't thank you enough for this, Sandra."

"Sure, sure. You just go have a good time tonight

and maybe bring home your Prince Charming." Sandra made a quick move, grabbing her dog by the collar as he wagged his tail and advanced towards me. "Don't you dare shed on her, Jax." Giving his flank an affectionate rub, she pointed to the front door with her free hand. "You better get going before he decides he wants to lick your face."

###

I splurged and took a cab to the restaurant. The driver was taciturn, maybe pissed that he had to work while the rest of the world partied. I sat in the back seat, alternating between ecstatic thoughts of being the belle of the ball and dreading that I would melt under the heat of that kind of scrutiny. It was a short trip and the cab pulled into the circular drive at the restaurant's entrance before the butterflies in my stomach had fully settled. Stepping out into the night, I shivered slightly. Maybe leaving my ratty coat at home was not one of my brighter ideas, but it ruined the outfit and I was hell-bent on having the perfect night out. Besides, this small chill was nothing compared to my recent dip in the icy stream.

The Meridian was packed with well-dressed

revelers and once I was in the thick of things, I blended right in. I was dressed well enough to get admiring glances, but then the admirer moved on to the next fashion-forward woman or man, typically someone more at ease in the role of the savvy style prophet. I walked the length of the long, narrow room looking for anyone I knew. The room appeared larger thanks to mirrors placed behind the infinitely long bar, elegantly reflecting the pattern of a Victorian-inspired wallpaper of striped dusty rose and burgundy. The walls were even decorated with sconces shaped to look like gaslights from the era.

Groups of strangers crowded around small tables that studded the area near the outside wall. Others sat along the gleaming, solid oak bar that traced the full length of the interior wall, resting their polished shoes on the brass foot rails. Music pumped with bass made my breastbone vibrate as I surveyed the faces and tried to disregard the discordance of modern music paired with Victorian décor that fed through my eyes and ears.

A gentle hand touched my elbow and I turned to see Lucas. He leaned close and spoke into my ear, so I could hear him above the music. “We’re over here.” Grasping my hand, he led me towards the bar and away from the thrumming speakers. Ron and Lenora sat sipping mini-drinks from small, plastic shot glasses, while Cam nursed a cup of coffee.

"Looking good, Fia." Cam raised his mug to toast me. "Whose closet did you raid?"

"Sandra helped me out. She made this by hand." I smiled and swept my hand over the outfit like a seasoned game show hostess.

"She does good work. The beading stands out." Lenora gestured toward the neckline. This was as close to anything flattering as I was likely to get, so I thanked her.

Ron handed me my own drink. "You cleaned up nice." He looked steadily at me for a moment and then raised his eyebrows and made 'gimme' signals with his hands when I didn't return the compliment.

"All right, all right. You're pretty too."

"Thank you." He smoothed back a lock of hair with an extravagant gesture, as Lucas watched our exchange, a thoughtful expression playing on his face. I raised my drink to salute Cam and Lenora and then touched plastic glasses with Ron, grinning and laughing at the tiny, complimentary beverages.

Lucas's eyes lingered on me as I extended my shot glass to also touch his before I took a sip. My eyes drank him in as I peeked over my cup. He wore his hair loose and it shone softly in the faux gaslight. His eyes were a stormy gray, reflecting the dark blue shirt that draped appealingly over broad shoulders. His gaze flicked briefly toward Ron and then settled on me with an intensity that took my breath away. A faint smile played on his lips as a blush rose to my cheeks. Waves of desire surged through me and Lucas was the moon beckoning this tide.

Forcing myself to look away from him, I pretended to people watch, so as not to stare so obviously and so hungrily at Lucas. The scent of ammonia told me that Hannah was near and hadn't missed the exchange. I ignored the smell and watched the crowd. A priest and a rabbi walked into the bar, accompanied by a large group of young adults and I wondered what that was all about. Surely, there was a joke in there somewhere. When Gander entered the bar escorting a handsome woman of a certain age, I waved to bring them over and made the introductions.

Gander presented the woman on his arm to the

group. “And this is Denise, my wife.” Glancing toward the door, he smiled. “And here comes Goose and JoJo.” Gander beckoned and Goose approached the group with a jaunty stride, JoJo bringing up the rear, grinning broadly. Arriving at the door, Rory saw the commotion and followed behind them, joining our group without invitation.

“Howzit, brah?” Goose greeted Gander with a modified handshake that ended in a shoulder bump. To cover his confusion and slight discomfort at this strange greeting, Gander started another round of introductions.

Cam stared fixedly at Rory when he was introduced in a perfunctory manner by Gander. No one seemed to notice as I moved to put Goose and JoJo solidly between us. When Lucas was introduced to the crew, the inevitable recognition of celebrity followed.

Goose’s eyes went wide and he jabbed his finger towards Lucas. “Dude, your show is epic, totally ballsatic.”

Rory shrugged and pursed his lips, looking like he’d just sucked on a lemon. “I don’t know. The show’s okay, I guess. But I don’t have time for that stuff. I’ve got more important things I have to do.” If he was hoping for someone to follow up on his self-proclaimed importance, he was in for a disappointment. Lucas merely gave him the non-committal head tilt, allowing for differences of opinion.

Goose continued with his commentary as if Rory had never spoken. “I’ve seen other shows like it, but they’re just bammerwee. I’d rather watch yours.”

Lucas squinted, cocking his head and listening hard, but no understanding reached his eyes. Lenora and Gander exchanged a look that seemed to say everything about how young people spoke their own language these days. Grinning, Cam finally offered a way out of the confusion with an impromptu translation. “Looks like you have another fan. He likes your show best.”

Lucas erupted in a million dollar smile when he caught on to what Goose was saying. “Well, thanks. That’s really kind of you. Can you tell me – ” Just then, Lucas’s phone rang and he was forced to excuse himself from the conversation to take the call.

After we’d consumed our allotted mini-drinks, we decided to move on to some old fashioned beer. Cam got the attention of the bartender, who informed us that the tap was broken and draught beer was out of the question. The crew exchanged knowing glances, all of us thinking that this might have been something that hadn't gotten sterilized in time for the big event.

As the bartender handed out a variety of bottled beers, Goose pumped him for information. "Dude, Angela around?"

The barkeep sized him up and decided he was okay. "Yeah, she's on break. You'll find her out back."

Goose asked for a bottle of something non-alcoholic for Angela, then laid down some bills and grabbed his bottles, waving farewell to the group as he made his way out. "Yo dog, latronic. I'm going to find me some sweet nectar."

Ron laughed. "That's a man on a mission."

"Yeah, he's had a thing for Angela since he first laid eyes on her." I raised my open beer at Goose's retreating back in salute and silently wished him well before sipping. The beer was good, and I was about to say as much, when a young woman approached our group and tapped Rory on the shoulder.

"My name is Suzie. Would you like to dance with

me?" She had sparkling blue eyes that were partially hidden by the epicanthal fold on the inner side of her eyes. Her words were slurred by a tongue that protruded slightly from her mouth, but she smiled widely, her face the picture of trust. The rabbi stood behind her, patting her back and telling her how well she was doing.

Rory returned her entreaty with a look of horror. "What? No way." He turned away to lean on the bar. "Get away from me, you freak."

Suzie's face crumpled and her whole body sagged as she turned to the rabbi's protective embrace. The rabbi could not even speak to comfort her. His face had gone white and his eyes glared at Rory, while he compressed his lips, maybe to prevent whatever bad words he was thinking from becoming audible. Those of us with the misfortune of being associated with Rory stood there shocked and unable to even apologize to the poor girl.

Ron took that moment to stand up, knocking Rory to the side and sending him staggering with only a twitch of his muscled shoulder. He grasped Suzie's hand and spoke gently to her. "Don't you pay any attention to that *mahtënu*. Will you dance with me? I think they're playing our song."

The rabbi smiled gratefully at Ron and encouraged Suzie to go and dance. After they departed, the holy man confronted Rory. "There was no need for that. You could have declined politely."

Rory's face was red and splotchy, his mouth hung open and spittle flew as he launched his retort. "She's a retard!" He did something spastic with his hands and contorted his face to convey what he thought about people with disabilities. "She has no business being here. Those people should be locked up."

Cam stood up and grabbed Rory be the collar. "Young man, you should go now or I promise you, there will be tears before bedtime." He gave a shove and sent the grommet off towards the exit. "Get on with you. You're not welcome here anymore."

Lucas did a quick side step to avoid the fleeing Rory as he walked back to the bar. "What was that all about?"

"Asshole. That's what that's all about." Lenora pointed towards the closing door as Rory departed. "But my grandson, he do me proud. I raised that boy." She patted her chest and nodded.

"And you did a wonderful job." The rabbi looked towards the dance floor and Lucas followed his gaze. "Father Garrett and I run a group home for young adults with Down's syndrome. We take the kids for a night out twice a year. It's something they really look forward to. I'm glad your grandson stepped up and saved the night for Suzie."

"Ron's a good guy," Lucas murmured, his eyes scanning the bar until he found the other people from the group home, huddled near the dance floor watching Suzie. Grabbing my hand, he pulled me towards the group. "Let's go find some dance partners." The rest of our group followed and we made some brief stops in the crowded bar as Lucas enticed other people to make the night out special for these kids.

I wasn't much of a dancer, but my partner was so delighted by the chance to show off his moves that I forgot my self-consciousness and enjoyed the moment. Cam, with his long limbs, looked like a spider on a hotplate as he danced, but he was completely uninhibited, grinning and really enjoying himself. Lenora shuffled with her cane, but kept good time with the music and JoJo, with all the metal in his body from the motorcycle crash, still managed to look like a bouncing sheepdog. The Ganders showed the kids how to groove old school and I tried to imitate how they just flowed with the music. I should have been utterly exhausted by now, after the experience with the Lenape family and my dip in the stream, but something about the joyous atmosphere was recharging my batteries. I danced with several of the kids from the home until the tempo of the music drifted into something mellow.

Lucas grabbed my hand and pulled me into a slow dance. “This was an interesting interpretation of a date.” He was smiling, so I could tell that he wasn’t upset.

“What, you expected one on one time? I’ll have you know that is third date stuff. The priest and the rabbi told me so.”

“Lucky me, more dates.” He pulled me in closer and I didn’t hear the rabbi or priest object, so I melted into his arms and put my head on his shoulder as we swayed to the music. Inhaling his scent, a different type of intoxication gripped me and my head swam with his nearness. As I turned to look up into his eyes, the glaring stench of ammonia suddenly filled my senses. I stiffened and my eyes went wide.

"What's wrong?" Lucas stopped dancing and held me at arm's-length to make sure I was okay. His eyes were full of concern and his hands held me gently.

I cursed silently and decided that I'd better create some distance between us before the situation elicited poltergeist activity. There were too many people on the dance floor to even consider this possibility. "I'm sorry. I got a little lightheaded." Stepping away, I let him see the regret in my eyes. "I better go outside and get some air."

Seeing Suzie, I grasped her hand. "Would you like to finish this dance with Lucas?" When she smiled and nodded, I walked off the dance floor, assured that he wouldn't follow me.

I ordered a bottle of coke at the bar and then went out the door to sit on the concrete wall at the entrance of the building. The cool air felt good after all that dancing and I greedily sucked down the sugar-charged caffeine to relieve my thirst.

Picking at the label on the empty bottle, I finally allowed myself to feel upset about Hannah's interruption. As I pondered exactly what could be done about her constant presence, I sensed someone walking towards me out of the darkness. When the figure stepped into the light of the parking lot, I recognized Rory weaving through the parked cars. He was drunk, holding a bottle in one hand and using the other to keep himself upright. Seeing me, he pointed and screamed something incoherent before staggering towards me.

The dead hand flipped the bottle so that it was holding the neck. Raising it up, I realized it was about to break the bottom of the bottle against the concrete to create a jagged-edged weapon. "Don't…you…dare." The dead hand stopped its action and then lowered the bottle, once again flipping it to grip the wide bottom. I considered going back inside, but I was still afraid of what Hannah might do, so I sat there and tried to look calm when he reached me.

"Hey! Hey, you bitch!" He was all up in my face and he reeked of alcohol.

I put my left hand on his chest and moved him back, making sure the dead hand was peacefully grasping the bottle. "What Rory?"

"I saw you dancing with them. You're just trying to make me look bad in front of Gander." His speech was slurred and his bloodshot eyes burned with hate.

"You made yourself look bad in front of Gander. Honestly, there's nothing I could do to make you look worse."

"You bitch!" He grabbed the neckline of my shirt, trying to haul me to my feet. I had no idea what he'd do if he succeeded, maybe try to drag me to the dark side of the building and – my mind stopped the thought as the dead hand shot up and buried the neck of the bottle in the armpit of his outstretched arm. The neckline tore as he crumpled to the ground, still grasping the fabric. He lay there gasping, his mouth opening and closing like a fish before he began retching and vomiting.

"I guess you don't need our help." Ron looked dazed for a moment as he stared at the suffering Rory. "We didn't like you being out here alone…"

Lucas stood there and blinked a few times, stunned and silent. I looked away and started adjusting the ruined neckline, trying to tuck the edges under my bra straps to keep it up. I heard Lucas's voice from a distance. "He won't be using that arm any time soon."

Others were approaching, but I didn't look up. I knew it wasn't my fault, but my cheeks burned with shame and tears threatened to spill from my eyes. One night out was just too much to ask for.

"Eww, grommet's gerbering everywhere. He dickfaced?"

"Yeah, dickfaced and Fia jammed a coke bottle up his armpit." Ron said this like he was proud of me.

Goose raised his eye brows. "Smooth move, Fia. Bastard had it coming."

"Fia, are you all right? Did he hurt you?" Angela bent down and looked up into my eyes.

"I'm all right." I stood up and she stood with me, brushing my hair out of my face and adjusting my shirt so it wouldn't fall.

Goose looked at Ron and Lucas. "Second time now that this eggo waffle tried something on her."

"Second time?" Lucas and Ron spoke the words simultaneously and then glowered at Rory, who lay curled into a fetal position. For a moment, I thought they'd kick him to the curb. For another moment, I was pretty sure I'd let them. I stopped my violent fantasies before the dead hand got any new ideas and took a deep, steadying breath.

"I'm going home." My voice was dull, my heart was heavy and I was done. This wasn't how my night out was supposed to end. Grabbing my phone, I called for a cab as I walked to the driveway entrance, leaving the others to clean up the mess.

CHAPTER 4

"So, he grabbed you and the dead hand leapt to your defense. Why isn't this a good thing?" Cam refilled my mug with more coffee and then sat down opposite me at the card table. Zackie circled near the table and then lay down. After a restless night, I had finally called Cam just as the sun rose and asked him to come over. I didn't want to have this private conversation in front of Ron and Lenora. To me, talking about the dead hand was like talking about venereal disease.

"It could have killed him. It was going to smash the bottle and cut him with it." I held up the dead hand wearing the neoprene diving glove, as if it were exhibit A, and then slapped it down on the table. Zackie yawned and smacked her lips before resting her chin on the floor, blinking lazily at me. I caught the gist of what she said and then compressed my lips and looked her in the eye. "I am not overreacting."

Cam shook his head and his brow creased. "But it listened to you when you told it to back off."

"And then it acted on its own when it jabbed him with the bottle." I rubbed my face with my left hand. "How is this supposed to be reassuring?"

"The way I look at it, it went after Rory twice, both times when he did something threatening." Cam leaned forward and tapped his forefinger on the table. "It didn't do anything when you were dancing with Lucas, so these defensive actions have nothing to do with people just being near you. It's only reacting when it thinks you're in danger." Cam sat back and folded his arms across his chest. "I'm starting to like this dead hand."

I gaped at him. "You're kidding, right?"

"No, I'm bloody serious." He took a breath and glanced away, squinting his eyes. "How do I explain it to you…" After a moment, he lifted his chin and looked back at me. His eyes were alight with mischief and a slight smile played at the corners of his mouth. "I've got it."

I sat back and shook my head slightly. "I'm not sure

I want to hear it. You're way too amused by this."

"No, just hear me out." He sat forward and pointed at the offending hand. "This dead hand is like having a badly trained Rottweiler. He's not too sure about other people, but he's completely devoted to you. It's up to you to keep him out of trouble and to train him how to respond appropriately to situations."

"So, I'm a hand trainer now?" I made a rude noise. "And how exactly am I supposed to do that?" I pointed to the dead hand as it lay on the table. "Stay, hand…good hand." I cocked my head at Cam. "Am I supposed to give it a treat now?"

Cam rolled his eyes and Zackie sneezed loudly at me. "It's an analogy, Fia."

"Look, I know it understands me because it didn't cut Rory into little pieces with a broken bottle." I rubbed my brow with my left hand and forced the bangs out of my face. "But it's not like it really listens to me. In the end, it just used the bottle in a different way."

"You didn't tell it not to."

"Cam, it was too quick. One moment, I was trying

to figure out what Rory's next move was and the next thing I knew, it was over."

"And no one died and no one was bleeding. I'd call that a success." Cam arched a brow, widening his eyes as if he couldn't believe I was this dense. "I think it has your best interests at heart."

"I'm not so sure. Just because it's attached to me doesn't mean it gives a damn about me. All the reactions to perceived danger might just be for its own self-preservation." I bowed my head and let my shoulders slump. "It's not like it ever does anything when Hannah goes after me." I slanted a look at Zackie. "And it's not like you ever do anything either."

Zackie flicked an ear and didn't bother to lift her head. After a dramatic sigh, she made a grumbling noise that felt to me like a warning to stop whining, grow up and deal with life.

Cam nodded. "You know it's not Zackie's purview to move them along. Zackie will take them if they want to move on. At the moment, Hannah will not leave Lucas." He took a sip of coffee and his eyes wandered the room. "The dead hand doesn't react to Hannah because it doesn't find her to be a credible threat, that's my take on it."

"You can say that after she dumped that tray on me in the restaurant? After she pushed me at Peyton's place?" I sat up, incensed that he wasn't taking my side.

"Oh, come on. It's not like she threw a steak knife at you or pushed you down a flight of stairs." He pursed his lips, shaking his head. "Yes, these were warnings to keep your distance from Lucas, but they were still on the level of pranks. These were not threats." Cam's eyes bore into mine as he traced a finger along his temple, just where the scar ran along my own hairline. "You know what a real threat looks like."

I swallowed hard and looked away, remembering the blood and the trauma. "Okay, I'll concede that what's going on with Hannah and the dead hand do not constitute emergencies – yet. But things could easily escalate with either of them. That's what I'm afraid of."

"And that is a reasonable fear." Cam leaned forward and jabbed his finger at the table top. "But be proactive and get in front of the problem. Prevent the escalation."

I heaved a sigh and tried not to feel persecuted. "So, what do you recommend? How am I supposed to get in front of the problem?"

"Communicate with them. Try to understand – "

I burst out laughing, but the sound was bitter. "Are you serious? Don't you think things might be just a little awkward with Hannah?"

Cam had the grace to look abashed, but then he rallied. "Well, yes, if you go to her asking permission to bed her husband." My face grew hot at his words and I stared at him open-mouthed. Zackie took that moment to declare she'd had her fill of my petty problems. Getting up, she shook herself and grumbled something before heading to the bedroom. A flash of light announced that she had departed through the portal. Cam shrugged and continued. "The conversation you need to have with Hannah should center around why she feels compelled to stay with Lucas when it's long past time for her to move on. It's not like he feels her presence in any way and is giving her a reason to stay." Cam pointed to the dead hand. "As for the dead hand, you know it's capable of writing. Why don't you try communicating through writing, so it's not a one-way conversation? I know we've talked about this before…"

I decided to focus on the dead hand and avoid any

acute embarrassment that might result if we pursued the topic of Lucas. “It wrote stuff in the past, but nothing of consequence, just a ‘thank you’ as I was writing a shopping list.” I shook my head. “Since then, I’ve had the incident with the burnt paper and knife. Why didn’t it leave me a note instead of giving me these hints of something that I can’t interpret?” I clenched my good left hand into a fist. “And nothing has changed since the last time we had this conversation – how can I trust anything that it might say?”

“I disagree. A lot has changed since the last time we had this conversation.” Cam sat back and crossed his arms over his chest. “The dead hand proved itself useful by finding Lummie’s journal in North Carolina. Without this help, we would not have been able to fill in the gaps to solve the haunting by Parmelia and Bodean’s ‘Anomaly.’” He paused and let that sink in. “The dead hand has protected you twice now with Rory, whether or not you appreciate it. And whatever it is trying to say with the burnt paper and knife, I think you’d better figure it out and listen.” Cam rubbed his jaw. “In my opinion, the evidence in its favor is mounting.”

I wanted to argue, but I wavered when he confronted me with the facts. I retreated to the one inconsistency. "Why doesn't it just write me a note instead of leaving these half-assed clues?"

Cam widened his eyes and angled his head to the side. "Why don't you ask it?"

"Fine." My jaw clenched as I got up and found a blank piece of paper and a pen. Sitting down at the card table again, I removed the neoprene glove and then held the pen in the dead hand over the paper. My throat felt tight, but I swallowed my misgivings, took a deep breath and then asked my question. "Who are you?"

The dead hand scrawled a name. *Lummie Sinclair.* The cramped handwriting was familiar to me from her journal. Sitting forward, I opened my mouth to ask another question, but the hand lifted and then set down a new line. *William.* This time, the script was flowing and ornate, what I'd seen on very old documents written on parchment. I shot a look at Cam and his face had gone white. Was this his lost William, the same dead William he loved so much that he was compelled to send him to the other side? While I stared at Cam, the hand lifted again and this time it inscribed a symbol that looked like a heavy cross on the paper. Of the next twenty names, most were not familiar to me, but interspersed among these were Amy Turpin, Peter

W. Parke and John Lewis Luckenbach – spirits we had helped to cross over. The hand was writing too fast for me to keep up, but the names continued to flow, written in block letters, graceful calligraphy and jagged script. There were symbols like the cross and symbols that I'd only seen on clay tablets in museums. There were names written with non-English lettering that may have been Arabic and Sanskrit and Korean. When the page was nearly full, as the hand lifted again and began to descend to write a new line, it wavered and appeared to struggle, waving the pen above the paper. At last, it made contact, and in a new script, the words '*We are many*' appeared on the paper. The hand threw down the pen and fell to the table, where it twitched and spasmed.

"Jesus Christ," I rasped. My eyes watered and I thought I would vomit.

"No, I don't believe He's signed, but then again, I don't know what Aramaic looks like." Cam's eyes were huge and his breath came in short hitches.

I looked at Cam, my face drained of blood and frozen in a horrified rictus. My mouth opened and closed a few times as I tried to get my numb lips to form words. In the end, I said nothing and just stared at the page for several long minutes.

Jarring me out of this state of shock, Cam held the neoprene glove in front of my face. “Here, put this on it.” My good hand shook as I took the glove and maneuvered the quaking dead hand into the thick covering. The hand quieted after this and I concentrated on breathing.

“You think it was lying about that?” Cam’s eyes flicked towards the paper. He looked gray and drawn, but a corner of his mouth curled a bit.

Still unable to speak, I sat hunched over and sluggishly shook my head. I stared at the sheet of paper out of the corner of my eye and a slow, but seismic shift in my thinking coalesced into a glimmer of understanding. Swallowing hard, I took another few moments for the words to organize themselves. “It’s all of them, Cam. Everyone who ever passed through the portal.” My stomach threatened to erupt like Mount Vesuvius and expel all the coffee I had drunk.

“I’m not sure what you mean. All of them, all at once using the hand?” He reached out impulsively to touch the dead hand, but then drew back without making contact.

“No… different one’s at different times, I think, just

like when they were writing." I sat up slowly and then pulled the page towards me with my good hand. "And not all of them are literate." Frowning, I traced a finger over the heavy cross. "That's the best this one could do to make herself known."

"You can tell that one was a woman?" Cam stared fixedly at me, his mouth slightly open.

I blinked owlishly a few times and then nodded. "Don't ask me how I know, but I'm certain." I pushed the paper to the center of the table and sat back, crossing my arms over my queasy belly and squinching my eyes as I tried to put it all together. "That display with the knife and burnt paper…whoever was running the show at the time, maybe couldn't write."

Cam rubbed his face and grumbled. "No, of course not. Why should things ever be simple?" He looked up and cocked his head. "Do you think we could ask it a few more questions?"

I shook my head. "Not today. It used a lot of energy letting through all of those souls just now."

"Oh come on, just one more question won't kill it." Cam looked at me with pleading eyes and I immediately thought of William. Before I could reply, the dead hand lifted, curled back all fingers except the middle digit and then collapsed back on to the table.

"I think you have your answer."

# # #

After the dead hand reveal with Cam, the whole day did not stretch out before me with a sparkling sense of hope and adventure. I was creeped out that the entire population of dead people could reach through from the other side using my hand as a conduit. It was like the whole world came to my house to use the bathroom. When it was just me using the bathroom, it was perfectly sanitary and there was nothing icky about it. After the whole world got through with it, the bathroom was now a polluted, misbegotten place that was rife with disease.

It seemed that the right way to spend the rest of the day was to cram into it as many masochistic activities as possible. I grabbed the mangled outfit from the previous night and headed for the dry cleaners. Sandra was going to be pissed when she saw what happened to the hand-sewn clothes she loaned me, but it wasn't like she was going to get any happier if I took my time getting the outfit back to her. Besides, delaying the return just meant more time to work on my guilt ulcer.

When the folks at the dry cleaners said they couldn't fix the neckline, I paid extra for the one day cleaning service, just so I could get it over with. I picked up some groceries during the hour the cleaners needed and bought Sandra a box of chocolates, as a way to apologize for ruining her clothes.

A text from Lucas – *You okay???* – caught me off guard as I loaded groceries in the back seat. I texted back that I was fine and that he shouldn't worry. Figuring that this was the end of the exchange, I returned the shopping cart to the corral and clambered into the car, only to have another text alert go off. Lucas wanted to meet for dinner and declared it to be our third date, counting the night out at the Meridian with the food avalanche as the first date. This being our third date, according to the rules set by the priest and rabbi, we would dine one-on-one.

I sat behind the wheel and drummed my fingers on my lips, not daring to answer before thinking things through. This was not what I expected. Between the possibility of a real date with Lucas and the revelation involving the dead hand, a sense of being overwhelmed made my head swim and I slumped down in the seat. I concentrated on controlling my breathing, so I wouldn't hyperventilate, and I forced myself to think rationally.

Nothing had really changed with the dead hand – I was just more aware of what was going on behind the curtain. I needed to be as cautious as ever with it and I didn't have to do anything different. But things with Lucas were suddenly moving fast and I wasn't prepared for it. If I were Lucas, I would be backing off after the incident with Rory. Why would anyone want to hook up with some violent lunatic? And what about Hannah? It had only been six months since she passed away and there was no way he was over the trauma of losing her. The only explanation I saw for the sudden uptick in Lucas's interest in me was Ron. It was possible Lucas thought he had competition and he needed to make a move before I rode off into the sunset with Ron. I shook my head in disbelief and decided to just accept my good fortune. But if things were going to work between us, I'd need to be more strategic in planning how events played out, including this upcoming date.

By definition, spending time alone with Lucas meant that Hannah was going to be an issue. I did not want to run off on Lucas again because she was threatening to throw a tantrum in a crowded venue. That sort of thing could eventually give Lucas a complex. I tapped out a message to let him know that I was all out of nice clothes, so we'd need to eat somewhere seriously casual. I suggested Hot Dog Johnny's in Buttzville and then sent the text. There was outdoor seating at this restaurant and the weather might cooperate, allowing us to sit outside comfortably with our jackets on. If the situation went south and degenerated into a brawl, I did not want to be trapped inside a small space loaded with innocent bystanders. Outside, I had more options where I could take the fight.

Lucas responded with a series of question marks, but ultimately accepted my dining recommendation and we set a date to accommodate his work schedule. Reeling between elation and dread like an emotional yo-yo, I put the key in the ignition with a shaking hand and drove back to the dry cleaners.

I was thrilled that Lucas was showing unambiguous interest in me and I could quit second guessing myself every time he smiled my way, but having a relationship with him might be like running an obstacle course. Aside from Hannah being near him every minute of every day, I also needed to consider his feelings for her. Love doesn't die just because a person does. Was he ready for a new relationship? Lucas was also a hardcore skeptic about the unseen world, always happy to do whatever mental contortions were necessary to make his observations fit the more limited reality he sensed. Maybe that would work in my favor where Hannah was concerned, but could I deal with constant disagreement? And then there was the dead hand. If things progressed in a natural way, this unnatural appendage was going to be a hindrance in a physical relationship. Fantasizing about being with Lucas was one thing. Experiencing the reality was going to take some creativity. Maybe I could keep the neoprene glove on and convince him I was kinky and this was just a strange fetish. Alone in my car, I blushed, then shook my head and admitted that I did not have what I needed to get through this life.

I hardly heard the cashier thank me for my business as she handed me the cleaned garment and accepted payment. With a head full of worries, I set off for Sandra's home and readied myself to be chewed out for ruining her clothes.

###

Cam opened the door and invited me in. “Sandra seems to have left you in one piece.”

I hung my head as I stepped over the threshold, still feeling guilty about destroying the borrowed clothing. “Yeah, but she wasn’t happy about it. She was just madder at Rory than she was at me, so that probably saved my hide. She said she could rework the neckline…” My voice trailed off as I noticed the aroma of frying bacon. Cam’s text inviting me for brunch came with perfect timing as I left Sandra’s house. No matter how crappy the day was going, a free meal always made things better. “Lenora’s cooking?”

“It was her idea to make brunch. Those mini-drinks packed a wallop, so no one really felt like eating breakfast.” Cam took my coat and then escorted me to the dining room. The table was loaded with fresh baked bread, fluffy scrambled eggs, crispy bacon and a steaming casserole dish full of French toast, the brown sugar, cinnamon and vanilla harmonizing sweetly with the savory scents and making my stomach growl with impatience.

Ignoring everyone, I piled my plate high with two helpings of everything and devoted the next few minutes to feeding the beast in my belly. Once my plate was empty, I sensed everyone was looking, so I put the plate down and resisted the urge to lick it clean. Instead, I sat back and sighed, mostly out of contentment, but also to give the food more room to settle.

Lenora handed me a warm wash cloth. “Napkin won’t cut it this time.” After taking her seat again, she propped her chin in the palm of her hand and watched me wipe the syrup and bits of egg from my face. “Why you eat like that, little girl? No one’s gonna steal your food.”

I shrugged and blushed. “I get really hungry after dealing with spirits. They drain my energy or something. And growing up in the institution, perfect etiquette wasn’t high on the list of behaviors they needed to see from me.”

Ron made a rude noise. “They were happy if she could go one day without bleeding. They thought she was doing it to herself.”

I grimaced and started fidgeting. Cam saw my discomfort and came to the rescue. “So, I looked up Tom Quick earlier. The Lenape family named him as their murderer, and it turns out, he was quite the sociopath.”

Lenora made a sucking noise through her teeth.

"Our people know this Tom Quick. He murdered many Lenape."

Ron's eyes blazed black fire. "He was celebrated for it by the white settlers. A hundred years later, they even put up a freakin' monument in his honor."

I gasped as the thought hit me. "Cam, do you think he's still out there? Wandering around in those woods?"

"Not likely," Cam said after a pause. "If he were earthbound, I think he would have tried to interfere when we released the family."

'Now, hold on there for just one second." Ron waved a fork with some French toast and then chewed it down before continuing. "Are you saying Tom Quick made it to the afterlife after all the evil he did, while He-Who-Counseled-the-Chief is still stuck on this side? How is that even fair?"

Cam and I exchanged a look. With a slight tilt of his head, Cam motioned for me to take the question. I rolled my eyes and said, "What does fair have to do with it? It just is."

Ron's eyebrows did a little dance of confusion and

surprise. "No, I can't accept that. There has to be justice after everything's said and done."

"Look, all we know is that spirits – good, bad, or indifferent – cross over to the other side. Sometimes it takes a bit of an effort to get them to go." Cam sighed and poured another mug of coffee. "What happens after that, we can't tell you. If it makes you feel better to believe that there is some kind of sorting or judgment, by all means, go with that."

"Besides, what do you really know about He-Who-Counseled-the-Chief?" Taking the coffee carafe from Cam, I topped off my mug. "He might have done some stuff he's not too proud of. He's still on this side, after all." Ron's face fell, distracting me and making me fumble as I replaced the carafe on the trivet. Ancestors were revered in his culture and I had just shat all over that. I clumsily babbled on and tried to cover my faux pas. "Or maybe there is something left unfinished and he needs to find closure. He led us to the Lenape family, but he didn't join them when they crossed over, so even though this was important, it wasn't the central issue for him."

Lenora spoke up, still holding her chin in her palm. "She-Who-Ate-Audachienrra was important to him. Why doesn't he go to her?"

"Good question," Cam said. "He's been dead and wandering since sometime in the sixteen hundreds and he hasn't tried to go to her. Obviously, we can use this lady to induce him to cross over." Cam sipped his coffee and considered. "He did seem excited when you spoke to him in his native tongue. He said he had been searching for you." When Lenora widened her eyes at this, Cam clarified. "Well, not you specifically, but probably other tribal members."

Ron shook his head, the corners of his eyes and mouth pulled down by sadness. "By the early seventeen hundreds, the Unami speakers like He-Who-Counseled-the-Chief were pushed out of New Jersey into eastern Pennsylvania. In the eighteen hundreds, our people were forced even farther west. We ended up as far north as Canada and as far south as Mexico and a bunch of places in between. It's no wonder he couldn't find his people when he searched the old tribal lands."

"That poor man…Can you imagine being abandoned, without your people?" Lenora put her knuckles to her mouth and shook her head slowly.

Sagging in his chair, Ron closed his eyes. "Yes," he said softly. Lenora reached over and put her frail hand over his large, meaty paw, saying nothing.

I looked away. I did not want to remember the feeling of isolation before I met Cam and Zackie. Clearing my throat, I brought up the other piece of the puzzle. "There's still the question of why He-Who-Counseled-the-Chief was with Maggie when she took her life."

"Who's this Maggie?" Lenora asked. "I remember you asked He-Who-Counseled-the-Chief what he did to her and it made him angry."

After we explained what we knew about Maggie's case to Lenora and Ron, she sat back with her arms folded over her chest. "Why'd you think he'd harm her? He'd tried to help her. It's obvious what he said was to stop her from shooting herself."

Cam sighed. "We don't know that. He might have been tormenting her in her last moments or he –"

Ron interrupted. "No, he wouldn't do that. He helped the Lenape family. Without him, they'd still be stuck here, trapped below the water."

"Dude, what if he only helps his own? He'd have no reason to have a soft heart for the people who invaded his land. And he saw what Tom Quick did to that poor family. That's not going to give him a good impression of white settlers." I forced the bangs out of my eyes and searched Ron's face for understanding. He looked away, unconvinced. "Look, I don't believe in my gut that he tried to harm her. But I have no solid evidence to tell me anything one way or the other."

Lenora uncrossed her arms and tapped the table top with her finger. "You talk to him again. Things'll be different for you now that you helped the family."

Cam shrugged. "You may be right. In any event, we do need to talk to him again, if only for his own sake. He needs to move on. But I'm not holding out hope that what he has to say can help us with Maggie." Cam gave me a probing look. "And we cannot do this today. Fia needs more time to recharge."

I nodded gratefully. If it were an emergency, I would have sucked it up to do what I had to do, but it would cost me. Another spirit encounter right then would probably be really unpleasant and possibly painful. "Maybe one more day. I think I'll be ready in another day." I looked for signs of disappointment and impatience, but the faces of my friends were understanding. I could take the time I needed.

###

The day had come and I completely lost any ability to focus. The date with Lucas preyed on my mind and any moments of soaring exhilaration came crashing down, brought to ground by the fears and worries of how reality might compare with my fantasies. I tried to watch TV to pass the time, but could not concentrate long enough to make it to a commercial break. It became background noise while I showered and then obsessed about my hair and clothes. Taking extra time and special care, I applied the mortuary makeup to the dead hand, blending the colors until I had a near perfect facsimile of life. I planned what I would eat because I wanted that first kiss to be perfect. And I wanted that kiss more than I ever wanted anything in my life.

The evening was unseasonably warm, more like a throwback to summer than an autumn night. I wore my finest black t-shirt, my best bet for hiding food stains, and rolled my windows down slightly during the drive to Hot Dog Johnny's. I couldn't risk getting my hair mussed, but neither could I arrive sweaty and sticky. Maybe I should avoid anything with onions or do without condiments to keep my shirt clean. I chewed the inside of my cheek, deciding. Maybe I wouldn't eat.

My mind churned uselessly, swarmed with trivial worries in an effort to block the true, core fears that slowly bubbled to the surface. What if I screwed this up, doing or saying something to make him think psychosis was a better explanation for who I was? It was different when Cam was there to back me up, but alone with Lucas, I was afraid that I'd bump up against his limits with the ghost stuff and he'd see me as the crazy girl. And what if he kissed me and I didn't measure up to Hannah? I would always be in her shadow. She was his first love, his wife, and I was certain he wouldn't have given me a second look if she were still alive.

I parked near the tree line and stilled the engine with a mindless turn of the key. A warm breeze blew through my open window, teasing strands of my hair to float softly around my face. I stepped out of the car and was greeted by the silvery sound of water from a stream rushing at the bottom of the hill behind the restaurant. He sat on a table, leaning slightly forward, his feet on the seat and his hands clasped loosely on bent knees. When he stood up and walked slowly towards me, his stride easy with its own unique rhythm, a bass line played soft as crushed velvet in my mind. It might have been my heart beating to match his pace as I stood unmoving, thoughts and fears stuttering to a halt, mesmerized by his animal grace. He wore faded jeans and a gray t-shirt that exposed the cut of his biceps below the sleeves. My eyes traveled along his form while the breeze swirled, pressing the soft fabric of his shirt against the muscles of his chest. I followed the movement of Lucas's blond hair as it swayed silkily around his shoulders, moved by the warm drafts, until at last I found his eyes. He looked back at me, gray as a winter sky and steady.

Stopping within inches of me, his unblinking gaze softened and delved into my eyes. His hands brushed the hair back from my face and then he brought his lips to mine. And I was lost in this purely sensual moment, with no room for thoughts or doubts. His kiss was soft and gentle, but there was nothing tentative. He smelled of clean soap and I tasted mint on his lips. I stroked his ribs and found the taught muscles of his back. With that small encouragement, his hands smoothed the contours of my body and pulled me in closer, his lips burning and insistent. My fingers tangled in the soft strands of his hair and my heart pounded, sending lava coursing through my veins. Like a scorching desert wind, his emotions swept through me, incendiary and wild, painting me with flame. Leaning into him, feeling the searing heat of his body, I deepened the kiss and savored the gift of this moment.

When he drew back, his eyes were dark and his hands stayed on me, keeping me close. My lips were parted, but I had no words. I was an artist's canvas that had never known color before this moment. A new world, iridescent with the vivid hues of autumn, welcomed me home and I inhaled the teasing, green tang of the fertile earth, feeling the lush susurrations of dancing leaves tingle on my skin.

My senses were overwhelmed by Lucas and when a powerful smell of ammonia wafted into my consciousness, I had no idea when the scent had started to build. The wind gusted and a tree groaned as branches rubbed, but I realized Hannah could do nothing while I stood so close to Lucas. Any harm intended for me would also reach him. I stood my ground, resting my head on his chest until the wind calmed. A wrenching sob echoed in my ears and I sensed the black hole of her despair as she departed.

Lucas took my good hand and led me to a picnic table. Sitting by his side, holding his hand in the warmth of the setting sun, I should have felt like this was nirvana. I had wanted this for so long. Instead of feeling content and joyful at this new beginning with Lucas, I hung my head, feeling like a rat bastard for stealing Hannah's husband.

With a crooked finger, Lucas lifted my chin and gazed into my eyes. "Have I done something wrong?"

"You did everything right. You're perfect." I said this with all the conviction I felt and a smile played on his lips.

"What's wrong then?"

I swallowed and screwed up my courage to tell him the truth. "Hannah…" My voice trailed off because I had no idea how to let him know that she haunted him. I didn't want to ruin our moment by getting into a discussion about the afterlife, his alternate explanations and different interpretations and the conflicts with my life's hardcore experiences.

"Hannah's at peace." Lucas's voice was strained and his body tense, as he willed this to be true. The grief was ever present just below the surface and it occurred to me that maybe her constant presence fed his grief, despite his lack of conscious awareness. After a moment, he appeared to relax and sighed sadly, a shadow passing over his eyes. "I think about her too." He looked away and took another breath. "I know you two were friends and this might feel like a betrayal." He shook his head, but the troubled expression stayed with him. "I also wondered if this might be too soon, but…" Lucas sat back and gazed into the distance.

"But what?" I stared at his profile and squeezed his hand.

"Ron's a really good guy and I like him. He'd be great for you, but…"

"But you thought you'd be better for me?"

Lucas smiled sheepishly, glancing back at me with sad eyes. "I wanted a shot, so sue me. I figured if I hung back and did nothing because I wasn't sure I was ready, you'd go with him. I had to let you know how I felt and then let you decide."

What I decided was that I really was a rat bastard. I never had these kinds of feelings for Ron, but I was okay if Lucas thought this was true and it encouraged him to want to be with me. And despite what Lucas believed, Hannah and I were never really friends. At best, we were frenemies, with Lucas always between us. Under other circumstances, I think we might have been friends, but as things stood, it was not a possibility.

Hannah was dead, but she was still here. Did staying earthbound give her the right to keep her marriage intact? Did I have the right to destroy that bond, simply because I had the advantage of drawing breath? If I were in her shoes, as much as I abhorred the idea of clinging to a half life on earth, I'd stay too, just to be with Lucas. I really couldn't blame her. Chewing on my lip, I wished my life was simpler.

When I didn't speak immediately, a crease formed on his brow and he turned his body towards me. "Tell me what you're thinking."

I took the coward's way out, sidestepping a serious discussion and deciding to fight the guilt. "I'm thinking you have an odd sense of timing. I thought this was the way a date's supposed to end." I grinned at him and poked him in the ribs with my elbow.

Lucas's expression relaxed. Consenting to this distraction, he settled his back against the table's edge. Bringing my hand to his lips, he brushed my knuckles with a kiss. "Let me put it this way – I hadn't planned on it. But once the idea crossed my mind, it seemed like the only thing to do."

"It does simplify things. I don't think I would have been relaxed enough to eat and make awkward conversation at the same time."

"Not eat? You?" He rubbed his jaw with his free hand. "Hmmm… Maybe you really do like me."

"You're making a pretty bold assumption there. What makes you so certain that we'd be talking?" I let go of his hand and slid my arms around him, pressing tightly against his body. "But I like you. A lot."

We sat quietly, holding each other until my stomach made loud, embarrassing growls to protest the newfound dominance of my heart in the body politic. Lucas sat forward, releasing me. "I should feed you. What would you like?"

I was happy to eat whatever he wanted. If we both ate onions, so be it, because I was pretty sure I wasn't done kissing him yet. The crowd for dinner had increased and it would take a little time to get through the line. While Lucas was occupied with getting our order, I called Hannah to me. It was the last thing I wanted to do on my first real date with Lucas, but Cam was right. Maybe if Hannah and I talked, really talked, we could work this out.

Hannah appeared from behind a tree. A black cloud of misery surrounded her and despite making the air around her crackle with the power of her growing rage against me, I felt calm and in control.

"So, you've won him to you. Did you call me to gloat about it?" She spit the words out and I understood in my marrow her feelings of betrayal and the injustice of dying so young.

I shook my head slowly. "Hannah, I am truly sorry. But this is why you have to move on. Lucas is still alive, with a lot of years ahead of him. He has no choice but to move on and whether it's to me or someone else, the result would be the same for you." I tried to read her reaction and stared with all my will into her eyes. "Staying here means nothing but pain for you. We can ask Zackie to help. She'll make it easy." No response from her, only her seething rage. I tried again to set her mind at ease. "You know how I feel about Lucas. I'll take care of him."

This was exactly the wrong thing to say. The dam broke and wind tore at the tree branches. The atmosphere took on a purple tinge and I tasted fire in my mouth as the smell of ammonia ripped my sinuses. A family crossing the parking lot cried out at the sudden storm and ran together to find shelter in the building. I hastily built my shark cage for protection from her, but I refused to run and I denied her a fight.

"Take care of him?" She shrieked the words, throwing her dark energy against the bars of the cage again and again, making my teeth rattle with each blow. Spinning like a whirlwind and battering the cage with the force of her emotion, she nearly broke through my defense before doubling over, her energy spent. She gasped out her final words before disappearing. "You are dangerous to him. You bring deadly things like me near him. I am his only protection."

I could no longer focus my will and the cage dissipated into nothing. Near to collapse, I put my head between my knees, concentrating on just breathing. Hannah was more powerful than I had anticipated and this all happened too soon after dealing with the Lenape family and letting the dead hand enjoy a moment in the light. I was drained empty and extremely ill.

"What happened? Are you all right?" Lucas set the tray of food on the table and helped me to sit up. A trickle of blood seeped from my left eye and I reached blindly for a napkin.

"Coconut water… in my trunk…" I forced the words out and pulled my keys from my pocket, dangling them in front of me for him to take. Seeing only hazy images, I was not sure where he stood, but I felt him grab the keys and take off at a run. I was shutting down just as he forced an open bottle into my hand. I drank most of the contents in one long pull and sat back gasping before forcing another bolus down my throat. More stable now, I finished the bottle and opened a second. "Thank you," I whispered.

Lucas sat next to me, his arm around my shoulders. "Better now?"

I nodded miserably, wiping the seeping blood from my eye. At least I wasn't throwing up on his shoes, but I hated to think what I might look like to him. I sipped from the second bottle as Lucas pulled out his phone and speed dialed a call.

"Cam? Something's happened to Fia." His voice was tense, but controlled. Lucas paused, listening to whatever Cam advised. "Yes, she's drinking coconut water, but her eye is bleeding." More tinny words came from the phone. "Right. Okay… okay, I'll do that now. Bye." A French fry nudged at my lips. "Here, eat this." This was followed by more fries as he encouraged me to keep drinking. When the coconut water was finished, Lucas handed me a coke to drink and then a hot dog. I ate mindlessly without tasting and with a grim determination as he continued to hand me food. In a short while, the tray was empty and Lucas was wiping something from my face with a napkin.

"I'm sorry, Lucas. I think I ate your dinner." I felt better, but my brain wasn't working right and my words slurred.

"That's all right." He disappeared for a moment with the empty tray and remains of the meal. When he returned, he slipped his arm around me and lifted. "I need to get you up now."

"Okay." I slumped against him and forced my lips and tongue to form words. "Where are we going?"

"I'm taking you to Cam's."

Lucas helped me to stagger to his car and loaded me into the passenger seat. Reaching across, he secured the seatbelt and then shut the door. The engine started and I felt the car pull out, just as I lost my fight to stay conscious.

# # #

"What were you thinking?" Cam paced the length of the room, throwing black looks my way as he vented. When I had first woken, Zackie shared my pillow, her wet nose breathing in my face. I had asked Cam if I were dying and he told me I would soon wish I were.

"I did what you suggested. I tried to talk to Hannah." After two days, my brain was back to working about as well as it ever did and Cam wasn't impressed. He stared at me like I had lost my mind. I pulled the blanket up against a chill and used my other hand to sip some coconut water.

Cam rubbed a hand over his face and then

attempted a patient look. "Had we or had we not just decided to put off meeting with He-Who-Counseled-the-Chief?"

"We had, but –"

"Did I not say that you needed more time to recover?"

"You did, but –"

"Then why would you decide this would be a good time to take on a really powerful spirit, directly after kissing her husband?" Cam's face was growing red and I felt a monster of a blush flare on my own cheeks.

"Oh, you spoke to Lucas, then…" I looked away and pretended to adjust the covers.

"Yes, he told me everything. Congratulations, by the way." Cam took another breath and was about to launch into the second half of his tirade, likely to detail all my faulty thinking and my inability to show good judgment, when Lucas poked his head through the door.

"I thought I heard my name." Squeezing past Cam, Lucas came to the side of the futon and knelt to get on eye level with me. "How are you feeling?" He had dark smudges under his eyes and I realized he probably hadn't slept in the two days I was out of it. I touched his cheek in apology. He had done enough of this when Hannah was dying and I regretted putting him through it again.

"I'm completely better. Thank you for taking care of me." For Lucas's sake, I needed to haul my sorry ass out of this bed and be healthy for him. "If you two would excuse me, I'd like to get up and put some clothes on."

Cam was about to say something to keep me in bed, but I gave him a pleading look and flicked my eyes towards Lucas. Cam pursed his lips, but understood why I had to get up. At last he nodded and said, "About time then. Come away, Lucas."

When the door shut, I sat up and was slammed by a wave of dizziness. I rubbed my face and grimaced as my mouth flooded with a bitter, coppery taste. Taking a deep breath, I gingerly put my feet on the floor and stood on shaky legs. Zackie came to my side and I kept my balance by leaning on her shoulders. A pile of my clothing sat near the wall in one of Ron and Lenora's open blue luggage bags. I took my time to get to the pile, leaning on Zackie the whole way, and found my keys sitting on top of the folded clothing. My hands fumbled as I pulled out what I needed, including, to my surprise, the neoprene glove and the mortician's makeup kit. Limping and leaning heavily on the psychopomp, I made my way to the bathroom on cramping legs to get showered and dressed. I felt better after the shower, but the cramping remained a problem. Before heading to the kitchen, I checked the dead hand. The fresh application of mortuary makeup looked okay and I figured I wouldn't make anyone throw up, so I was good to go.

Hobbling down the hall with Zackie at my side steadying me, I heard noise from the dining room and changed course. Everyone was seated at the table, eating lunch. The dizziness had returned as I tried to take my seat and the effort of pulling the chair back proved too much. Lucas was seated across from me and stood to help, but Ron, seated next to me, reached over and drew the chair back without getting up.

As Lucas returned to his seat, Ron gave him a look of challenge. "You need to take better care of your woman."

Meeting Ron's eyes squarely, Lucas replied with sincerity. "I intend to." They held this eye contact for a breath and then Ron grunted approval before helping himself to a plate of fried bread. If Ron wanted to play big brother, he could be my guest. I didn't have the energy to even roll my eyes.

Lenora plunked down a bowl of thick lentil soup in front of me, put a spoon in my hand and then poked Ron as she moved back to the kitchen. "You give her some bread."

Ron did as he was told and Zackie shot up from under the table, grabbing the first piece that was offered. After accepting the second piece of bread, I tucked into my food without being prompted, quickly finishing everything in front of me. When Lenora returned with more fried bread, hot and straight from the pot, Lucas motioned to Ron to put more on my plate. I greedily ate the fresh bread and then put away two servings of chocolate ice cream for dessert.

"How come you don't eat like that?" Lenora prodded Cam as he cleared dishes from the table.

"I do eat like that, and more, but you expect that from a man of my size. No one ever bats an eye." Bringing back a carafe of coffee, napkins and some mugs from the kitchen, Cam continued. "But I'm neater about it, so there's less evidence." He tossed some napkins my way and I put them to use.

Ron also felt the need to comment on my eating habits in front of Lucas. "She eats like her life depends on it."

"People, I'm sitting right here." I tried to get them to stop before they made Lucas calculate what his new food budget might be. Zackie made a chuffing noise and nudged me under the table, amused by my embarrassment.

Cam shrugged, ignoring me. "Her life probably does depend on it. Our metabolism is different from most people. I like to think it's the extra needs of our brains for additional calories."

Wonderful. They were dissecting the minute details of my freakishness. Right in front of Lucas. I wanted to bury my head in my arms and hide. Instead, cheeks burning, I changed the subject to distract them. "Speaking of brains, do you think the fact that a bullet destroyed Maggie's brain affects her ability to think and process now? That's maybe why everything's so garbled and mixed up with her?"

"I think it's more a function of being newly dead," Cam said. "Spirits who do not cross over immediately tend to require some time to adjust to their new situation and there is initially a profound sense of disorientation. In my experience, the manner of death does not ultimately affect their abilities, provided the spirits are willing to accept the fact that they no longer live and need to accommodate a mortal wound."

Ron shrugged as he toyed with a teaspoon. "I guess that makes sense. Look at He-Who-Counseled-the-Chief. His head was crushed by a bear, but everything you've told us about what he says seems reasonable and makes sense for the most part. His brain seems fine."

I frowned and shook my head, still confused. "So, why doesn't he show up with a crushed head? Why does he look undamaged to me when so many other spirits are really physically messed up from whatever killed them, even some of the old ones?"

Cam sighed and his eyes looked distant and sad, like he was remembering all the souls that crossed his path. "I think for the most part, spirits display their death wounds as a way of telling us that they suffered, that they are suffering. He-Who-Counseled-the-Chief is not suffering because of his manner of death. Something else is causing his pain and preventing him from moving on." Cam's words made me think of Hannah and how she manifested with chemo tracts on her arms, her body emaciated and weak.

Lucas sat with his arms crossed, maybe not one hundred percent buying everything we said, but listening and processing the conversation. “You’ve built an entire mythology around this phenomenon. I have to give you kudos for creating internal consistency in your arguments.”

“You call it mythology, I call it observation.” Cam shrugged, unwilling to be drawn into a debate.

“Tomatoes, to-mah-toes…” Lucas flipped his hand back and forth, smiling tiredly and letting it go. He was also lacking energy and appeared to be in no mood for a rigorous discussion of our differences in opinion. I must have swayed in my seat from my own fatigue, because his eyes suddenly darted to me and he stood. “I think Fia needs to get some more rest.”

He came around the table and helped me stand, keeping his hand under my elbow to make sure I didn’t fall over. “Come on, let’s get you back to bed.”

I refused to be an invalid in front of him. “No, I’m not tired. I don’t want to go back to bed.”

"You sound like a two year old," Lucas said as he led me away.

I dug in, but played the role to amuse him. "Please? Just five more minutes?"

He could tell I wasn't going to go peacefully and just gave me a tired look, filled with infinite patience. "Okay, how about we just sit on the couch and watch a movie?"

I was agreeable to that and snuggled close when he put his arm around me. I saw maybe five minutes more of the movie than him before we both fell asleep.

# # #

"That is an excellent idea." Cam lit up, his eyes wide as he nodded vigorously.

"What are you talking about? That's a terrible idea." I wasn't having it and my face was set in my most devastating scowl. Hannah's warning repeated in my mind, that I was dangerous to Lucas, and now, here he was, wanting to be there every time we went out to deal with spirits.

Ignoring my objection, Cam flew into planning the logistics of how this would work. “It would be like having a flanker on a SAR mission. Lucas could –”

“Lucas could get in the crosshairs of something really bad.” I shook my head and crossed my arms.

Ron rolled his eyes. “Lucas has experience in ghost hunting. He can take care of himself. Listen to them.”

“Common sense, little girl. More people, more eyes. It’ll be safer.” Lenora looked impatient, like she was dealing with a child who didn’t know what was good for her.

“Come on, Fia. This makes sense. You and Cam are vulnerable to environmental influences that can impair your reactions. For whatever reason, I have immunity. I can get you out if things go bad.” Lucas watched me closely, maybe looking for a tell that one of his arguments was hitting the mark.

“You don’t have immunity if they go poltergeist and things start flying.” I tried to stare him down, but it wasn’t working.

“Neither do you. And you always seem…” Lucas’s

brow furrowed as he searched for the word. "… distracted – yes, that's the right word – distracted when this sort of phenomenon occurs. You don't have the sense to get out of the way or seek cover."

I compressed my lips, irritated by his choice of words. I was distracted because it took enormous concentration and will to muster and direct the energy to fight back. He made it sound like I was unfocused, my attention claimed by shiny things. I slammed my palm on the table. "Look, I'm not defenseless when this sort of thing happens. You can't sense it, but I'm working to shut it down."

"And while you're working, you need someone to watch your back." He cocked an eyebrow at me as he waited for the next volley.

We sat in the dining room with Ron and Lenora at the far end of the table, nearest the kitchen, and Cam at the other end. Lucas and I flanked Cam on either side. Cam turned his head from one to the other of us as he followed the exchange. "Point, set, match, Lucas." Cam gave Lucas a high five.

They were ganging up on me and I wasn't going to

win this one. Lucas sensed that I was angry at their collusion and he reached over the table to touch my hand. “Fia, I don’t want anything to happen to you. You scared the hell out of me with this last one. What would have happened to you if I hadn’t been there?” He stared steadily at me, his eyes worried.

I looked down at the whorls in the wood of the table, unable to meet his gaze, my head heavy with the desire to lie down. This last one was the worst I’d ever experienced. I had probably been a hair’s breadth from going into a coma and organ failure, and my gut told me I would have died if I had landed in a hospital. Lucas had the good sense to bring me to Cam, so the fact that I recovered was thanks to him. I don’t know if it was the vigilant nursing care from everyone, or something that only Cam and Zackie could do, or all of the above that pulled me through. At least I was still around to wonder about it.

But that was me getting myself into trouble. I made my own choices with eyes wide open. Lucas couldn’t possibly understand what he was getting into. If Cam and I were dealing with a dark spirit and things degenerated into the fine print of Murphy’s Quantum Law, I’d need all the help I could get if Lucas was caught in the crossfire. And

Hannah would do anything and everything to keep Lucas safe. It was a deal with the devil, but actively trying to move Hannah on was now completely out of the question. I trusted her to keep Lucas out of harm's way, but there were some serious downsides to my plan. Aside from the dubious ethics of not doing everything in my power to help Hannah find peace, it was also extremely uncomfortable to know she was around, probably watching everything I did with Lucas. But I'd suffer the sin and deal with the lack of privacy if it meant keeping Lucas safe.

"All right. You win." Lucas looked relieved and squeezed my hand. Cam gave a skeptical tilt of his head, surprised that I appeared to give in so easily, but then followed that up with a speculative look. Maybe he figured out what I had in mind or he thought I was just too weak to put up a good fight.

Lenora turned to Ron, pleased with the outcome. "She's stubborn, but not stupid. That's good. I like stubborn, shows you have backbone. Don't like stupid."

Ron grinned. "Yeah, she is stubborn. Bossy too."

"No, bossy's no good. Don't like bossy." Lenora got up and made for the kitchen to start dinner.

###

A week after my collapse, I was fully charged and fit for duty. The muscle cramps had gone, my strength returned and I was able to focus again without being dragged under by exhaustion. Lucas had negotiated with his job to work remotely and was with me for every step during my recovery, cajoling me into eating one more bite or enforcing rest periods by starting with a kiss and then holding me until I slept. Occasionally, the mask would slip to show a tense and frightened expression and I'd know he was remembering how it was when Hannah died, fearing things would also go sideways with me. If it hadn't been for that, I would have milked the situation for all it was worth, enjoying every minute of being the center of his attention. As it was, I bulled my way through my convalescence to ease his worry and reassure him that I would recover. To his credit, he did not go running for the hills to get away from painful memories or an uncertain present. He stayed.

The best part of this time together was that Hannah never made an appearance. I was pretty sure that, like me, she had taken a hit from our last interaction. It takes energy to manifest and however she was able to siphon that energy from either Cam or me, it's possible that process was broken for the moment. Either that, or whatever energy she was able to draw was being used for repairs. That's my best guess for her absence.

The halcyon days did not last and, too soon, Cam asked if I was ready for another meeting with He-Who-Counseled-the-Chief. I had no real excuse to put this off and no desire to prolong his suffering. Tamping down on my fear of having my life force drained again, I told Cam I was ready.

We returned to the clearing near the stream where we had last seen He-Who-Counseled-the-Chief. The charred remains of the fire was the only evidence of our previous visit. The atmosphere had cleared and no psychic remnants of the centuries old slaughter contaminated the area. We called the spirit to us, but my effort was half-hearted. A small part of me hoped that he wouldn't show up and I'd be spared another round of energy depletion because of an unquiet spirit. Maybe that was selfish of me, but the experience with Hannah had left me skittish.

This new attitude did not go unnoticed. "You need to get back on the horse." Cam gave me a little shove towards the woods where He-Who-Counseled-the-Chief had disappeared into the last time we were here. "Go on, then. Call to him."

"Fia, are you sure you want to do this? Are you really ready for it?" Lucas spoke from somewhere behind me and he sounded worried.

Squaring my shoulders, I responded without turning around. "Born ready." I put on the false bravado for his sake, but I knew Cam was right. I had to pull myself together and do what needed to be done. I called to He-Who-Counseled-the-Chief, withholding nothing this time, but whether he would answer was another story.

The scent of tobacco smoke, at first faint, wafted around me and then coalesced into the figure of the Lenape man. "Why do you summon me?"

"Is he here? I thought I felt a chill." Ron rubbed his arms and looked around without being able to pinpoint the area occupied by He-Who-Counseled-the-Chief.

Cam indicated the ground near the remains of the fire. "He's standing there." Turning to face He-Who-Counseled-the-Chief, he began the interview. "Thank you for coming. We would like to better understand your circumstances, to see if there is anything we can do to help you continue your journey."

The Lenape man grinned, white teeth flashing through the red pigment on his face. "I have walked on, but I have not gone far. This is true." I took on the role of interpreter for the hearing impaired, repeating his words so Ron, Lenora and Lucas could understand. Lucas switched on a digital recorder to capture the conversation, placed it on a rock in the middle of our group and then indicated that we should sit.

"Why're you staying?" Lenora sat on the camp chair Ron had brought, while the rest of us took seats on the ground. Her eyes soft with concern for the man she could not see, and she waited to hear his answer.

"I needed to help the family and the others Tom Quick had murdered. The family had been trapped for so long…" His eyes winced with pain and his shoulders sagged with the weight of centuries. "I had tried to free them for as long. But it was beyond my strength. It required the strength of many and I am grateful for your help."

"Are there more victims? Can you show us?" Cam urged him to continue, to let us know where to look.

"These were the last. Tom Quick had killed many

Lenape. Some walked on, but some needed this ancestor spirit to help them rise again and walk."

"And that's why you stayed? To help these people?" Lucas cocked his head, as if he could hear the response.

"Not at first. I wandered heartsick and confused for some time after the bear took me. When I looked up again, the world had changed. My people were dying from the sickness brought by the whites. The tribes grew smaller and smaller and then it became difficult to find the very few of my people who were left."

"But you continued to search. You needed to find your people again." Ron leaned forward, encouraging the spirit and probably sympathizing with his plight.

"I searched. I walked many, many miles looking for Lenape. Years passed and I would find a few, scattered here and there on the old tribal lands. And then Tom Quick came, murdering the few of my people who remained. I clutched him to me and would not let go, so I could try to prevent his killings. But I was a weak spirit then." He held up his hands, palms up with the fingers slightly bent. "I learned to devil him, shaking his bed when he tried to sleep, spilling his water when he drank. I would nudge his rifle when he took aim and rattle the branches where he waited in ambush. Some he chose to kill were saved because of this, but not all. I could not stop all the murders, but I could help those that he killed to walk on. So, I vowed to stay with Tom Quick until he died. And I rejoiced when they put him in the ground."

Cam began the process of moving this spirit on. "But why did you not go to your afterlife then? Tom Quick was dead and would kill no more. Why did you stay?"

"His family lived and his evil could live on through them. I stayed with the family, to watch and to try to stop them from harming my people. My strength had grown by then. But the family did not have his bloodlust."

Cam continued to remind the Lenape man that he was free to move on to the afterlife. "If no more Lenapes were being murdered, you could have moved on then and –"

"No. The people from my tribe were still trapped in the water. I would not leave them. But I could not bear their suffering for long, so I would come and try to free them, failing again and again and then return to watch the children of the children of Tom Quick."

A thought niggled at the back of my mind. "And are you still watching the descendants of Tom Quick?"

"Yes."

My eyes widened as the thought coalesced. "Peyton?"

"Yes." He waved his hand impatiently. "I am with her a while, but then I wander."

This information put a whole new spin on events. He-Who-Counseled-the-Chief had been haunting the family for generations. This was not a case of him recently latching on to Peyton, finding her during the foray into the woods to locate Maggie. Peyton had brought He-Who-Counseled-the-Chief to Maggie.

With this on my mind, I asked the next question. "So, you came to the search with Peyton and then found Maggie when you wandered. Why did you tell Maggie that she gave up too easily?"

"Because she was trying to die." He began to sweat and shifted uneasily. "I could not let her die. She-Who-Ate-Audachienrra died too and it should not have happened."

“So, you were trying to get Maggie to stop, to not take her own life? You were trying to encourage her not to give up?” I already knew the answer, but I needed him to know that we understood that he had tried to do something good for Maggie, but he was having none of it.

“She used the gun after I spoke to her. Because I spoke to her. It was my fault… my fault again.” The Lenape man was becoming increasingly agitated and leaped to his feet, pacing and grimacing as tears streaked down his cheeks.

“Who was She-Who-Ate-Audachienrra to you?” Because we were finally making progress, Cam fired off the question to keep the spirit off-balance and to keep the information flowing.

“I loved her. We were to be married.”

I followed up quickly with the next question, deliberately not giving him time to think. We had to get to the full truth of his condition. “How was it your fault that She-Who-Ate-Audachienrra died?”

He-Who-Counseled-the-Chief stopped pacing, bowed his head and then shook it slowly. “This was a bad time.” His voice was ragged – he was near a breaking point.

"Did someone harm her?" I spoke softly this time, trying to change the pace and ease the story out of him.

The Lenape man looked up and his eyes were fierce, but full of sorrow. "It was me. I harmed her."

"Did you poison her?" Cam asked.

He-Who-Counseled-the-Chief pounded his chest with his closed fist. "It may as well have been me, but I did not give her the Audachienrra."

"Did someone else give her the root of the may-apple?" I stood up and faced him, wanting to watch his expression as he answered.

At first, his face closed and I thought he would not answer me. I stepped closer, staring him in the eye and demanding an answer. He closed his eyes and spoke through clenched teeth."No one gave it to her. She ate it to get away from me."

"Why? What had you done?" Lenora spoke up, her voice full of dismay at this admission.

"I was young and stupid and full of myself. I

counseled the chief and our tribe prospered. I was vain. When other women in the tribe paid me compliments and admired me, I would preen and posture for them. Eventually, I would go to them."

"And She-Who-Ate-Audachienrra found out." Lenora crossed her arms and her lips became a thin line as she waited for his answer.

"Yes. I turned from her and did not marry her. She ate the Audachienrra to punish me."

Cam's eye lit up with an epiphany and he raised a finger as he asked the next question. "And after she died, you went hunting."

"Yes. Brother bear had a good hunt that day."

Cam nodded. "So you've said…And did you bring your best knife?"

"No…" The Lenape man's eyes shifted, as if he were looking for a way out.

Cam was relentless as he zeroed in on the confession that needed to be said for the spirit to find peace. "I see. And did you arm yourself appropriately for the hunt?"

"No. It would not have mattered. The bear was too strong." He-Who-Counseled-the-Chief half turned away and did not make eye contact as Cam continued his questioning.

"Did you fight back when the bear had you?"

He-Who-Counseled-the-Chief repeated the same words as before, but he was close to yelling this time. "No. It would not have mattered. The bear was too strong."

Cam muttered to me, "Suicide-by-bear, but he's not admitting to it." Turning his attention back to He-Who-Counseled-the-Chief, Cam doggedly pursued the truth behind the bear attack. "Did you allow the bear to end your life because you had caused She-Who-Ate-Audachienrra to end hers?"

The Lenape man buried his face in his hands, breathing hard. Thunder rumbled from somewhere near us as energy from the spirit's emotions spilled over into the environment. Looking up at last, his eyes were wild, but he had made his decision. "I will speak the truth at last. I gave myself to the bear because of what I did to her. But I still could not make it right." He swallowed hard and tears dripped from his chin. "In dying, I made another mistake because my tribe needed me and I had abandoned them. I should have hunted and brought them food to keep them strong. I should have tended the sick to help them get better. My tribe weakened and died because of my vanity and stupidity. I do not deserve to live in the house of the Creator."

He was trapped in a never-ending cycle of guilt. The guilt from She-Who-Ate-Audachienrra's suicide had driven him to end his own life, but he believed that in doing this, he was not there when his people needed him. The double suicide, although separated in time, also explained his connection with Maggie. Confronted with another young woman who was about to take her own life, and knowing how suicide could affect those left behind, He-Who-Counseled-the-Chief must have tried everything in his power to prevent her death. But in the end, his efforts backfired. We all sensed the hopelessness he felt.

Ron cleared his throat, but his voice was rough with emotion. "You need to understand that the tribe lives on. Yes, most of our people died during your family's time because of smallpox, cholera, whooping cough – diseases that they had no immunity for, diseases that they could not fight. Those that were spared no longer had the numbers to defend the land from the whites and the Iroquois. They were forced to move west, out of the tribal lands." Ron took Lenora's hand and his voice softened. "But we live on and hundreds more like us keep the traditions alive. We speak the language and we know the names of our father's fathers. We are proud to be Lenape."

Cam sighed and looked at the spirit, his eyes brimming with compassion. "You could not have stopped what happened to your tribe, even if you had lived. She-Who-Ate-Audachienrra made her own choice. She could have decided otherwise, maybe married another and moved on with her life. In the end, even though you acted badly, it was her choice. You need to absolve yourself of this guilt."

"And what of Maggie? If I did not exist, she might still live." The spirit was on his knees, broken by the emotional catharsis and weeping openly. Zackie came to him, nuzzling his face to offer him comfort.

Cam spread his hands, palms up, in a gesture of helplessness. "We don't know anything about Maggie. We don't know why she felt she needed to die. If it wasn't your words, something else might have triggered her to end it."

I felt terrible about it, but despite the spirit's

anguish over what happened to Maggie, I was obligated to pursue answers for her. "One thing we do know is that Maggie kept telling us that she needed to protect the baby from them." I squatted down to get on eye level with He-Who-Counseled-the-Chief. "Do you know anything about 'them?' Who are they and why did they want to harm the baby?"

The spirit swallowed and wiped hard at the tears on his face, trying to regain his composure. "They were children once." His shoulders slumped and he shook his head with sorrow. "Now, they are like leeches. Sucking life from the living. They are greedy for life. They have lost…" He paused and looked at the ground, concentrating to find the right word. "They have lost their humanity. Their eyes are empty and full black, and they have no memory of kindness or mercy anymore."

The small hairs on the back of my neck stood up as he described these beings. I shot a worried look towards Cam, but then forced my full attention back to He-Who-Counseled-the-Chief. "Did they come to Maggie because she was contemplating suicide, and they were attracted by these dark thoughts? Or did she suicide because they were tormenting her and draining her will to live?"

In a low voice, Cam offered a another explanation . "Or maybe she had the gun for self-defense against them and she hadn't originally intended suicide."

The Lenape man shrugged his shoulders. "I know not. They scattered like leaves when I approached and then Maggie put the gun to her head. I should not have spoken to her, but I wanted to stop her."

Cam sighed. "Again, not your fault. From what you've told us, it was just bloody awful timing. The one thing we know for sure is that Maggie was suffering. And we will try to help her to move on. Will you let us help you?"

"But what of Maggie? She will be left here, still suffering."

Cam shook his head. "We will help her. You need to trust that we will not abandon her and we will keep trying until she is free. Will you let us free you?"

Zackie nudged He-Who-Counseled-the-Chief with her muzzle and he turned his head to look at her, his features drawn down by sadness. Their eyes locked and a moment of understanding passed between these two. At last, the yoke of guilt fell from his shoulders and he nodded. Getting up, standing straight, He-Who-Counseled-the-Chief placed his hand on Zackie's shoulders. "I will go now."

Still holding hands, Lenora and Ron chanted the plaintive strains of the funeral song we had heard when the family crossed over. Zackie led He-Who-Counseled-the-Chief out of the clearing. The flash of light was enormous as he passed through the portal, the heat penetrating my cells and making me cringe as I protected my eyes. Before the portal closed, the rich, earthy aroma of tobacco surrounded us and a legion of voices chanting the funeral song reached my ears, the voices rising and falling like the cry of the wild wolf. They were calling him home.

# # #

"How did you find out?" Peyton flushed and picked at her nail polish, avoiding making eye contact with anyone. "That's not exactly something I want to broadcast."

"He-Who-Counseled-the-Chief told us." I carefully placed my bottle of coconut water on her table before continuing. I knew all about having private information that you didn't want to share with the world. "And don't worry, it's not like we're going to tell anyone."

Lucas caught her eye. "No worries, Peyton. This isn't going to end up on the show. You have every right to privacy."

Peyton pushed her chair back, her eyes roaming through the family pictures hung on the walls of her cheery, yellow kitchen. The silence grew and the sound of a barn owl hooting floated in from the woods. Softly, she made her admission and there was a tightness around her eyes as she spoke. "I am a descendant of Tom Quick, but I'm not proud of it. He was a nasty piece of work."

Sipping his bottle of coconut water, Cam asked the question gently. "You don't think having his father killed and scalped by Delaware Indians could be considered extenuating circumstances?" Cam's expression was mild and I think he was trying to offer Peyton a way out of her multi-generational guilt. Living her entire life in the shadow of He-Who-Counseled-the-Chief must have had some influence on her views of the past.

"No." Peyton shook her head, her jaw set. "I can see going after the Delawares that took his father out, but vowing revenge on all of them? His own mother said that seeing his father murdered turned his head and he wasn't responsible for anything he said or did after that." She savagely swiped a stray curl from her face and then folded her arms over her chest. "When he died, he admitted to killing ninety-nine people. They say he begged his friends to bring him one more Indian to make it a perfect hundred. Tom Quick wasn't right in the head. That's not something that should be glorified with a monument."

Ron sighed and rubbed his face. "The monument's a freakin' nine foot tall obelisk. And one inscription on that monument actually pays homage to his killing." He used his hands to frame the view like a movie director. "Tom Quick, the Indian Slayer."

Peyton flashed a grim smile. "Not anymore. I smashed the fucker with a sledgehammer back in '97 before I joined the military. They repaired it, but they never put it up again."

"You done good to smash that fucker." Lenora reached over and patted Peyton on the knee.

"Be that as it may," Cam interjected, "Did you ever wonder why you had such strong feelings for something that happened hundreds of years before you were born?"

Peyton cocked an eyebrow. "Um, mainly because it was wrong?"

"Quite." Cam rolled his eyes. "But while many people would agree that it was wrong, few people would take up a sledgehammer to make the point."

I touched Peyton's hand, curled in a fist on the tabletop. "What Cam's getting at is that He-Who-Counseled-the-Chief has been with you your entire life. He was kind of passed down from your ancestors." I paused to let this sink in. "It began with Tom Quick. The spirit witnessed the murders of his kinsmen and decided to haunt the guy. When Tom Quick died, he stayed with that family to keep an eye on them because he didn't much trust any of the relations either."

Peyton's brow furrowed. "So, he didn't just latch on to me during the search for Maggie?" I shook my head. "Then why didn't I know anything about him until then? What made him start pounding on the trailer?"

I paused and chose my words carefully. He-Who-Counseled-the-Chief also had a right to privacy and I didn't feel justified in blurting out the whole story of She-Who-

Ate-Audachienrra and his subsequent suicide. “We think he was distraught because of Maggie’s suicide and the pounding was some kind of outlet. He had tried to stop her and it affected him deeply when she chose death.”

Peyton stared at me, dumbfounded. “So, he wasn’t all bad then, if he tried to help her.”

“No, he wasn’t a bad sort at all.” Cam hitched a shoulder. “Most of them aren’t – they’re just stuck.” I had to agree with Cam. He-Who-Counseled-the-Chief had helped so many of Tom Quick’s victims and he never meant any harm to Peyton.

Somewhere in the house, a clock ticked. Soft rain began to fall, streaking the window and I looked passed the slowly coursing rivulets of water to the trailer. Quiet and empty, it lay in repose like a slumbering bear in the back of the property.

“You know, there was this thing that happened when I was a kid.” Peyton spoke hesitantly, biting her lip as her eyes drifted to the trailer. “We had a fire in the middle of the night. The smoke alarms hadn’t gone off because the fire was still really small and there wasn’t enough smoke built up. Something pushed me out of bed and I landed in a heap on the floor. That woke me up and I smelled something burning, so I went to investigate." She rubbed her nose, maybe remembering that night. "I started screaming for my folks and they were able to put the fire out before anything really happened. I always thought I just dreamed the part about being pushed out of bed."

CHAPTER 5

I returned home to spoiled milk in my refrigerator and a keen sense of isolation. A leaky faucet in the bathroom dripped in a monotone as I surveyed my barren domain. Compared to Cam's crowded house, my home echoed with emptiness. Sighing, I accidentally inhaled the stagnant air, redolent with the odor of sour milk and quickly busied myself with opening windows. I next managed a half-assed job of dusting surfaces, but I was highly unmotivated and soon gave up. The main thing wrong with my world was that after such close and constant contact with Lucas, being alone felt like an amputation. Time promised to drag until I saw him again that night. We were going to have one final dinner together to say farewell to Ron and Lenora before they went home to Oklahoma. Sighing again, I thought how I'd even miss Lenora when they left.

A text from Gander saved me from spending the

entire day wallowing in self-pity. We had another job, this time for a classic car, a vintage Mustang. A pregnant woman's water broke while she was on the way to the hospital. She had insisted to her husband that she wanted to go in style, and so, the 1965 Ford Mustang Shelby GT350 had been pressed into service. Many tears had been shed by the new father, both in celebration of the birth of his first born and for the awful mess left in what had been his most treasured possession.

I had a moment's hesitation in accepting the work. Rory might also have been called to the job and I had no desire to see that little schmuck. On the flip side, I could not let that jerk dictate what I would do in my life, whether I would work or take a day off. My rent was coming due, so that decided it for me. I sent a text to Gander to let him know that I'd be there to help with the job.

Parking my car in the far end of the lot, I took care to keep a significant distance from the assortment of Porsches, Maseratis and the sprinkling of other even more exotic cars staged in the lot and under a protective canopy. There was no sign of JoJo and the white BioSolutions truck, but the van was parked in the lot, so I wandered to the building in search of the crew.

The open garage bay doors showed a spotless, white interior lit by strategically placed suspended lights with brushed nickel drum shades. Immaculately clean tools were sorted and placed in cabinets or arranged in aesthetically pleasing displays along the walls. Bent over protective velour blankets covering the chassis, mechanics in pristine, powder blue coveralls peered into engines, while others stood by and updated tablets with diagnostic details related to the vehicles in their care. The disturbing absence of grease made me think that the environment more closely resembled a surgeon's operating theater than a garage.

I found Gander and Goose in the adjacent office area, speaking to a man in a charcoal gray suit. They stood under a chandelier, drinking from tiny espresso cups and appeared to be perfectly at ease in this chi-chi, frou-frou environment.

Gander waved me over as I hesitated near the door and then introduced me to the guy in the suit. "Javier, this is Fia. She will be helping with the Shelby Mustang."

I declined the espresso that Javier offered and shifted from foot to foot until Gander told me to go outside and wait for our truck at the driveway entrance. Within minutes, the white truck appeared and I pointed to some open space away from the valuable cars where JoJo could park. Jogging over, I got there just as he killed the engine and clambered out of the truck.

"Hey JoJo, everything okay?"

"Yeah, sweetie, freakin' accident on I-80. Everything's backed up for miles. Welcome to Jersey." He threw up his hands and grinned ruefully before walking to the back of the truck to unlock the door.

As I was about to go in and change, JoJo touched my arm. "I asked my brother-in-law to look up that Rory guy. Kyle's a private detective. After what happened at the Meridian – and I heard about the coke bottle incident, by the way – I'm thinking something's not right with that kid and I wanted to know what, before he shows up at work and starts shooting or something."

"What did he find?" I swallowed and took a shallow breath, coloring slightly at the mention of the coke bottle.

"Rory's some kind of trust fund kid. He's had all sorts of trouble with the cops, but nothing that stuck." JoJo made a sour face and shook his head, spreading his hands. "Family connections and money. Whatcha gonna do?"

"So, what – he's slumming it? Why's he working this job if he's rich?" I leaned my back against the truck and crossed my arms.

JoJo hitched his thumbs in his pockets and spread his feet to center his mass. "The little shit was living the high life until a couple of months ago, and then he had another run in with the cops. The kid got caught trying to burn down the house of a girl who had refused to go out with him. Got off, as usual, but this time, looks like the family had enough of his crap and cut him off."

I was slack-jawed and I stared in horror at JoJo. The susurration of traffic passing in the distance and the faint smell of car exhaust filled the silence while I processed this disturbing facet of Rory's personality. I had thought he was definitely irritating and the classic bully, but overall, not a significant threat to me. Maybe I needed to re-think that assessment. "Arson? He could have killed that girl."

"Her and her family, but yeah, nothing came of it because he couldn't get the fire lit and then his family probably paid them off not to press charges." JoJo shook his head in disgust. "Anyways, Kyle found an investment account with the kid's name on it, but no withdrawals. I'm thinking he's just making do 'til he's old enough and that money falls into his lap."

I looked down, concentrating on the blackened fingernails of the dead hand. Because she rejected him, Rory was willing to seriously harm a girl for whom he presumably held an attraction and possibly, a budding fondness. Where I was concerned, he had nothing but animosity after the dead hand had publicly humiliated him on several occasions. That didn't bode well for me. I shook my head, not wanting another problem added to my life and my lips compressed in distaste. "Do you know if Gander called him in? Is he coming to work today?"

Gander appeared from around the side of the truck, with Goose a step or two behind. "Rory? I did not call him. This is a three person job and I'd like to end the day not feeling irritated."

Hearing this, I instantly relaxed a notch. JoJo filled the other two in on what Kyle had uncovered about Rory and finished with, "So, not exactly the kind of thing HR would have found doing the usual background check."

Gander's forehead wrinkled as he took in this new information. "No, not something they would have known when they on-boarded him." Looking down, he blew out a breath and rubbed his forehead. After a moment, Gander raised weary eyes to JoJo. "Would Kyle be willing to share what he found with HR? 'Cause if I just stop calling Rory in for work, he stays in the pool of available and could just end up on a different crew. He's too much of a liability for the company. Probably just a matter of time before something happens."

"Before something else happens, you mean." Goose shot a meaningful glance my way. I chewed the inside of my cheek, wanting to be rid of Rory, but not wanting to raise red flags with my employer. I was too new and no one in the company knew me besides the people on this crew. It would be bad for me if I got sucked into Rory's drama and was tainted by association.

JoJo eyed me speculatively and seemed to reach the same conclusion. "I'll talk to Kyle. I'm sure he'd be willing to help."

"Okay, then. I'll reach out to HR to give them a heads up after we finish this job." Gander popped the door on the truck and motioned for us to get a move on.

We suited up and spent the next few hours doing ATP tests on the upholstery. Whenever we found signs of biological activity from bacteria working on the residue of amniotic fluid, we cleaned what we could to preserve the original materials in the car. Despite our best efforts, the passenger-side floor mats, seat leather, and cushion had to be stripped out and put in biohazard bags. We wiped down and sanitized what was left, deodorized the surfaces and then performed one final ATP test to certify that everything was clean. It was then up to Javier to work his magic and restore the vehicle to showroom quality.

By the time we finished with the Shelby Mustang, the sun was setting and I showered quickly, not wanting to be late to the farewell dinner. After roughly toweling my hair dry, I jumped out of the truck and told everyone I'd see them on the next job. Wet hair dripped on my t-shirt as I jogged to my car and I regretted not taking more time to properly dry my hair. Rolling in from the west, forbidding dark clouds massed overhead and a slight frisson gripped me as the wind picked up, chilling the wet spots on my shirt. An autumn storm would rule the night and I hoped there was a jacket or sweatshirt rolling around in my trunk, because I didn't have time to stop at home.

# # #

"No, it's okay. I stay here." Lenora waved off Cam's well wishes for safe travels. We had finished eating the meal she prepared and I was slumped in my seat, contentedly holding my belly to keep it from exploding. I was stuffed with fried bread after setting a new personal record in consumption.

"Eh? What's that?" Cam's face fell and he set down his coffee mug midway to reaching his lips.

"I had a dream –" Lenora was about to continue when Cam interrupted.

"What, you're bloody Martin Luther King Junior now? And you've decided to 'occupy' my house?" Cam formed air quotes to draw our attention to his double entendre. When no one reacted, he leaned forward, placing his forearms on the table and frowning ferociously.

Lenora smirked. "Maybe I decide to reclaim my ancestral lands here. How 'bout that, Kemosabe?" She refilled his coffee from the carafe and then got up to put the kettle on. Returning to her seat, she picked up where she left off. "What I was about to say, I dreamed of my grandfather. He told me don't leave before helping

Maggie."

Cam shifted uneasily. "Lenora, I appreciate your willingness to help, but things could go south on this one. It could be dangerous."

"Doesn't matter. Grandfather said to help Maggie, so that's what we'll do." Lenora met Cam's eye squarely, unmoved by his warning. "I'm a doula – a midwife," she repeated when she saw the blank looks. "Maggie's pregnant. Makes sense."

Ron shrugged and then crossed his arms over his chest. "It's settled, then. We stay until Maggie crosses over."

Cam sat back and surveilled the remaining people at the table, maybe hoping he could put it to a vote. Lucas raised his mug in salute and mumbled, "Cheers, Cam." No help there.

The room was cozy as bursts of wind threw a cold rain against the windows. I was drowsy and half way to a food coma, but I rallied long enough to smile sweetly at Cam as I posed my question. "Do you want me to pick up some more flour, Lenora?"

"No, it's okay. I have more in the luggage."

Cam eyed us wearily. "Right…Maybe we should discuss logistics."

"I think we're good. She has enough flour." I slouched down a little lower in my chair and closed my eyes. Under the table, a chuffing sound let Cam know that as long as we were well supplied with fried bread, Zackie was in favor of the living arrangements.

Cam rubbed his face and expelled an exaggerated sigh. "Not that, you muppet. I'm talking about how we should approach Maggie."

I forced my eyes open, sat up and stopped kidding around. It was time to get serious. Reaching for the carafe, I filled a mug with coffee to fuel the thought process. I took a hit and gave it a moment to circulate. "Okay, go ahead. Shoot."

Cam took a look around the table. "Let's start with a review of what we know, since I'm not sure everyone has all the details." Lucas pulled out a small pad and a pen and prepared to jot down notes. Everyone else looked similarly attentive, but not quite to the level of Lucas's studious type A personality. "To the best of our knowledge, it started with a car accident that killed Maggie's husband and left her with a severe head injury."

I glanced at Ron and Lenora and added, "It wasn't that long ago. She was pregnant at the time."

Cam folded his hands on the table and continued. "The head injury caused her to hear disembodied voices. She tried to get treatment, but nothing helped."

"Maggie told us that she heard a male voice say that he would take the baby. She also said a male voice told her that she gives up too easily, but she said this in Lenape." I jabbed my index finger at the table surface to emphasize the point. "That made me think that He-Who-Counseled-the-Chief was somehow involved in Maggie's death."

"But that wasn't true," Cam continued. "He-Who-Counseled-the-Chief was trying to stop her."

"I think we only have his word that this is what happened." Lucas flipped through his notes and then grunted an affirmation when he found the record. "Can we rely on this?"

Cam's eyes drifted as he considered the question. "Yes…yes. I think we can."

"I believe him." Ron raised his eyebrows, daring anyone to contradict him.

Lenora slapped the table with her palm. "Me too. He was a good man."

"What about you, Fia?" Lucas turned his gaze to me.

I nodded. "I didn't have a good first impression of him, but I have to admit he won me over. I think we can trust what he said."

"Which brings us to the next part of what He-Who-Counseled-the-Chief told us." A shadow passed over Cam's eyes and a furrow formed between his brows. "Some sort of dark spirits surrounded Maggie in her last moments, but they scattered when our Lenape friend approached."

Lucas consulted his notes. "He said they used to be children, but now they drain the living. And there's something weird about their eyes." He looked from me to Cam, serious and concerned. "Do you want to explain to me what the hell that's all about?"

"Wow, you almost look like you believe this stuff."

I tried for a joking tone to ease his worry, but it didn't work.

Lucas's mouth turned down at the corners, not appreciating my attempt at humor. "I don't have to believe these are ghosts in order to attempt an understanding of this phenomenon." He put his elbows on the table and leaned in. His shirt sleeves were rolled up and I stared at his bare forearms, tracing the taught contours with my eyes and nearly missing what he said next. "Ignorance is never bliss if you're trying to prepare a defense. So, tell me what you know."

I could feel the heat of his skin from across the table and found myself leaning towards him. To keep from crawling over the table to draw closer to him, I wrapped my hands around the coffee mug and concentrated on formulating a reply. "Okay, I get that. I also try to plan ahead when I can."

Cam snorted. "What utter rubbish. You are one of the most impulsive people I know."

"I said 'when I can.'" I sat back and glared at him, feeling exposed. "You can't always plan ahead. Sometimes you just have to act."

"You will learn that you don't always have to act. If you can take a moment to think, do it. You might live a little longer." Cam was about to say more, but Lucas was determined to bring us back to the main subject.

"Excellent point, but in the spirit of thinking first, can we get back to planning how we're going to deal with Maggie?" When we each grumbled our assent, Lucas circled back to me. "You haven't answered my question. What do you know about the beings the Lenape man described?"

I stopped trying to come up with a witty retort to Cam's nagging and focused on what Lucas wanted. "No idea about these things. I've never run into anything like them."

My comments didn't seem to allay his fears and his mouth turned down further. "Okay, so Fia has no experience with these black-eyed kids. How about you, Cam? Have you ever dealt with them before?"

"I have." Cam became subdued and picked at non-existent crumbs on the tablecloth. The air in the room grew still and close as we waited for Cam to gather his thoughts. A floor board creaked in the hallway as the house settled.

The only other sound was the wind buffeting hard against the windows and rattling the door.

“They’re nothing to be trifled with,” he said at last. His brow lowered and he stared at his hands, grasping the coffee mug. “You can think of them as black holes. If you get too close, everything that you are or might become gets sucked into them. These were children whose lives were cut short and they have a voracious, insatiable hunger for life.”

“Have you ever succeeded in getting one to move on?” The room had grown chilly and my skin prickled. The many loaves of fried bread sat uneasily in my gut and I shifted to ease the discomfort. The rustle of my movements were loud in the still room and I stopped fidgeting.

“Not me personally, but I’ve seen it done and it had a very steep cost.” Cam glanced up and his eyes flickered with remembered pain. A low howl from the wind sounded from the eaves of the house as we stayed quiet, not pushing him, waiting for Cam to find the words. “I was still a lad and my grandmother was teaching me the sibyl’s craft. Granny was called to Ireland to deal with a rash of deaths of young adolescent boys. The local constabulary thought nothing of it – aside from the tragedy – because, of course, boys will be boys. But a sibyl from the area thought otherwise and notified Granny."

"How did these boys die?" Lucas flipped the page on his pad and poised his pen to record the answer.

"Various ways, each one more foolhardy than the last. That's why these fatalities never raised a red flag with the authorities. There was no pattern." Cam grimaced as he ticked off the causes of death. "One died playing at dodging traffic on a busy road. Another raced his bike down an embankment to leap over a fast running stream. A third boy decided to play matador with a farmer's bull." He rubbed the back of his neck and grit his teeth. "It was all hijinks and mischief, the sort of things boys might do on a dare."

Ron quirked an eyebrow and nodded knowingly. "So, just high-spirited boys who took it one step too far."

"Exactly," Cam agreed.

Lenora grunted and pointed a gnarled finger at Ron. "Could have been you, boy. Damn near gave me a heart attack with your games." Cam tensed and gave her a sharp look, but Ron just shrugged.

I encouraged Cam to go on with his tale. "So, what happened?"

"My granny figured out that the epicenter of these accidents was an ancient ruin. It had once been a great fortress in the dark ages, but it was largely reduced to a pile of rubble in the present day." He rubbed his jaw and shook his head slightly. "Although you could still climb the battlements and one of the towers was still intact.

"And that's where my granny found me – forty feet up, balanced on a parapet along the battlements. While she was trying to call the spirit to her, I had foolishly wandered off and inadvertently drawn his attention. To him, I was irresistible. Just the right age and powerful enough to give him form."

"Who was he?" I was completely drawn in and I sat on the edge of my seat, tunnel vision collapsing on Cam and the story. Shattering the stillness, the tea kettle shrieked and I jerked towards the sound, gasping as I almost fell out of my chair. I scrambled to regain my balance, my heart going into overdrive before I realized the source of this noise. Lenora stood to silence the kettle, while I looked down and shook my head, embarrassed by my over reaction because of the damned PTSD.

Cam waited to continue until Lenora returned, carrying a fragrant pot of brewing tea and fresh mugs. My heart was still racing when he finally spoke. “Obviously, he was a black-eyed child. He looked to be a boy my age, but his eyes were empty, all black instead of the normal iris and whites of the eyes. In life, he had been the youngest son of a noble family in early medieval Ireland. The family aspired for more lands and more power and the High King at the time was threatened by this naked ambition. He demanded hostages after a minor, testing skirmish between his troops and those of the family.”

Lucas interrupted. “Don’t you mean the king ‘took’ hostages after the skirmish?”

Cam shook his head. “No, in those days, hostages were provided to seal the peace after terms were negotiated. If one side reneged on the agreement, it put the hostages at risk and so, more or less enforced good behavior. It was also a way to create a lasting peace, since hostages were frequently the sons and daughters of noble houses. They were well-treated, according to their station, and educated in the traditions and ways of thinking of the captors. So, hostages became a bridge between two peoples and prevented misunderstandings from developing into new conflict."

"I would think hostages would have been killed most of the time, given how violent it was in the Middle Ages." Lucas cocked his head, looking for confirmation.

Cam shook his head again and took a sip of coffee, making a face when he discovered it was cold. "Quite the opposite." Reaching for the tea pot, he poured the liquid into a fresh mug and the spicy aroma of bergamot filled the room. "Most people in power were reluctant to take this step, even if the other side had blatantly welched on a deal. This was especially true when the hostage was a child."

"So, the black-eyed child had been a hostage?" I asked, trying to draw Cam back to the story.

"Yes, but his father overplayed his hand, pushing things too far. He rebelled against the High King – repeatedly. On the first occasion the king warned that he was risking his son's life." Cam looked down sadly. "On the second occasion, the king simply sent him the boy's head."

"That's terrible." Lenora looked aghast. "That poor boy."

Cam continued with his eyes downcast, speaking softly. “This boy had lost all trust. First, his own father had placed ambition above the life of his son and then, the king, who he had come to trust as a surrogate father, orders his death for an offense that was not his doing.” Raising his gaze and his voice, Cam described the consequences of this cruelty. “As a spirit, the boy would replay the loss of trust again and again by luring other boys to commit highly dangerous acts and then, at first, saving them at the last minute. He would do this once, twice, but then the third time, allow them to die with the expectation of rescue. While it lasted, it was exhilarating for these boys and it gave the spirit a taste of life at its sweetest.”

Ron’s eyes were huge as he took in the story. “When your granny found you on the parapet, was that the first death defying feat?”

“First and last. Granny grabbed me down from the ledge by my belt and then used the full extent of her power to influence the spirit to stay and tell his story. He had his hooks in me and she wasn’t going to give the spirit a second chance after that close call. He very nearly drained her dry in the hours it took to convince him to step through the portal.” Cam stared glassy-eyed into the middle distance. “She stood at his shoulder to make sure he went.”

“Whoa, seriously? She was right there, up close and personal with the portal?” I shivered. I knew exactly what that entailed, and it only happened to me because I was ignorant and stupid when I did it. She must have gone into this knowing exactly what she would face and she did it anyway. That was raw courage in my book.

“She was never the same after that. The act blinded her and made her heart weak. She aged suddenly overnight.” Cam swallowed. “And it was my fault. Because I was careless. I forced her hand and she had to rush the process.” He shook his head to clear the memories. “What you all need to understand from this – Granny was the most powerful sibyl that I ever met and laying this black-eyed spirit nearly did her in. We are going to have to proceed with the utmost caution.”

The blood drained from my face and I nodded meekly. Cam was not one for hyperbole, so I knew what he was saying was dead on. The thought of being drained again terrified me and I was suddenly really glad that Lucas would get me out if things went beyond my pay grade. The stark terror must have shown on my face because he reached across the table and covered my hand with his.

Without saying anything, I felt he was making me a promise. Forcing myself to relax, I took a deep, cleansing breath, but my shoulders reflexively shot up around my ears as the scent of ammonia shocked my sinuses. My eyes went wide and I froze.

"Lucas is true as the tide." Hannah whispered in my ear and then she was gone as suddenly as she had appeared. The only aroma remaining was a soothing combination of coffee, bergamot and the leftovers from dinner. I looked around, confused and on my guard, waiting for her to reappear. A few thumps from a wagging tail under the table let me know that Zackie had sensed her and Cam raised an eyebrow at me in question. His eyes shifted as he scanned the room for any evidence that Hannah was somewhere nearby, but then lifted a shoulder as he came up empty. I could only shake my head, that I couldn't feel her presence anymore either.

"What?" After listening to Cam's story, Ron sat uneasily, hunched forward, his eyes darting around the room. "Something just happened. What are you not telling us?"

I shot a quick glance at Lucas, knowing it would not go over well if I said anything about Hannah being around.

"I thought I felt something, but there's nothing here."

Cam backed me up. "I don't feel anything either." Looking around at the tensely drawn faces, he tried to calm the group. "Look, we're all feeling a bit edgy right now, knowing what we're up against. Maybe we should just call it a night and leave it for tomorrow to sort this out."

"No," I said, surprising myself. "Let's keep going. I'm as freaked out as everyone else about the black-eyed kids, but prolonging this is just going to give me more time to stress about it."

"I agree." Lucas squeezed my hand and glanced at me before continuing. "Being proactive, planning our next move, doing anything but being passive right now will help us feel more in control and less fearful."

"Take the bull by the horns," Lenora chimed in, her jaw set stubbornly.

Ron assessed the strength of that set jaw and then sighed. "Okay. How do we get to Maggie?"

"She's in Worthington State Forest. Off-trail, about a half mile in, overly fairly rough terrain." I watched Ron's face fall, so I tried to make him feel better. "We found the best way in and flagged a path."

He shook his head. "I can't carry *Uma* that far. There's no other way in?"

"Nothing closer and nothing easier to walk. Sorry." I leaned my head on my fist and tried to think of a solution.

"Are we sure we need a doula?" Lucas ventured. "Even if Maggie's pregnant, that doesn't mean she'll – " He stopped himself and breathed out heavily through his nose. "Look, I'm having a hard time with this. How does something dead procreate? That's kind of the definition of life." He sat back and forced a hand through his hair, making it stand up in an appealing way.

Lenora leaned towards him and rapped her knuckles on the table. "I take care of pregnant women before, during and after their births. Maggie's gonna need me no matter what happens." She sat back and crossed her arms, case closed, ignoring the deeper questions of life and death and everything beyond these borders. Lucas opened his mouth like he was going to say something, but then thought better of it and stayed silent, placing a crooked finger over his lips.

I took up his question because I felt his misgivings

were valid and I didn't want him to feel like his opinions on this case were being ignored. "We don't know, Lucas. We'll try to figure it out on the fly and just respond to things as they come up. That's the best we can do." He nodded, but I could tell he didn't find this satisfying.

After a moment, Lenora murmured, "How about a horse? I could ride in." This little old lady was tough in ways we hadn't considered.

Ron lit up and looked like this could solve the problem. "*Uma* was a trick rider on the rodeo circuit when she was a girl. She's good on a horse."

"No, won't work." Cam frowned and shook his head. "It's too dense and there are lots of low hanging branches. You could barely walk a horse through that, let alone ride." Tapping on his chin with a finger, his eyes shifted left and then right as he thought through the dilemma. "How about giving us remote support? We have radios we use for search and rescue. We could keep in contact and you could tell us what to do to help Maggie."

Lenora cocked her head and pursed her lips. "Might work. Better if I'm there, but… " She shrugged, accepting the limitations of what could be done.

"Okay, here's another thing that's bothering me." Lucas was flipping through his notes again. "He-Who-Counseled-the-Chief said the black-eyed kids scattered when he approached. Have either of you ever seen or sensed these presences?" His eyes flitted back and forth between Cam and me. When we both responded 'no' simultaneously, he continued with his line of questions. "So, what's going to keep them from running off this time? If they're dangerous, they can't be allowed to keep doing what they're doing."

"We could send Zackie ahead," I blurted, thinking of sending her zipping through the portal, emerging at Maggie's clearing and surprising whoever might be there.

Lucas cocked his head. "How are you going to do that?"

When I stammered uselessly, trying to come up with something plausible, Cam picked up the question and prevaricated brilliantly. "Well, she's a trained search dog, right? You know that Astro collar we used to locate her when she ran through the woods after He-Who-Counseled-the-Chief? She's trained to follow stimuli transmitted from the handheld to the collar. We use that to direct her to specific coordinates. She gets another signal from the collar to let her know where to stop and wait for us." Zackie let him finish his explanation before having a sneezing fit under the table. I got the feeling she thought this was funny. Cam must have thought this was ill-timed, because he gave her a nudge with his foot to get her to stop.

Lucas continued with his perfectly reasonable questions that I didn't want to answer. "Okay, that should work. But what's she going to do when she gets there? How does having her in the clearing affect anything the black-eyed kids might do?"

Cam chewed his lip and tried to come up with another whopper. "Dogs have a way of sensing these psychic disturbances and, er – "

"The spirits will respect the dog." Lenora interrupted, not realizing what a keen sense of timing she had. "Dog tells them to stay, they'll stay, or the dog won't let them cross the bridge to the afterlife."

Lucas stared at her for a moment, unblinking. Mind blown. We had reached his limit.

"Look," Cam said. "If the black-eyed kids are there when we arrive, we deal with them first. They're the real danger to life and limb. If they're not there, we do what we have to for Maggie to get her to cross over." Cam tilted his head and tried to catch Lucas's eye. "And you can film anything you want for the black-eyed kids, but we've agreed that Maggie's off limits because it would upset the family. Does that sound right to you?"

Brought back to the present by the mention of his ghost show, Lucas finally responded. "Yes, that sounds reasonable." Catching himself, he rolled his eyes and muttered, "And now they've got me saying this sounds reasonable, as if none of this defies reason."

# # #

The windshield wipers slapped away the streaks of rain as I headed home. The group had decided to go to Maggie's clearing first thing in the morning and I needed my beauty sleep if I was going to be ready for this. It was a short drive and after parking, I hustled through the rain with my key at the ready, already groggy and wanting nothing more than to just lie down and close my eyes.

I poked at the area around the lock a few times before getting it right, clumsy with the need to sleep. A quick turn of the key and I pushed through the door and got out of the rain, realizing that while the place had been aired out and no longer reeked of spoiled milk, I had forgotten to shut the windows when I left and there were likely some wet spots I'd need to clean up before I could sleep. I fumbled around the wall for the light switch until it flicked on to reveal a folded piece of paper on the ground, just at the threshold. It was a note from Joel, my landlord, telling me to knock on his door when I got home and not to wait until morning, even if the hour was late when I arrived. Despite this open invitation, I pulled my phone out to check the time – it was late – and then realized that the windows were closed. Upon closer inspection, not only were they closed, they were locked. Still grasping the note, I went outside again and walked quickly through the rain to Joel's door. I was no longer sleepy, my adrenaline was pumping and I was on high alert.

Before I could knock, I heard the deep barks of Heckle and Jeckle on the other side of the door and Joel telling them knock it off. The door opened and Joel stood there in a ratty, navy terry cloth robe, holding a mug. "Come on in."

I stepped in and wiped my feet on his welcome mat. "What's up, Joel? Why'd you leave me the note?" The dogs snuffled at me, wagging their tails and whacking my thighs hard when they turned around to let Joel know they were delighted to see me.

"Come on over to the couch. I just made cocoa. I'll get you a mug."

I sat stiffly on his couch, knowing he wouldn't take no for an answer and petted the dogs while I waited for the cocoa. Once he handed me the mug, he sat down in the big reclining chair facing the couch and began talking. "So, the dogs suddenly started barking like crazy a few hours ago. It wasn't the normal bark either. You know them, they're a bunch of knuckleheads, wouldn't hurt a fly. This was a 'I'm going to tear your throat out' kind of bark."

I took a sip of cocoa and rubbed my upper lip to clean off the clinging froth. "What were they barking at?"

"That's what I said. So, I opened the door to take a look around. It was just getting dark, but I see this guy over at your place, messing with a window. The dogs, they just pushed passed me and took off like they had no manners, barking like hell hounds. The guy musta heard them coming and he took off running. They chased him into the woods and I thought they'd bring me back a bloody carcass, but then I hear a car door slam and the guy gunned the engine and peeled outta here." Joel chewed on his lip. "He musta parked on the street and then come through the woods to your place. It was too dark to see what kinda car. I called the cops, of course, but I didn't have much to tell them, other than some guy trying to break into your place."

"Could you tell what he looked like?" I felt cold and then hot. My dead hand clenched hard. I put the mug down on the coffee table, so I could put my good hand on top of it to keep it still.

Joel shook his head and scratched at his beard. "I dunno. Like I said, it was dark. I could tell it was a guy cause of how it moved, and kind of average height, but that's about it." He drank some cocoa and his brow furrowed. "So, I went into your place to lock the windows after the cops left. Hope that was okay with you."

I nodded absently. "Yeah, thanks for doing that."

"Probably just trying to steal stuff, but lock your door and your windows from now on. He probably won't be back, now he knows about the dogs, but you never know."

I told him I'd be careful and thanked him for

waiting up to tell me what happened. He held the door open for me as I left and stood watching on his threshold until I had made it safely to my place and closed the door. I turned all the locks on the door and then double checked the windows to make sure they were secure. The floors were dry, so everything must have happened before the storm broke and I didn't need to clean up any puddles.

With nothing left to do, I grabbed my largest kitchen knife and went to my bedroom. I put the knife on my nightstand, got out of my clothes and into some comfortable pajamas. I picked up the sleeping glove and then decided against it, leaving the dead hand exposed and within easy reach of the knife.

# # #

The parking lot at Worthington State Forest was empty aside from Cam's white pickup truck and Lucas's car, a red Nissan. I pulled in and updated everyone on the prior night's events. I had slept well, secure with the idea that the dead hand was on guard duty and ready to respond if needed. As it turned out, it wasn't needed and the night had passed uneventfully. Despite a restful night's sleep, I was jumpy, my senses tracking any small movements or sounds in the woods. I had no proof, but my gut told me that Rory was behind the break-in attempt. I didn't voice this suspicion, but everyone else immediately leapt to the same conclusion.

"Can you get a restraining order?" Cam sat on the tailgate, fiddling with the Astro collar.

I bit my lip and considered the idea before shaking my head. "I kind of doubt it. I don't have any proof of anything."

"Maybe I should go pay this guy a visit. Just have a little conversation until he sees things from my perspective." Ron casually leaned his shoulder against Cam's truck, but his eyes were flat, black and cold.

Lucas grinned without humor. "I like your thinking, but even if we pooled all our money, I don't think we'd be able to scrape together enough for bail after your little social call." Turning his attention to me, he said, "Maybe you should stay with Cam again."

When Cam started nodding, I shook my head. "I just moved out…And seriously, for how long would we be doing this? And based only on a suspicion?" Lucas opened his mouth to say something else, but I made a slashing motion and nixed the idea before he could get a word out. "No. I am not staying with you either." It was way too soon for that and I didn't want to jinx the relationship. Besides, hiding the dead hand would become a huge issue in such close proximity.

Lenora looked at me with respect, and I almost laughed out loud when I realized she thought I had made this decision to safeguard my virtue. "Good girl. How 'bout you get a gun or a dog. Maybe get both."

The gun was probably an idea to save as a last resort, given my PTSD and a propensity to have a hair trigger when I got hepped up. Joel would get upset if I shot a bunch of holes through my walls.

Before I could voice this concern, Cam spoke up. "The dog is a good idea. It was Joel's dogs, after all, that stopped the break in. You should have Zackie at your place."

I wanted to argue, just because I had gotten into the habit of naysaying, but given the other possibilities for security and the fact that I did feel vulnerable, this was the least of all evils. Zackie had stayed at my place before when Cam had been in the hospital with a badly broken arm and nothing terrible happened. Maybe this would work and it wasn't forever, just until – until what? Until I felt secure again? More likely, until we got on each other's nerves.

I stopped trying to map out all the possibilities when Cam called Zackie over and buckled the Astro collar around her neck. The mission was starting and needed to get my head in the game. While Zackie took off into the woods, Cam made a show of fiddling with the handheld device and I popped my trunk. Reaching in, I grabbed my multi-tool and hung it on my belt. Next, I found two radios and programmed each with the frequency we would use. I handed one to Ron and we did a quick radio check, making sure each of us could transmit and receive. Satisfied that the radios were working, I stuck my unit in the leg pocket of my cargo pants and then rummaged through the trunk again to find some prophylactic coconut water. I handed a bottle to Cam and then chugged down the contents of my bottle. While we waited for Zackie to get in position, I put on eye protection, gloves and then a baseball cap to cover my hair. In reality, Zackie could appear in the clearing nearly instantaneously, but for the sake of the other observers, we needed to make it look like she was running through the woods to get there.

After a few minutes, Cam indicated that Zackie had reached the clearing. I felt like I ought to gear up, as if this were a SAR mission, but what could I bring that would be of any use? As a last minute precaution, I put another bottle of coconut water in my other pants leg pocket and threw one to Cam, who did likewise.

“Wait,” Lenora said. Reaching into my trunk, she pulled out a twenty foot length of purple tubular webbing that I used for tying a Swiss seat harness so I could clip to a rope. “Take this.” Without asking why, I grabbed it and daisy chained the length before finding a carabiner in the trunk to attach it to my belt loop.

We hit the trail, with Lucas following, and then cut into the woods when we found a branch tagged with our flagging tape. Cam had outfitted Lucas with spare equipment, so he was able to move through the thicker woods at a good pace. While capturing some of our trek with a handheld video camera, Lucas became tangled in briars. I grabbed my multi-tool and cut him out, watching with sympathy as tiny splotches of blood formed on his shirt from the thorns. Those little wounds would hurt later.

"Be careful to follow Cam's path, or you'll get caught in another briar patch," I cautioned him.

We set off again and soon reached the clearing. As we broke through the brush, the sound of Zackie growling brought us to an abrupt stop. The sound roared, echoing and reverberating through me, making my eyes tear and my breast bone vibrate. Yellowed leaves rained down from trees and brush that circled the clearing and the air was freezing. My ears clenched with pain and my hands jerked up to cover them. I ground my teeth and locked my knees, so that I would resist running from this terrible onslaught to my senses.

Maggie sat on the edge of the clearing, her knees up and her arms protectively circling her belly. She stared with a horrified concentration towards the middle of the clearing, where three children clustered together, two boys and a girl. Panic etched their faces and when one or another tried to break and run, Zackie proved too fast for them. A reddish blur, she sped to where the child took a step and they would immediately retract the offending foot. If they were a micro-second slow in withdrawing, she slashed with her teeth at their ankles and they wailed in fear.

"What's going on? Why's she running circles?"

Lucas trained the handheld on Zackie to record her frenetic movement.

I stood rooted, afraid to do anything to distract the psychopomp. “She’s got the black-eyed children trapped. I’m not sure where we go from here. Cam, what’s next? What do we do?”

“Remember when we talked about moving children on? How they’re very trusting and you just have to tell them to find their mum and they’re off? Well, none of that applies here.”

Something clicked in my brain. “Because they’re like that Irish boy hostage and they’ve lost all trust?”

“Exactly. It’s good to know my lessons aren’t going to waste.” Under the strain, Cam looked pleased with me. “Something happened to these kids during their lives and deaths, something that robbed them of their innocence. Because they are unable to trust, it’s hard to have the conversation necessary to convince them to move on.”

“So, how did your granny convince the Irish boy?” I asked.

Cam frowned, his brows creasing. “I’ve told you.

Her talent was influencing spirits."

My brain gave another click. "Ohhhh, I thought you meant that she was just a persuasive person, that she knew how to say just the right thing and make a connection."

"She did do that with spirits, but there was an undercurrent of power that they could rarely resist, especially if she'd hit on the reason for them remaining earthbound."

"Too bad your granny's not here right now." Lucas spoke softly, keeping the camera focused on Zackie as she lay down facing the kids, daring them to make another move.

Cam sighed. "There's nothing for it. Let's go and talk to these kids."

We walked the short distance from the periphery of the clearing and stopped just behind Zackie. The children were very pale and painfully thin. Their clothing was tatty and stained, the boys in short pants and suspenders with slouching caps perched on their heads. The girl wore her hair in braids and a too-big gingham dress hung loosely on her frame, coming just past her knees. They were barefoot, their legs also bare and their feet dirty. The children's eyes were dark pits, but instead of malevolence, they radiated despair.

Cam studied the children and then dipped his head towards the psychopomp. “I don’t suppose you’d consider going with Zackie, here.”

“Give us the baby. We’re bored,” the older boy said.

The other boy chimed in. “Yes, give us the baby, a new little sister.”

“We’re lonely. All we want is the baby. Then we’ll go.” The girl whispered the words and then reached toward Maggie, eliciting a warning growl from Zackie.

“You’re not getting the baby.” Cam’s mouth formed a grim line. He waited until the children quieted down before continuing. “Tell me how you died.”

The older boy smirked and raised a pale hand to point at Lucas. “I will tell you how he will die.” Turning back to Cam, he showed more teeth. “And you, old man. You’ve lived long enough, don’t you think?”

“The girl… tell that story. That’s the best of them all.” The younger boy spoke excitedly, hopping from foot to foot like an imp. His eyes lit up with delight.

"Shhh…don't tell. It's a secret." The little girl giggled and hunched her shoulders, pulling a braid in front of her smiling lips.

The air chilled further making my scalp contract and the hair stand on edge. As the children played their game, pointing at us and whispering to each other, sniggering and joking, vitality poured out of me like blood from a mortal wound. Thoughts of death and the futility of life flooded my mind and I looked to Cam to give me a reason to keep going. His face crumpling, Cam drew his hands up to cover his eyes. I bowed my head in defeat, my hands clenching at my sides. Our future was bleak, with no escape from demanding spirits who would feed on our energy like worms on a corpse until it was our turn to join the danse macabre.

"Bloody useless. It's all bloody useless." Cam muttered from behind his hands as he swayed forward, bending at the waist.

I lacked the energy to speak and would have sunk to my knees if it hadn't been for Lucas. Grabbing both of us by an arm, he turned us away and pulled Cam and me towards the edge of the clearing. We had no will and obediently staggered on feeble legs from the miasma of despair flowing from the children.

"Look at me." Lucas touched my cheek and forced me to look up. Reaching into his pocket, he pulled something out. "Lenora said to give you this if things got bad." He put a small, drawstring pouch into my hand. Grabbing Cam, he forced another pouch into his hand.

The pouch was warm and surprisingly weighty. An herbal scent wafted towards my face and slowly engulfed me, displacing the miasma and giving me a sense of comfort. Doula, herbalist, rodeo trick rider – what else could this woman do? I immediately felt stronger and shook off the last of the dark thoughts from the recesses of my consciousness.

Cam put the pouch in his shirt pocket and squared his shoulders. "Ready?"

I nodded and did the same with my pouch. We approached the children again, but this time with a weapon to combat them. The giggling stopped when we returned to our place behind Zackie and they shifted uncertainly when they saw the thunderous expression on Cam's face. He was out of patience and done with their games.

"Tell me how you died." Cam growled the question to the older boy and then crossed his arms, waiting for the child to answer.

After a moment, the child was compelled. "It was the kiss of death." The older boy shrugged as if he didn't care, but a tear leaked from his eye.

"What do you mean 'kiss of death?'" I took a step towards the children and they flinched, raising hands to protect themselves. I froze, suspicious of this response, and asked the next question softly. "Did someone beat you?"

The girl raised her chin defiantly. "Sometimes. We worked in the wool mill. If we were too slow or if we fell asleep, the man would hit us. He said it would make us learn."

"You'd fall asleep? How long did they make you work?" I worked three jobs at one point to make ends meet. It was exhausting and I was tired all the time, but I never fell asleep at work. What had they done to these kids?

The older boy scuffed his foot in the dirt and put his hands in his pockets. His brows came down angrily over his eyes. “We worked twelve to fourteen hours a day. Every few minutes, we had to suck the thread through the hole in the shuttle.”

“It made me cough all the time. I’d swallow lint and dust and I’d cough.” The other boy patted his chest and his face contorted. “It made me sick.”

“No one cared.” The girl crossed her arms and scowled.

“I’m sorry.” Cam’s features softened and he reached a hand towards the children. “Let us help you.”

The children exchanged uncertain glances, but then the older boy shook his head and glared. “No, you’ll send us back to the mill.”

“We won’t do that. I promise, we’ll never send you back to the mill. You can trust us.” I said this with every ounce of truth in me, to get them to believe, but they stared stubbornly back.

“No, adults can’t be trusted.” The girl’s eyes grew even sadder as she said this and I imagined she was thinking about her parents, how they let her work in such a hell hole, probably for pennies a day. Cam had been right –

forget trying to send her to her mom.

"You said you wanted the baby because you were lonely and bored. If you go with Zackie, there will be other children there. Would you like that?" Ever resourceful, Cam tried a different angle, but his efforts were met with defiant stares.

The older boy huffed out the group's response. "No. There were other children at the mill too. That didn't make it a good place."

I caught Cam's eye, hoping he had some other ideas. He gave a tiny shake of his head, that he had nothing. "They're too dangerous. We can't just leave them here, Cam."

"We can't force them either. They have to go of their own free will." Cam put his palms up helplessly and was about to say something else when a blast of light from behind caught us by surprise.

My hands shot to my eyes and I gasped as my body reflexively hunched forward in a protective posture. Recovering as quickly as I could, I spun around to see what new threat was emerging. Striding out of the woods, He-Who-Counseled-the-Chief approached. He looked resplendent in his buckskin and his red face was radiant.

The children murmured excitedly and the girl said, “Oooh, it’s the Indian man.”

“What? You again?” Cam was as surprised as I was. “I thought we’d done with you.”

The Lenape spirit grinned and shrugged.

“What the f– Can he do that, Cam? Can he come back? I thought this was a one way trip.” I looked rapidly back and forth between my mentor and He-Who-Counseled-the-Chief, confused as all get-out.

“What’s going on? Something’s happening.” Lucas looked like he was about to burst. He had waited patiently as we talked with the children, hearing only one side of the conversation, but now he could no longer hold back his curiosity. I quickly filled him in before his head exploded. “Why’s the Lenape man back?”

I whispered to Lucas that I had no idea what was going on and then handed him my radio and told him to keep the others updated. This gave him something else to keep him occupied, instead of asking questions. As grateful as I was for the initial intervention, I needed a bit of peace to sort this out.

"I've come to take the children across." He-Who-Counseled-the-Chief assessed the children with a scowl on his face. "Do not try to run from me again." When they nodded submissively, eyes downcast, he turned to Zackie. "With your permission, Ancient One?" Zackie favored him with a long gaze and then stood and shook off. Stretching first, she loped off to sit with Maggie.

The children found their courage and stared openly at the Lenape man, eyes wide with wonder. The older boy stammered out a question. "Are you with Buffalo Bill's Wild West show?"

He-Who-Counseled-the-Chief raised an eyebrow and cocked his head. "I do not know this man. But I will take you to the Land of the Spirits, in the country of good hunting. Would you like that?"

The children glanced at each other with wrinkled foreheads, their hands twisting together nervously and their feet shuffling as they fidgeted. At last, the girl spoke. "We're afraid."

"I will take you to live with my people. You will join our tribe."

The older boy took a tentative step forward. "Will you teach me how to ride bareback?"

The Lenape spirit smiled gently. "We will teach you many things."

The other boy joined the older boy, holding his hand. "Well, that's good. 'Cause I only ever wanted to go to school and learn."

Still not convinced, the little girl looked at the Lenape man from under her brows. "You won't take us back to the mill, will you?" Crossing her thin arms, she stood her ground, testing him.

He-Who-Counseled-the-Chief curled his lip. "No. No mill ever again." He reached out both hands to the children. The little girl shyly took his left hand and the older boy, still tightly grasping the other boy's hand, took his right. He smiled gently at the children, and together, they walked out of the clearing.

Knowing what was about to come, I swung away and shielded my eyes just before a blinding bright light erupted. Standing straight after the blast, I stared at Cam. My eyes must have been as big and bright as the full moon. "Is he a psychopomp now?"

Cam bit his lip and nodded, also stunned by the turn of events. After a moment, he expelled a deep breath. "I guess we shouldn't be that surprised. He was following this path when he helped all the victims of Tom Quick make the journey. I've just never seen this happen before, but I suppose he's been training at this for centuries."

"But why would the children go with him? Why did they trust him?" I was thrilled that the children would find peace and the baby was safe from them, but none of this was making sense to me.

Cam's eyes became serious and the fine lines stood out as he squinted. "I think he was so far outside of the children's experience that they saw him as first and foremost a tribal man. The fact that he was an adult did not register because he was not from their culture." Cam threw his hands up. "That's the best I can come up with. Let me know if you think of something better." He turned and marched towards Maggie and Zackie.

Maggie sat with her arms wrapped around Zackie, who lay companionably at her side. I took a quick survey of my energy and then opened the bottle of coconut water, taking a slug before handing the other half off to Cam to finish. The black-eyed kids had taken their toll and we weren't anywhere near done yet.

We squatted down to get on Maggie's level and after a moment of wobbling, I sat to keep from falling over.

"Good idea," Cam grunted, as he joined me.

Maggie's face looked worn, but her relief was evident. Her posture was relaxed and the wild, tortured look was gone. It seemed that her eyes were clearer and her thoughts more coherent. Maybe it was because she'd had time and wasn't newly dead anymore, or maybe it was the absence of the black-eyed kids. She looked from me to Cam and breathed, "Thank you."

"No need to thank us. It was He-Who-Counseled-the-Chief who brought them over, after all." Cam quirked his lips. I took that expression to mean that he was still getting used to the idea that we had one more psychopomp in the world. The idea was giving me the shivers, but we had to concentrate on Maggie now.

"How did these kids come to be with you?" I asked, genuinely curious.

Maggie's eyes drifted and she sighed. "It was at Greg's funeral. We were at the cemetery and that was the first time I heard the voices. They were coming at me from all sides and I thought I was losing my mind because of the stress." She swallowed and a shadow of the terror from that day passed over her face. "I held it together for as long as could, but Katherine had to get me out of there as soon as the minister finished speaking. Once I was away from the cemetery, the crowd of voices stopped, but the children's voices stayed with me." She rubbed her arms. "It was chilling, what they said."

"So, you went to doctors to find a cure?" I didn't have to think too hard to imagine how awful this must have been for her.

"Yeah, but it didn't help." Maggie shook her head and then eased the hair from her face with a shaky hand. "One night, I felt them right next to me. They said they were going to take the baby, that they would kill me to take the baby. I could feel her ¬¬– the baby –¬ kick and fight them, but they were so strong." A tear rolled down Maggie's cheek and she buried her face in her hands for a moment. She was crying in earnest when she looked up and she sobbed with naked grief as she told us the end of the story. "She fought them to keep me alive. She fought until the life went out of her." Maggie collapsed forward and pressed her cheek against Zackie's flank, breathing hard. "I felt her die and go still and I think I lost it then. I remember grabbing Greg's gun and running into the woods because I didn't want Katherine to find me. I remember a voice telling me I was giving up too easily, but I couldn't let them have her. I thought if I died too, I could protect her in death because I didn't protect her in life."

Tears streamed down my face as I listened to Maggie. I wanted to hate the black-eyed kids, but they were the product of an uncaring and miserable world. My mind went black, filled with the thought that in this world, suffering bred only more suffering and there was no end to it. Lucas touched my hand and then put his arms around me. I buried my face in his shoulder and, between sobs, repeated what Maggie had told us. He held me, purging the darkness and giving me the strength to keep going, to finish the task. After a few more shaky moments, I wiped my face and asked him to tell Ron and Lenora. Then I willed myself to finish this. The suffering had to end.

"Maggie, will you allow Zackie to take you and baby through the portal?" Cam absently wiped at his eyes. He had also been affected by the tragedy of her story.

"I would go. I want to be with Greg, but the baby

won't go." Deep lines of stress showed around Maggie's eyes and turned down mouth.

"Why won't the baby go?" Cam frowned with confusion.

"I don't know why, maybe those kids…" Maggie sat up and then rubbed her belly in a soothing circular motion. "Maybe they infected her somehow? They wanted to stay here to taste life and maybe she feels like she's missing something." Maggie looked down sadly at her belly. "I know about life. I had my experiences, but this baby never even had the chance to set her feet on the earth."

I thought maybe we could get at least one of them to go. "We have a midwife with us on the radio." I pointed towards Lucas, who was holding the device at the ready. "She can help you deliver the baby." At least, I hoped so. We were in unchartered territory and lost in the wilderness. "You could go ahead and we would help the baby move on."

Maggie compressed her lips and shook her head. "No, I won't go without the baby."

Cam made an exasperated sound with his lips. "But

don't you see? If you go first, we can convince the baby to go through to be with you. It will all work out."

Maggie chewed her lip, her eyes wide and frightened. "I'm not sure…"

"Do you trust us?" I put my hand on hers and looked into her eyes.

"I –I do," she stammered. "But what if I'm not enough? What if the baby still wants to stay here?"

Cam ran a hand impatiently through his graying mop and expelled a heavy breath through his nose. "Then we'll take care of the baby until she's ready to move on." Casting an uncertain glance my way, he looked for me to add my support.

I rocked back on my heels and sat down hard on my rump. I knew nothing about taking care of babies and maybe this was entirely different, but the prospect scared the crap out of me. "We're doing what, now? What the hell, Cam." My voice rose shrilly as I searched for a way out of this.

"Look, I think the odds are in our favor that the baby will want to follow her mum. If she doesn't go right away, we need a Plan B." Cam silently pleaded with me to work with him.

I narrowed my eyes at Cam, resenting being put in this situation. But then I thought about the baby and what she had been through, how brave she was to fight. And when I looked at Maggie. Her expression was desperate, but there was also a grim determination in the set of her shoulders. If worse came to worse, she would stay here for all eternity to make sure the baby was not alone and was cared for.

My mind raced, trying to find another alternative. Maybe if I had a few days to calmly think this through, I could come up with a solution that worked for everyone. But right here, right now, my thoughts kept hitting a brick wall. Rubbing my face, I mumbled through my hands. "All right." Looking up, bleary-eyed, I made sure Cam understood how this was going down. "I'll do it, but you are the primary caregiver."

"Is this all right with you, Maggie?" Cam asked. When she nodded, he turned his attention to Lucas. "She's ready."

Lucas held the radio close to his lips and depressed

the button to speak. “Ron, can you hear me?”

There was a little static, then we heard Ron respond. “Go ahead, Lucas.”

“Looks like we’re going ahead with the…with the, um…birth?”

“Okay, hold on.” The channel went dead for a moment. “*Uma*? See, hold the button like this and then talk. Here, just–” A loud siren alarm broadcast from the speaker and a light on the radio flashed urgently.

Lucas fumbled with the radio and then stared wide-eyed at it. “Here, you take it.” He sat down next to me and handed over the blaring mess. I held the radio at arm’s length and plugged the ear nearest to it with a finger.

After a few seconds, the noise stopped and a voice came through. “Sorry, she hit the panic button.” Ron’s voice shook with laughter. “I’ll just hold it while she talks. Go ahead, *Uma*.”

“…stupid piece of…Hello?” Lenora sounded a little far away, but we could hear her.

Cam made a rolling motion with his hands, for me to get moving with this. “Lenora? Maggie says she’s ready.

What do we do?"

"You find a tree branch and throw that purple belt over it."

I unclipped the webbing and threw it to Cam. "Okay, Cam's going to do this."

Cam grabbed the loose strand of the daisy chain to unknot the end and then flung out the webbing to release its full length. He gave his hand to Maggie to help her stand and they walked to the nearest tree. Cam threw the webbing over a stout branch and after centering the loop to make sure he had equal lengths on both sides, he called over to me. "Now what?"

I relayed our progress. "Okay, we have it looped over a tree branch. What do we do now?"

"You don't do nothing. Maggie's gotta grab the ends and use the belt to pull hard when she pushes. She's gotta pull, bend her knees and squat until the baby comes."

My brow furrowed and I clicked the button to talk again. "Really? She doesn't have to lie down or anything?"

"No, that's a dumb way of doing things. She's gotta use gravity to help her."

Maggie rubbed her belly and said something soothing to the baby in a low voice. Zackie ambled over and stood before Maggie, gazing expectantly up into her face. After a moment, Maggie got a good grip on the webbing, doubling it around her hands, and stood with her legs braced and apart. Her face took on a look of intense concentration and she began pushing. Her knees bent and she grunted with the strain. Lenora kept up an encouraging chatter on the radio.

Three times, she pulled and strained. “Please…please…” she muttered, as sweat poured down her face. Cam stood helplessly by, his face was pale and his hands occasionally shot out as if he would catch her if she lost her balance. On the fourth push, Maggie bent deeply and moaned, her chin tucked into her chest. Zackie extended her muzzle towards the distended abdomen and lunged through the spirit’s substance, her head disappearing into the mounded belly.

When Zackie pulled back, Maggie let out a relieved sigh and the baby emerged, gently held in the psychopomp’s maw. The little limbs flailed and a cry of triumph came from her tiny throat. Maggie sank to her knees, letting go of the webbing and sobbed joyfully.

"What's happening?" Lenora demanded from the radio.

"The baby's here," I breathed.

Ron came over the speaker. "That was quick. I've birthed livestock that took longer."

I felt a little giddy and started babbling. "Nothing happened the usual way, but–" I let go of the button, not sure what else to say.

After a beat, Lenora spoke again. "But nothin'. Dead woman's having a baby. Nothin' usual about that." The radio was silent for a few beats and then we heard Lenora again. "Tell me everything that's happening."

Zackie lay down with the baby between her paws, nuzzling the little one until she squealed with delight, kicking her feet and waving her hands. The psychopomp looked up at Maggie, tail wagging and displaying a toothy grin. It occurred to me that perhaps Cam would not be the primary caretaker for this baby. Maggie reached out with her hands and lifted the baby, cooing and cuddling it to her breast. Cam joined them on the ground. Looking immensely relieved, he extended a finger for the little one to grasp.

I described the scene over the radio. Lucas, listening in, shook his head in wonder. “What’s the baby’s name?” he called to Cam.

Maggie stroked the soft cheek. “I’m calling her Katherine, after my sister.”

“She says it’s Katherine, like her sister,” Cam called back, grinning like the psychopomp.

As I turned to Lucas, I caught a whiff of ammonia and my smile faltered. Standing a little apart, Hannah watched the mother and baby. Her face was drawn down with sadness and she began to fade almost immediately. I had the urge to reach out to her, but it was too late. She was gone.

“What is it?” Lucas tensed and his eyes scanned the area where Hannah had been.

“It’s okay. No danger.”

He looked relieved and then the corners of his mouth turned up a little. “This mission was unexpectedly calm. I’d understand it if you docked my pay.”

“Count your blessings. I think this is pretty rare, so treasure the moment. And you did give us Lenora’s gift when we really needed it."

Lucas laughed. "I gave you placebos. You believed it would make a difference, so it did."

I was about to argue the point when Cam motioned for us to come over. Lucas stood and offered me his hand and together, we approached the happy group surrounding the baby. The handholding worked in our favor, since I was able to stop Lucas at a respectful distance before he interfered with Maggie's space. "What's up?" I asked.

Maggie still held the baby and her face was serious. "Katherine wanted to be an independent being before we transitioned. She's told me that she's ready to go, but wants one more thing before she leaves this earth."

A wave of relief washed over me. Up close, Katherine was a cute little thing, but I still felt jittery about taking on responsibility for a baby. I was deeply grateful that she would go on with her mother. But my moment of gratitude dissolved, replaced by uncertainty, as I followed up on Katherine's request. "What's the one more thing?"

Maggie looked from Cam to me, her face solemn. "Can you both promise her that her name will be on the headstone?"

I stalled for time and explained the situation to Lenora, Ron, and Lucas before answering her. "Isn't that your sister Katherine's call?" Shifting uncomfortably, I made eye contact with Cam and raised my eyebrows. I didn't want to promise anything if I couldn't pull it off.

"I wrote it on my arm with a Sharpie before I – before I…" Maggie paled and the corners of her eyes turned down as she recalled that awful night. "I wanted Katherine to know I'd named the baby after her. She'll believe you if you tell her this."

"That should help. We'll talk to her and try our best."

Cam was more optimistic. "We'll make it happen."

Zackie stood and nudged Maggie to her feet, cradling little Katherine in the crook of her arm. "Thank you both. And please thank the midwife for all her help." They walked into the woods and Cam and I turned away as the bright light flashed, temporarily bleaching the colors out of the foliage. The last thing we heard was Maggie's ecstatic cry, "Greg!"

###

Katherine stalled for time and offered us some more cookies. We sat in her living room and stayed quiet, giving her time to process what we'd told her. The conversation had been careful and gentle, telling her nothing about the time Maggie spent in the clearing or her suffering. Katherine was still fragile and the grief weighed heavily on her. We mentioned the message written in Sharpie and that Maggie would be pleased if Katherine included this name for the baby on the headstone. It would be a few months yet before the headstone could be erected, so she had time to think about it.

"I thought there was something about you two when we met in the church." Katherine concentrated on pouring tea and spoke softly. "I will, of course, give the baby a name on the headstone. I lost both my sister and my niece that night." She put the porcelain teapot down with shaking hands and stared almost desperately into our faces. "Is Maggie at peace?"

Cam held her eyes with a steady gaze. "Yes, she and the baby are at peace."

Katherine nodded and appeared to relax. "Thank

God for that." She sat back in her chair, the tension rolling off her shoulders. She closed her eyes briefly and repeated those words like a prayer.

After we ate all her cookies (we were still depleted from the recent spirit work), she saw us to the door. She seemed to be breathing easier and a weight had been lifted from her. Katherine's eyes shown as she bid us good-bye. "Thank you both for coming here."

# # #

Living with Zackie was proving to be a chore. She spent the nights popping in and out and I thought I was going to have a seizure from all the blasting light. I suspected she was visiting baby Katherine. When I complained to Cam, he said it couldn't be helped and I needed to suck it up.

It was the third night with my unwanted roommate. We were going to the final farewell dinner for Ron and Lenora. Zackie stood next to me yawning, as I secured all the newly installed locks on my door. She pointedly ignored me as I groused about her nocturnal habits and my voice rose with my growing anger at being disregarded.

"Hey, you can't train a dog by just yelling. You gotta look for the behavior you want and then reward it." Joel climbed out of his red truck. "How you doin'?"

"Doing okay, except for dealing with Zackie. She's keeping me up at night."

"Pfft…you'll do all right. The important thing is, you got the dog with you at night." He pulled out some gum, took a stick and then offered me one. When I shook my head, he continued. "So, remember the Roseberry Homestead I was tellin' you about?"

"That really old house you're restoring? Yeah, how's that going?"

"Great. We got the architectural historian coming in tomorrow. Thought you might wanna come and see the place with your master stonemason friend." He snapped his gum and grinned.

"Awesome! I'll give her a call. She's still studying, she's not at the master level yet, but I know she'll want to see this." I was glad for this distraction. It would be a good thing for Peyton. She'd been through the grinder these last few weeks and having something fun to do would cheer her up. Joel gave me the details of when and where as I turned the key in the last lock. "We'll be there. Right now, I'm late for dinner at Cam's. See you tomorrow?"

A short drive later, I arrived at Cam's house and let myself in because no one heard the doorbell over all the yelling. Zackie and I went straight to the dining room, where she planted her front paws on the table and grabbed some fried bread. She went under the table and I waved at the combatants, trying to get their attention.

"—no more spirits left to free." Cam's face was red and he slapped his palm on the table.

"And I'm telling you Grandfather said we're not done yet." Lenora also slapped her palm down.

I gave up trying to get their attention, grabbed some fried bread and sat in my usual spot across from Lucas. "Should we be yelling too? I think I'd like to eat my bread first."

"Go ahead and eat. They're doing enough yelling for everyone." Lucas took some bread and followed my lead.

Ron frowned at the empty bowl. "Looks like I'm going to have to add to the noise pollution." Holding up the empty bowl, he roared, "We need more bread."

That request brought a temporary cessation in hostilities as Lenora got up to fry more bread. "You also want more bread?" she asked Cam, crossing her arms and leaning her hip on the table.

"Yes. Please." Cam growled the response and looked like he wanted to say more. Probably in the interest of hastening the bread delivery, he held his tongue.

"We do still have the Scotland trip hanging over our heads." Lucas said the words mildly, but there was a twinkle in his eye as he waited for the response.

Cam placed his elbows on the table and glowered. "*Et tu*, Lucas?"

"What'd I say? We're not done yet." Lenora grabbed the bowl and stalked out of the room.

I sat back, contentedly chewing my bread and took a good look around the room. Whatever my condition, whether I was hungry, sick or frightened, these people had my back. Maybe they were a bit loud on occasion, but hearing loss was a small price to pay to be among people I trusted. I'd found my family, and all was well in my world.

****

If you enjoyed reading SOUL SCENT, please, please write a short review on Amazon and/or Goodreads. Your review is incredibly important—it is the currency that establishes a book's worth to other readers and also enables indie authors like me to qualify for desperately needed promotional opportunities. Please make the next book possible by leaving a review now.

Many thanks for reading and reviewing.

www.reynafavis.com

*************************.

ACKNOWLEDGEMENTS

Nothing in this world happens without the help and support of others. I would like to express my undying gratitude to the Schooleys Mountain Writers' Group at the Washington Township Public Library, the Phillipsburg Free Public Library Writer's Group and the Belvidere Writers' Group for their unstinting support in reviewing early versions of this work and offering helpful feedback. Thanks also to beta readers Dana Geissler, Sara Ehrlich, and Rich Kliman (note the Oxford comma, Dr. Kliman) for generously donating their time and providing critique on the overall story structure, as well as catching those pesky typos. The librarians at the Phillipsburg Free Public Library were instrumental in providing key references for this story and I am grateful for their help. I would also like to thank Loren Spiotta-DiMare for her words of wisdom and Laura Reilly Salmon for sending me a dragon when I really needed it.

AUTHOR'S NOTES

Lenape

I hope you enjoyed meeting Ron Falling-Leaf and Lenora Ottertooth. My intent was to make these characters human and relatable, while highlighting the story of the Lenape people in New Jersey. While I thought that like Parmelia and Bodean, Ron and Lenora would depart at the end of the story and return to their home, they surprised me by wanting to stick around.

The history of the Lenape and their cultural beliefs were gleaned from Kraft's tomb of a book. This is truly the definitive guide.

Kraft, H. C. (2001). *The Lenape-Delaware Indian Heritage 10,000 BC to AD 2000*. Lenape Books.

All dialogue written in the Southern Unami dialect was taken from this source. Any errors are my own.

Lenape Talking Dictionary. (2002). Retrieved January 23, 2016, from http://www.talk-lenape.org/sentences.php?resultpage=2&

Current and historic Native American views on suicide were derived from the works below.

EchoHawk, M. (1997). Suicide: Individual, Cultural, International Perspectives. In A. A. Leenaars, R.

W. Maris, & Y. Takahashi (Eds.), (pp. 50–59). New York, NY: The Guilford Press.

Lester, D. (1997). Suicide: Individual, Cultural, International Perspectives. In A. A. Leenaars, R. W. Maris, & Y. Takahashi (Eds.), (pp. 53–38). New York, NY: The Guilford Press.

Please note that the use of a rope or sash belt (or webbing, in the case of the story) during the birthing process is likely not a Lenape practice. In the article below, the sash belt is referred to as a common Native American tradition and the Navajo are specifically cited as using this as an aid during child birth. Modern hospitals near reservations even install sash belts in the ceilings of the obstetric units to help the mothers. I thought this idea had a lot of merit and wanted to include it, despite the fact that this was probably not historically or culturally accurate. However, it did not seem beyond the pale that displaced tribes meeting in Oklahoma might share ideas and certain practices might be adopted.

https://www.scienceandsensibility.org/blog/series-welcoming-all-families-supporting-the-native-american-family

Crime Scene Clean Up

Much of the details for Fia's new job were taken from the book by Reavill about the crime scene clean up company, Aftermath. The cleanup process for the fancy car was taken from Aftermath's website.

Reavill, G. (2007). *Aftermath, Inc.: Cleaning Up After CSI Goes Home* (Hardcover). New York: Gotham Books.

http://www.aftermath.com/crime-cleanup-services/vehicle-blood-bio-cleaning-car/

Coffin Birth

Holy crap, it's real. If you would like to learn more about this interesting phenomenon, please refer to the citations below.

Hawkes, S. C. (1975). An Anglo-Saxon obstetric calamity from Kingsworthy, Hampshire. *Medical and Biological Illustration*, *25*, 47–51.

Wikipedia Coffin Birth. (2016). Retrieved from https://en.wikipedia.org/wiki/Coffin_birth

Tom Quick

The story of Tom Quick and how to interpret his murderous actions were taken from the articles below. Being that a descendant categorized him as a psychopath, I felt no qualms in also doing so. The story about the butchered Lenape family was taken from "Tom Quick Indian Slayer, Hero or Serial Killer." The quote from Tom Quick's mother (about how he couldn't be held responsible for his actions because witnessing the killing of his father "turned his head") is real. The obelisk dedicated to his memory as an Indian Slayer is also real, as was the damage inflicted upon it by parties unknown. The repaired monument remains in storage.